11. AUG 08   30   LATEST

AUTHOR   PRUNTY, M.

CLASS   F

TITLE   Poison arrows

Lancashire County Library

30118091512297

Lancashire
County Council

LANCASHIRE
COUNTY LIBRARY
Bowran Street
PRESTON PR1 2UX
Recycled

D0993816

poison arrows

London-reared of Irish parents, **Morag Prunty** edited several young women's magazines in London including *More!* and *Just Seventeen* before moving to Ireland in 1990 to relaunch *Irish Tatler*. She is now a full-time writer and lives in Dublin with her husband and son. *Poison Arrows* is her third novel.

Also by Morag Prunty

Dancing With Mules

Disco Daddy

MORAG PRUNTY

poison arrows

PAN BOOKS

First published 2003 by Pan Books
an imprint of Pan Macmillan Ltd
Pan Macmillan, 20 New Wharf Road, London N1 9RR
Basingstoke and Oxford
Associated companies throughout the world
www.panmacmillan.com

ISBN 0 330 42031 3

Copyright © Morag Prunty 2003

'I Will Survive' words and music Dino Fekaris and Freddie Perren.
© 1978 Perren-Vibes Music Co./ Polygram International Publishing Incorporated, USA.
Universal Music Publishing Ltd. Used by permission of Music Sales Limited.
All rights reserved. International copyright secured.

The right of Morag Prunty to be identified as the
author of this work has been asserted by her in accordance
with the Copyright, Designs and Patents Act 1988.

All rights reserved. No part of this publication may be
reproduced, stored in or introduced into a retrieval system, or
transmitted, in any form, or by any means (electronic, mechanical,
photocopying, recording or otherwise) without the prior written
permission of the publisher. Any person who does any unauthorized
act in relation to this publication may be liable to criminal
prosecution and civil claims for damages.

1 3 5 7 9 8 6 4 2

A CIP catalogue record for this book is available from
the British Library.

Typeset by SetSystems Ltd, Saffron Walden, Essex
Printed and bound in Great Britain by
Mackays of Chatham plc, Chatham, Kent

This book is sold subject to the condition that it shall not,
by way of trade or otherwise, be lent, re-sold, hired out,
or otherwise circulated without the publisher's prior consent
in any form of binding or cover other than that in which
it is published and without a similar condition including this
condition being imposed on the subsequent purchaser.

for my cherub,

Leo

LANCASHIRE COUNTY LIBRARY	
09151229	
H J	21/07/2003
F	£6.99

SOUTH LANCS LIBRARIES
SEU SET SB SCG
1/04 4KY 1/05 7/06

PART ONE

missive impossible

CLASS ONE CONFIDENTIAL MISSIVE

To: Archangel Gabriel, department of
         Renunciation and Hope
From: God

Ignatius Anum, a fallen angel made flesh in the Year Of Our Lord nineteen hundred and seventy-five, having been expelled from this Kingdom in contravention of the Poison Arrow Act 1547, is nearing the end of his mortal existence. I am instructing you to take charge of this matter in the strictest confidence – not even my left and right hand are to be informed. The agent deployed must be engaged on a need-to-know basis only and I am relying on you to select the best angel for the job. I am sure you appreciate the urgency of this mission. The Sacred Mystery of this realm is at stake and must be preserved at all costs.

Keep me informed.
   God

This missive will self-destruct in ten seconds.

Prologue

One of the very worst things about being God is that sometimes you get it wrong. Or rather, sometimes one of your employees fecks things up so badly and God, being, shall we say, the most supreme of the deities, gets to take the rap. I'm not going to even start with the whole famine/war/pestilence thing. I'm not far enough up the scale to be qualified to comment on that class of a problem. But as a senior cupid at OHF's (Our Heavenly Father's) Ministry of Love, I can tell you that on a day-to-day, affairs-of-the-heart basis, when it comes down to bad matchmaking, it is more often a case of sloppy marksmanship and poor attention to detail.

Of course, there are cupids out there who will blame the system, who say they are poorly paid, that the perks aren't nearly enough to compensate for the hassles of the job. Few of them would have the gall to blame the boss Himself, but then when you're working for a guy who can conjure up hellfire and brimstone quicker than you'd flick a Zippo, well, put it like this, unionizing the workers is a *definite* no-no. In any case, I've been in this job for the best part of two hundred years and I would have to say that most of the gripes you hear these days are basically unfounded.

OK, so cupids are born gay. Big deal. Now, in this day and age is that a hardship? Maybe once upon a time, when you might have been picked up for a bit of sex slavery by a corrupt pope or a pack of, God forbid, Romans, but what with the pink pound and gay pride, have we really anything to complain about? As angels, we don't need to eat, so we are cheap to run and always stay slim. Each cupid has been blessed with astonishing good looks, so that there is always some needy old queen willing to provide us with a roof over our halos, and there are no restrictions on wardrobe in this job. You can go around dressed like a Spice Girl and no one is going to object as long as you get your allocated punters fixed up with somebody suitable.

And perks? Don't be talking! Just last year, a brave posse of middle managers called for an audience with OHF. Results have been seriously down decade on decade. Bugger all solid marriages to speak of, men out there spreading it around until their mid forties then turning out to be so emotionally incompetent and beer-bellied that no one will have them. Fussy women niggling right through their thirties about not getting their 'needs met'. You fix them up with some perfectly compatible specimen – then six months later they ditch him because, oh I don't know, he couldn't cook, or he looked glad-eyed at one of her friends, or he wasn't Leonardo di Caprio. You want to say to them, 'Look – there's only so many

Leonardo's to go around, honey. Can't you make do with a standard issue male, for this life anyway?' But then they are like, 'Oh, Chris, you're so good looking and you understand me, such a shame you're gay,' and you are like, 'Stop whinging, woman . . .' Heads full of mad romantic notions. It is making our job almost impossible.

Anyway, matches are down and the field workers are getting antsy. We've looked into all sorts of ways to get motivation levels up: monogrammed leatherette arrow pouches, special issue servile seraphims – but it wasn't enough. Eventually God, as ever, came up with a scorcher of a scheme. One-to-one advice for cupids in distress, from the Deity Himself. But (and this is why they call Him God *Almighty*) understanding that not everyone wants a visitation from some old guy with a navel-length white beard, He came up with this thing where you could call Him into your presence in the image of whoever you want. Yes. That's right. Got a tricky case and searching for some extra inspiration? You can call Barry White right into your own living room and be assured that any words from the Walrus of Love's mouth are coming straight from above. Of course the scheme is not without its problems, but overall we find it works very well. (See *Heaven Knews* on page 366.)

And I'll tell you one thing for nothing, was I glad of it when I got my promotion assignment through to that pot-holed corner of Hell I grew up in.

Quick recap. Born in arse-end of nowhere – west coast of Ireland – town called Gorrib. He spat me out in 1847 just in time for The Great Famine. What with your rotting tubers and all that, it was death by starvation all round and a lean time for matchmaking. When poverty comes in the door, love flies out of the window, as the saying goes. So after learning the basics under the most difficult of circumstances (man, woman, meet, marry, breed – none of your mucking around with hearts and flowers, just bog-standard matching the bit of land with a pair of child-bearing hips) it was down to Cork, onto a boat at Cove and off to America with me to help build the brave new world. Had fab time for next century or so. Was in on the ground floor with the whole Hollywood hype thing which, as everyone knows, was the start of clueing the world up on the concept of true romance as we know it today. Oh, and the whole Scarlett/Rhett drama of she loves him/she loves him not was fabulous, as was the great amnesty when Himself decreed that mixed race/religion marriages were no longer to be considered exceptions but positively the 'in thing'. Then, after the Second World War, I was sent to dreary old England to jiz up the quota over there. It was fine, but frankly the Brits are a stoic and reserved race and it seemed we were filling the suburbs with Doris Day wannabes and grey nine-to-five dullards for aeons before the Paddies and the West Indians started to arrive and shake things up. I got lucky with the whole free love, Beatles thing, which the powers that be decided I had a hand in, and was promoted and given charge of the whole of the UK and Ireland. Nice enough job but, you know, when you get to be my age, which you won't, things like the weather start to get you down. London is all right but Paris is better – and that's why I went after the CEO of Europe job, which is based in the world's romance capital. But Mr Hilarious upstairs decided that in order to prove myself eligible for the job, I had to go back to that ghastly hole Gorrib and sort out an unholy mess.

1

'What did you say?'

Brian Fitzgerald did not move his head from behind the paper. That was not a good sign.

'I called you a racist.'

At fourteen, Davy Fitzgerald was Gorrib's only anarchist. Given the lack of a monarchy in Ireland, his railing against society largely took the shape of smart-talking his father. A normal symptom of teenage rebellion perhaps except that the self-important bigoted businessman was such an apt target. Brian Fitzgerald carefully folded the paper across the article, 'Refugees Welcomed in the Town of Gorrib', about which his comment had caused the outburst, and gave Davy a hard Gestapo glower.

'Not that bit, the *other* bit.'

Davy wriggled in his seat with discomfort before deciding that principle took precedence over politeness, and spat, 'A fucking racist. I called you a *fucking* racist, all right?'

'How dare you use language like that in my house?'

'It's not your house, it's Mum's house.'

Brian's temper was fit to take flight, but he knew from experience that losing the rag would take his attention off more important matters – like this business with the refugees.

'All the more reason to not say that word.'

'So it's all right for me to call you a racist but it's not all right for me to say "fuck"?'

'I have explained to you a thousand times before, I am not a racialist, I have no objection to foreigners—'

'As long as they stay in their own countries.'

'Now the little shit has it!' Brian declared to nobody in particular. Nobody being his daughter Mary who, along with his wife, Rose, he had long since considered invisible.

Mary was sitting at the table reading *Bridget Jones's Diary* and trying to fathom what a nine-stone publishing PA with access to Chardonnay-stocked Notting Hill wine bars could possibly have to complain about. She herself was pushing the ten, spent eight hours a day in filing and photocopying purgatory in the local Town Council offices and, lacking wine bars, all that was on offer in Gorrib was the Dubonnet Eddie Doran – proprietor of the 'hippest pub in town' – kept behind the counter on the off-chance that some female glamorous enough to appreciate it might sweep into town one of these days. To add insult to injury she was not even to be left alone in her self-pity; instead she had to endure father and son cawing and scratching at each other like a couple of hungry hens. As if anything that happened in this miserable rural hole mattered in the great scheme of things. She hated the pair of them.

Her mother wasn't much better. Silently shuffling through the chaos, her only mission in life to keep her family happy, and failing miserably at that. She was such a bad role model, Mary thought. All drab slacks and blouses, with her three days a week in Cooneys Superstore; fifteen white sliced loaves out the door on a good day, packets of chocolate digestives stacked carefully at the counter like they were gold dust, and ferrety-faced old farmers looking for something 'different' in a tin for their tea. Nothing very 'super' about that.

'Why don't you go after the manager's job?' Mary had suggested to her mother when they were running ads in the paper for staff at the new eight-aisle supermarket.

'I like the bit of chat with the regulars,' Rose had said, her voice full of apology. 'Besides – what would they be wanting with me at my age?'

'You're only forty-five!' Mary had screamed at her, too often to be bothered any more. Besides, Rose would always look at her daughter then as if she were still a child and didn't understand what it was like to be ancient and unlovely and only fit for picking tins off shelves for farmers. Perhaps, thought Mary, if her mother had some get up and go in her, she might have been a potter or an artist like her friend Ella's mum. Then she might have been given a name that meant 'beautiful fairy princess', instead of being fobbed off with the glum 'Mary' which, while it was the Mother of God's handle, held the meaning 'bitter'.

'Are you surprised?' Ella said when they looked up their names on the net one night. 'I mean, pregnant without so much as the benefit of a bit of sex? I'd be bloody bitter! Just as well Mum put me on the pill at fifteen. In this town with my track record. I have to say, though, Mary – if you don't get a move on, the aul Immaculate Conception will be your best hope.'

Ella was the only person who could say stuff like that to Mary without making her feel like a wimp. But she was a wimp and she knew it. Saving herself. Holding out – at her age. And for a man who had seen so much action in his thirty-seven years he'd probably want to send a friend in first to make sure the coast was clear.

Ahhhh Theo. Theo Malone. Theodore. Theo for 'you', and dore for 'adore'. I adore you, Theodore. Mr Theo Malone. Mr and Mrs Theo Malone. Mrs Mary Theodore Malone. Morning, Mrs Malone, and how are you today? Just picking up a few groceries for the tea there and what will it be tonight? Pasta Bolognese and a nice bottle of Chardonnay to go with it or something 'different' out of a dusty tin, given that you are fifty years of age and Gorrib's only existing spinster?

That was what was ahead of her if she carried on like this. She knew that for sure. And yet, even though good sense decreed otherwise, it seemed impossible for her to let go of him.

The irony was that Mary had gone after him in the first place because she thought nobody else would want him. Theo Malone had been one of those wiry weird-looking young men, always slingeing around the town in a long black coat with a notebook full of his own, fairly dreadful poetry. The girls in Gorrib didn't go in much for 'arty' types, so as a plain and uninspiring-looking sixteen year old, Mary had set her sights on what she thought was going to be an easy option.

Mary was friendly and open to the ostracized twenty-something son of Regina Malone (a snooty confection of a woman who considered herself a cut above and was easily the most unpopular snob in the town) and they became friends, which *Company* magazine had assured her was the best place to start a relationship. Mary waited and waited – then one night her moment came. It was a Saturday in Bosanova, Gorrib's 'premier' (read only) nightclub. Being the Christmas holidays, the place was packed with returned emigrants and a smattering of English cousins. Eddie Doran had just put Dexys Midnight Runners to rest, and shoved the microphone half-way down his throat to announce he was 'slowing things down here, folks' for what was all too aptly named 'the erec-shun sec-shun' of the night – as he had done at the same time with the same conviction every Saturday for the past ten years. Mary looked across the room as the lads who had up to now been pogo-ing with great confidence shuffled about looking guiltily for their girl-friends or trying to decide whether they were drunk enough yet to risk asking one of the English girls up. Theo would never indulge in anything so obvious as a slow dance, he was far to discerning and complex a creature for that 'country matchmaking crap', and Mary trod a fine line between agreeing with him and living in hope. In any case she was relieved that she didn't have to watch him sway, with his long arms dangling around another girl's waist, to Crystal Gayle's 'Talking in Your Sleep'. Mary wouldn't have been able to take it. So Eddie Doran's throatal pronouncement was usually a cue for them both to meet at the bar and discuss the latest Smith's album, which she had to pretend she liked. But this night, Theo didn't come to the bar and as Mary scanned the room she noticed his shoulders sloping out of the fire exit on the other side of the dance floor. Something was wrong – or perhaps this was a cue for her to follow.

She found him sitting on a stack of crates in the alley out back. He looked morose and pensive, but that was nothing new. Mary remembered that moment as the peak of her longing for him. Before she had felt only teenage infatuation and since her feelings for Theo had been no more than a kind of terrible habit. Saying nothing she stood and touched him with her eyes, letting them wander across the landscape of his face: three trenches dug into the smooth plain of his forehead, now bent with some secret worry; black curls furled down over his ears, his sideburns straining towards his chin. His mouth, too broad and gaping when he laughed, was set tonight in a soft-cushioned pout. After a few moments he raised his head and looked up at her. His eyes were watery with something that looked like sorrow, but could have been something else. The blue of them seemed to pierce her very skin.

'Can I read you something, Mary?'

She nodded, afraid her voice might break the spell she felt sure the silence had woven over them both.

He took the notebook out of his pocket and began to read. It was a love poem. Mary shivered as she noted the long whiteness of his fingers against the black wool, the hilly knobs of his knuckles. Her whole body seemed to blush and yet she felt strangely calm, as if she had known that one day this would happen. Her reward for loving him had finally come and she was ready.

It was a long poem, and Mary had tuned out in the third verse whilst she tried to concentrate on setting her face into an expression which was appreciative of its content, whilst at the same time pretty enough to still be deemed worthy of such accolade. When she tuned back into it (in preparation for being asked questions later) it became apparent that the poem was not about her at all. It was about some girl called Sandra (rhymes with Lycra and love-ya, aside from that he had struggled) an English whore of a name if ever there was one. A 'bitter' fact that Mary was only to feel subsequently, for in the immediate wake of this terrible realization she was too crushed by the obvious competition. Visiting English girls were of an exoticism way beyond the most attractive females on offer in Gorrib, a list numbering some hundred or so on which Mary had long since placed herself in the low twenties. They wore the kind of clothes Mary had only ever seen in magazines and strutted about the town with a city-girl confidence, thinking nothing of indulging in a holiday dalliance with some poor lad then heading off back to London or Birmingham leaving him behind to deal with his broken heart and, more than a few times to Mary's knowledge, a broken engagement. And now one of them had muscled in on her Theo. Or hadn't. For the poem was undoubtedly redolent, in spirit if not language, of Yeatsian unrequitedness.

Mary was devastated. If she hadn't had that third Cinzano and 7UP she might have held it together, but the shocking contrast between expectation and reality was too much and she burst into tears. Not pensive dribbly tears that pride might hide beneath a carefully positioned sleeve. No. Out came a dramatic involuntary howl, followed by racking snotty sobs over which she appeared to have no control. Had she been more subtle in her sorrow, Theo would almost certainly have been too absorbed to notice, but as it was he got stopped short in verse thirteen and found himself gripped by that terrible masculine compulsion to stop a woman crying. He put his arms around her and got a good grip of her, praying silently that she would soon get a grip on herself. He knew, of course he did, that Mary was in love with him. But he had never assumed it would affect their friendship, or stop him confiding in her about his passions and dreams. After all, she was a plain girl and unpretty girls were, he assumed, by virtue of their misfortune, pragmatic. But the harder he held her, the more racking her sobs became. Then he did what any man would do when nature decrees he must, at any expense, stop a woman from crying. He kissed her. On the lips. He didn't mean it, and Mary knew that, but it did stop her crying.

It also gave her something to hold on to. Something

to remember when the dark years came after Theo announced he was off up to Dublin to try and make it in 'the arts'. A nebulous term that more or less covered his need to wear long black coats and and indulge in writing poetry. Mary heard nothing from him until he turned up one terrible night on the weekly farming soap *Down the Country*, where he had reinvented himself as the brash and womanizing Jerome Nolan. Week after week Mary tortured herself watching him trudge around some fake field in Co Wicklow before engulfing some fake female into the expanse of his Aran-jumper clad arms. After a couple of years, Theo was killed tragically in an accident with a thresher (showbiz code for we're not renewing your contract) and Mary's heart turned sideways in her chest as she heard of his imminent return to Gorrib.

'Got fed up with all that celebrity rubbish, Mary. Means nothing me. My heart's in Gorrib. Always has been.' That was just like Theo, Mary thought. Bursting with humility. Theo could have disappeared off and become a movie star like others before him. But he didn't. He came home. With his big lump of TV money, he shunned Hollywood and fulfilled his modest dream of opening a record shop in town. Swoon.

Mary had been about to leave for London where she had got a place at college to study beauty therapy, and Rose's sister had the room ready for her in Kingsbury. But, if Gorrib's good enough for Theo Malone, she had thought, then it's good enough for me. So she stuck around, got herself a job for life with the town council and started to wait again. Only this time it was different.

There was not a female in Gorrib under the age of forty who did not long to be taken into the jumpery arms of TV's favourite rogue farmer – many of them more than happy to allow events to go further than the censors of early evening television allowed. To put it crudely (as many of his contemporaries were happy to inform him over a pint) Theo Malone was getting more ass than a toilet seat.

As a woman who had been close to him before his current incarnation of returned celebrity, Mary was relegated to the back of the queue.

She knew it. He knew it. But Mary was too far gone. All of the regular samples of Gorrib male who had shown an interest in her in the past (and there weren't many) were long since hitched, and any that weren't had long memories and weren't going to stick their oar in again after she'd relegated them to the 'less interesting than Theo Malone' pile, especially given his new glam status.

All hope was gone, and even though Mary knew some healthy anger might propel her into action, still she couldn't hate him. For the time being, at least, she had to content herself with hating her family instead.

FIELD REPORT ONE

To: Christian Donnelly, Officer in Charge of
         Romance, Britain and Republic of Ireland
From: Archangel Gabriel, Director of Conjugal
         Relations, department of Renunciation and
         Hope, Heaven

Ref: Implementation of Service Operational Plan in town
of Gorrib, west coast of Ireland – informed by Corporate
Objectives as stated in (Year of Our Lord) 2002 Annual
Report under Strategic Development Plan, sub-section
six.

It has come to our attention that many people who
live in remote areas are currently being under-serviced
by cupids, due to the modern angel's reluctance to
work in 'unfashionable' areas. This is a state of affairs
that OHF is extremely unhappy about and He has
therefore decreed that by end of (Year of Our Lord)
2002, this situation be universally rectified. Where the
human soul has misguided an individual, or individuals, into an unhappy union and/or a situation of

unrequitedness with regard to the heart, the officer in charge of that region must prioritize action by either servicing the area himself, or in cases of particular unrest applying to Officer Saint Joan of Arc for a special Field Unit of God's Army of Angels. However, military action will only be sanctioned under the most extreme of circumstances – the so-called 'human touch' being the preferred solution.

To: Archangel Gabriel, Director of Conjugal
        Relations, department of Renunciation and
        Hope, Heaven
From: Christian Donnelly, Officer in Charge of
        Romance, Britain and Republic of Ireland

Arrived in Ireland yesterday via aeroplane as decided best start as mean to go on (see attached expense sheet). Intend to stay overnight in Dublin as have located a place called Cupids and am curious to see what contained within. Am concerned about my position in Gorrib. Applied two days ago to Saint Joseph in Industry and Fortitude but have heard nothing back. Perhaps should have gone straight to Peter in Divine Recruitment? Please advise correct department. Either way, you might see what's available. Still have the highlights so if possible I'd like to avoid anything too manual; e.g. turf cutting or herding cows. Job in bar or disco would be nice.

Christian

Expenses

Heathrow Express: £10 (one way)
Aer Lingus flight: £190 (Economy)
Taxi from Airport: €20
Please advance:
Two nights Jury's Hotel: (pending your reply) @ €90
   per night.
Subsistence: (drinks and entrance fee to Cupids's night
   club) €150
Bus fare to Gorrib: €45

Please forward to Saint Peter in Finance and Penance.
Ask to send courier-dove to pick up receipts.

   Note: unable to calculate total as Ireland now euros
but UK not (!!!!Why????)

   Will be registering complaint with J. Escariot in dept.
of Retribution, as he surely had hand in this.

2

'Ah-testing, one two, one two . . .'

Moses McGreavy was not a tall man. Or a handsome one. Standing at just five foot four in his mail-order stacked heels, his naturally curly hair (with the aid of a volumizing root perm) helped add another half inch. A short upper body and the addition of hair gel, of which he was inordinately fond, helped complete the impression of a wet wig on legs. But Moses was popular. Since the death of old Johnny, Moses was heir and proprietor of McGreavy's Bar on Church Street, and his family had been in the business of dishing out drink to the population of Gorrib for three generations. So by birth alone, Moses had it all going for him. Being an only child, he had inherited the family business and within a couple of years of taking it on was able to afford a modest refurb in the L-shaped bar, including a small stage and state-of-the-art karaoke equipment – an addition he had been fighting old Johnny over for years. With Karaoke Klassics jamming him solid every Wednesday, on quieter evenings, Moses could leave his mother Margaret attending to the smattering of regulars while he indulged in his true passion, song writing, in the comfortable parlour upstairs. As the man who had bought karaoke to the inhabitants of Gorrib, when hitherto their sole source of entertainment in the winter had been the annual performance of *The Playboy* by the local Am. Dram., he was something of a hero. The few bob from the bar, a comfortable home with a mammy still there to throw out the odd dinner, in Gorrib terms Moses McGreavy had it made.

But some nights, as he looked out over his empire, side booths full with regulars who were smart enough to get there early, then small tables brought in from the back grouped across the floor, each groaning with drink and faces earnestly selecting their croon for the evening from the photocopied sheets, Moses wondered if there wasn't more. Tonight was 'country' night – but there would be few surprises. Each Wednesday rotated a different theme: sixties, soft rock, ballads/old time and country. Moses had tried to up the ante by introducing eighties and indie nights, but his customers were having none of it – seeming to have an endless appetite for 'Rock Around the Clock' and 'The Coward of the County' – each old time night ending with Cozy Maloney's operatic rendition of 'My Way'. For all his efforts to jazz up the entertainment scene in Gorrib, it seemed the locals were, after all, creatures of habit. At one time Moses had hoped to use McGreavy's as a vehicle in which to perform his own music. Modest by nature, he had never wanted more than a small appreciative audience with which to share his self-penned folksy ballads. He knew that the *Late Late Show* and *Top of the Pops* were never going to be on the agenda, but all the same, there was a yearning in him to perform which, for the time being at least, had to be satisfied by his customers' regular cry of 'Mo-ses! Mo-ses!', his cue to get up and sing a Christy Moore cover.

It was nine forty-five and the place was filling up. There was Regina Malone, sitting in her regular seat underneath the red scalloped lampshade, which she had long since discovered showed her fifty-something pan-caked skin in a particularly flattering light. 'All done up like a kipper!' was his mother's favourite insult, the meaning of which he had yet to decipher as kippers, certainly in his experience, had no particular facility for elaborately appliquéd low-cut jumpers, in the likes of which Regina was currently displaying her wares.

The special guests (that is punters who could sing) were all up at the back bar looking for their complimen-tary drink of the night. 'Cider' Murphy had his teeth out to prepare clear passage for his pint. He was about to perform his weekly trick of swiftly wrapping them in a beer-logo bar towel and slipping them into his pocket when Mammy McGreavy caught him and administered a swift and unreserved smack to his knuckles.

The young crowd were in too. Ferdia from the post office was wearing the Elvis wig. Moses picked 'In the Ghetto' out of his collection – they'd start with him tonight. Clancy's daughter from Ballykenny was also in for the night, she did a magnificent Dolly Parton, and Theo Malone had also put in an appearance. He wouldn't sing – although Moses knew he could. He was on the other side of the room from his mother, eyeing up any fresh farming talent that might be in with her proud daddy for a family night out. He'd leave the girls alone tonight, but at least he'd have a better idea of what might be on the menu when the country bus ferried them in to Bosanova that Saturday. Theo and Regina always made a point of not appearing publicly in close proximity; 'Lest we might guess from his scraggy format what age the Duchess thinks she isn't.' Another home truth from the mouth of the irrepressible Mammy McGreavy. Near the door, which Moses could see from the stage, was that unspeakable bollix Brian Fitzgerald spouting forth to an audience of McGreavy regulars. These were the four or five 'unfortunates', as the landlady called them, who kept the daytime trade going. Each of the front bar stools was indented with their individual arse prints as they sat mute over their pints gazing at the television Johnny had installed above the pine counter. They indicated to Mrs McGreavy their requirement of a 'fresh one' with the merest alteration in expression, the exact change always left in a small pile in front of the empty glass for her to swipe, without comment, into the till.

Rose wasn't in yet. Moses only noticed her absence vaguely these days. That was the way it had to be. For years after their split he had waited for her to come through that door, so often that he knew every notch and scrape on it. He had loved her for so long, even after he knew there was no point, that eventually the pain had just crumbled into a sighing acceptance.

Moses had considered himself so unworthy of her beauty in the first place that when she went off and married somebody else he had thought himself at least part protected by the inevitability of her rejection.

It was the summer of 1973. Rose Davitt lived alone with her doting parents at number nine Church Street, five doors down from the pub. Being only a couple of years older than her, and also being an only child, Moses and Rose had played together as children until the buds and neurosis of adolescence had deemed it inappropriate. Then one day she had come into the bar with a rhubarb tart from her mother. He remembered even to this day what she had said.

'My mother said the rhubarb has gone wild out back and she's after cooking a rake of tarts. She thought Margaret might use one for the tea.'

She was wearing a white cotton dress, and the sun coming in from the open door behind her set her body beneath it into a glowing silhouette. Her long dark hair was lying down along her shoulders in a glossy curve. Although Moses was an innocent twenty year old who didn't normally register such things, he could not help but notice that she was wearing make-up. Her eyes were blackened with kohl and her lips dribbled with pink lipgloss. The young neighbour thought to himself, What is Rose Davitt doing coming down here all done up in a see-though white dress and made up all sexy like a Pan's

Person when she's just come five doors down the road to deliver a tart? So he asked her, 'Are you going up town?'

'No,' she said coquettishly, 'Why?'

'Only with you being all . . .' He thought better of it then. He knew little enough about girls but was aware that they were sensitive to the way they looked.

She put the tart down and slowly spun around. As she turned towards him, Moses could clearly see the outline of her breasts swaying. No bra.

'Do you like the dress? I got it up in Galway last week.'

Then she finished him off altogether by saying, 'I might go up town if I'd someone to go with.'

It seemed too much to bear thinking that Rose Davitt might have dressed up like this for his benefit. That a creature so lovely as she might be trying to inspire his affection. So he said, 'Right so,' took the tart off the table and turned his back on her. As he reached the door to go upstairs he turned around and she was still standing there. With the light he could not clearly see her face, but he fancied it might have fallen slightly.

'Be sure to thank your mother,' was the best he could manage as a parting.

Margaret McGreavy went stone mad when he handed her the tart and told her about Rose's calling by.

'Well, where is she?'

'Downstairs.'

'Did you not bring her up?'

'No.'

'Well go down and get her.'

'She'll be gone now.'

'Did you not ask her up town for a coffee?'

'Why would I do that?'

Margaret McGreavy and Rose's mother were great friends, and there were clearly plans afoot.

'Well, you ignorant fool, sure I don't know where you came out of at all. You're to go down to that house tonight and apologize for leaving that poor girl standing in the bar of a farmers' pub in the middle of the day.'

Moses knew that argument was pointless. News that Rose had a liking for him was taken with a pinch of salt. Moses knew that his mother harboured the misguided belief that every woman in the town was falling over themselves to get at him. She was an Irish mammy. That was her job. All the same, she might have been privy to some exclusive post-Mass gossip that he had missed.

So that evening he ironed out his flared denims and his flower-patterned shirt, flicked back the side panels of his mullet and went down to ask Rose out to the pictures. He could hardly believe it when she said yes, even though her mother was hovering threateningly at the parlour door.

They were inseparable for two years, long enough for a comfortable fondness to develop, but not so long that Moses ever grew used to the willowy curve of her neck or the languid watery way she smiled at him after they'd kissed.

Then that terrible night. She had been clearly preoccupied all through their evening walk. At the second bridge they stopped, as they always did, to watch the family of swans glide through the white reeds then potter up to the scruffy bank.

'Look there, some bastard's thrown a trolley over the bridge,' he said, as an experiment in breaking the heavy silence.

'I'm pregnant.'

She said it out – just like that. Looking back, Moses supposed there was no other way of doing it, but the shock was something he would never, not to this day, forget. It went some way to explaining his response.

'How?'

Her dark eyes flicked up at him briefly, then looked away. Moses realized then that she hadn't looked him straight in the eye for, how long now? Three weeks? How could he have been so stupid? How could he have not noticed there was something wrong? The only thing he knew for sure in that moment was that he was not the father. Not without divine intervention and Rose was a good girl – but she wasn't that good.

'Brian Fitzgerald.'

Oh the rage then. Fuelled by every snide comment he had endured from smart-guttys about the town teasing him about his height; 'Look there goes Leo Sayer – give us up a song there, ye mouldy wee midget!' – that Fitzgerald being the worst of them. He remembered nights when, mossy with drink, he and Rose had fumbled wildly at each other, trying to find another way of loving without breaking the codes of modesty they had been reared to. Always him. Always Moses breaking off and saying, 'We'll wait.' Protecting her. His precious Rose. Loving her the very best he could. Walking a tightrope across his passions so that she would stay true to the innocence that had needed the delivery of a rhubarb tart to initiate flirtation. Then this.

For two weeks he avoided her, then one day marched up to her door. His face still bore the stoic hurt of his rage and he came straight out with it.

'I'll marry you. I don't care. I'll raise the child as my own. I'll love it and I'll love you. I'll see the priest and get it fixed up tonight. No one will know.'

But it was too late. Rose was starting to show and her father had been to see the Fitzgeralds. Brian had denied it at first, but the Davitts were respectable Mass-goers and Rose, for all that had happened, was known to be a sensible, straightforward girl.

'You could do a lot worse, son,' Brian's father had consoled him. And that was that.

But it was not the half of it for Moses.

After the Fitzgeralds returned from their honeymoon in Cork, Moses was looking out of his parlour window and saw the two of them walking along the river. Rose stopped at where the swans were, and Brian tugged at her to hurry along. As she took her new husband's arm, Moses had a long hard look at Rose's face. He was searching for some retribution. Misery, regret, a slice of pain perhaps tinting those brown, almond eyes; evidence that she knew she had taken a wrong turn. What he saw there hurt him more than the pregnancy; more than her marrying the arrogant rugby-loving shit Brian Fitzgerald. It was a look of unashamed, tender admiration. Adoring – as if she was locked in a spell. The look that Rose Davitt gave her husband demoted the way she had looked at Moses to a brotherly fondness. He had kept on loving her after that. Holding on in that tragic, despite oneself way, which happens when love is given, then taken away without consent or apology.

In a way Moses was glad knowing that Rose loved Brian because, over time, it had helped to kill off his own hope. He wanted her for years afterwards, but he never hoped for her – and without hope he knew that at least his pride was intact and he'd never be made such a fool of again.

Twenty-odd years on he could tolerate Brian standing at his bar, knocking back pints and giving out about refugees. Rose would come in later and sing a Crystal Gayle song, and Moses would think that she was lovely in that way that he thought Crystal Gayle was lovely, but it wouldn't hurt. Not any more.

Rose was a fine woman, too good by far for Brian Fitzgerald, but then the world was filled with women like that. In his own way, Moses was grateful for the life he had – what with the bar and being generally liked in the town and his mother still alive. Things could be a lot worse, he thought to himself as he twiddled with the knobs on the karaoke system and worried vaguely about his mother belting around behind the bar like a youngster, than the habitual comfiness of everyday life in Gorrib.

3

Sandra tapped the black box to the side of the stage with the toe of her thigh-high boots and waited for the coloured lights to explode into action before sliding over to the pole. She needed all the help the disco lights could give her tonight to help disguise the botched Brazilian wax she'd had earlier that day. She was still getting used to the facilities in Dublin. There wasn't a city in Britain where she didn't know where to get the fastest most meticulous, relatively painless, head-to-toe wax job. Birmingham, Manchester, Glasgow, Wigan, for God's sake; she'd done stints in all of them, but never had she had this trouble scoring the right clobber or getting a decent set of acrylic nails. First up – none of the other girls working here were local so she had no one to show her around. They were all from Eastern Europe and holed up en masse in houses way out of town. Ten girls to a four-bed semi in characterless estates in Lucan and other suburbs. They brought their 'wardrobes' with them (nasty gold bikinis and the like) and did their own waxing and nails. Never leaving the house until the drivers came to ferry them to the clubs in the evening. Saving every penny to send home to their families, poor sods.

Sandra was having none of it. She believed in contributing to the local economy, and wanted to get out and about and see the sights. Turning down Randy Mulligan's offer of a house share, she'd told him straight, 'You can put me up in a B&B in town. Nothing fancy, but clean if you don't mind. It's only for three weeks and you can afford it. Besides, I'm worth it.'

And she was.

Sandra 'Valentine' Gallagher was quite simply the best lap dancer north of Watford. Born and bred in Neasden, north-west London, of good Irish stock, she had terrified her parents by simultaneously developing breasts and an unseemly level of self-confidence at the age of fourteen. She failed, in the conventional sense, at school, but excelled in extra-curricular activities such as disco attendance, smoking, Babycham consumption, kissing, 'necking' and worse. Frankly, by the time she turned nineteen and announced that she had answered an ad to become a professional dancer in a club up north, her parents were glad to see the back of her.

Sandra hadn't looked back since. She loved her family, and sent them regular postcards from wherever she was working. Stints in Russia and Japan last year had paid great dividends, and while she knew that her parents held their heads low over her career choice, she wasn't going to lie about who she was just to make them feel better. The money sent to cover the cost of double glazing for their modest three-bedroomed semi had helped ease the

Gallaghers' shame. Sandra hoped to have their kitchen extension paid for by the spring, which should, after ten years in the business, finally convince them that their daughter's voluntary, nay, enthusiastic public displays were not such a waste of time after all. Her mother, certainly, was coming around as last Christmas she had received a home-made fruitcake posted all the way to Alaska, where she had been working on what she called an 'out-post mission'. Most girls balked at the idea of dancing in an area where the men had been starved of female company never mind a come-on vision in a latex-G, but Sandra considered such gigs as her Christian duty. 'I've been so fortunate in my career,' she would say to her nonplussed agent who was used to lying through his teeth to get dancers for middle-of-nowhere spots, 'I want to give something back'.

Being the place where she had spent her summer holidays as a child, the decision to take up Mulligan's offer of work in Ireland was a sort of experiment in the same. But, the lack of proficient waxing facilities aside, Dublin was certainly not what she had been expecting. Cupids was jammed to the gills with just the sort of subdued be-suited sophisticates you might expect to find in New York. Not a sex-starved farmer in sight. Still, she thought, as she slipped out of her zipped leatherette corset and wrapped her left leg around the pole, might as well get on with it.

As she slithered down the pole, Sandra's eyes scanned the room for punters to target for a private dance. It was all very social here, she had discovered. None of your pointing out girls to the bouncers then the first thing you know you've got Attila the Hun leaning back on a sofa waiting for you to do your thing. The men here were easy enough to chat up, largely polite and often shy. Although it was early yet, and the loutish stag nights didn't usually appear until after the pubs closed. Even so, security was tight, Sandra had been pleased to note, and very few drunk and disorderlies got past Randy's dicky-bow boys at the door. The place was only three-quarters full, and the clients gathered around the stage looked harmless enough. Plump-faced accountant types; too many dinners and not enough of the other, thought Sandra, not for the first time. A couple of them were gripping onto their single twenty-five-euro voucher trying to decide which girl was worth spending it on like they were shopping for a wife. They were of no use whatsoever to any experienced lap dancer. 'Chit-huggers' Sandra called them. They were hoping that if they laughed loud enough, puffed their chests out and bought enough cocktails then one of the dancers might volunteer her services. Dreamers, God bless their sorry little socks. Some of the less-experienced foreign girls were chatting to them and Sandra made a mental note to put them straight in the small room at the back where they changed into their slinky socializing dresses.

'You'll waste an hour talking to some loser, and all you'll get is a fruit cocktail and ten euros. Cop yourself on and spread yourself around. The best punters are the quiet ones who'll take six or seven different girls a night.'

Then, over by a corner booth, on his own, Sandra

came across something rare. A looker. Thirty-odd, certainly never forty, not even in this light. He was well dressed, and subtle enough that he might even have the few quid. Most of the clients like to show it all off. Arms outstretched and legs akimbo, the low tables in front of them littered with wallet, keys to the Audi, rounds of drinks and vouchers so there was hardly space for a girl to perch a neat sequinned bottom. This guy was different. Tight. Huddled into a dark corner with nothing in front of him only a short. Malt whisky, Sandra thought. Not cheap in an establishment like this. Class. Loaded too, she had no doubt. I'll just get this set over and done with, whip on a black number and slip myself in there before the others spot him.

He was hard work, and after twenty minutes when he hadn't asked for a dance, Sandra was beginning to think she had made a mistake. She couldn't figure him out. She rarely got these guys wrong, and the Tag on his wrist, which he kept, rudely, checking, attested that money was not a problem. She'd done all the usual chit-chatting – where are you from, do you come here often, blah-blah, who gives a shit? – and while he was making some of the requisite noises he seemed somewhat uncomfortable. She noticed this because his fine, long fingers were playing with a single ring on his right hand and his transparent blue eyes were darting around the room and wouldn't hold her best seductive gaze. Or rather, Sandra noticed he had transparent, blue eyes and fine, long fingers and that the ring was not on the wedding finger. Sandra never normally noticed such things, and she began to feel a tad uncomfortable at noticing that she was noticing them. She was about to call it a day, and had stood up to go across and give a hand to poor Tatiana, who had been trying to entertain a gang of tight-fisted no-hopers clearly in from the suburbs for a Big Night Out, when the sandy-haired looker said, 'Let's get on with it then.'

She had heard more engaging invitations in her time, but she had just spent twenty minutes chatting him up, and he had a voucher in his hand, so it would have seemed odd of her to turn him down. Although, and here was the funny thing, she wanted to. Despite, or perhaps because of, the blue eyes, long fingers, etc., Sandra did not feel in the least bit like dancing for this man.

His reaction to her charms during 'Love To Love You Baby' by Donna Summer did nothing to contradict her initial reluctance.

He was like stone.

Now, understand this. Lap dancing is not always the overtly sexual act it is advertised as, and no one knew this better than Sandra Gallagher. Of course, you'd get the odd sorry fellow who nearly goes off his head at the mere sight of a baby-oiled diddy, and in some clubs where the security is lacking, you might be unlucky enough to land a hand on your arse. But in the main what a good lap dancer can expect from her audience is a genuine smile, the occasional erection (which experience can deftly avoid) and between a five- and twenty-euro tip accordingly.

And Sandra was good all right. She was the best and she knew it. Sandra danced like she meant it, the difference being that she did. It was not uncommon for her to become more hot and bothered than the clients she was dancing for, and the flattery of that usually paid off. The very least she extracted from the coldest of lap-dancing aficionados, businessmen who socialized in such places week after week and were usually just partaking out of a sense of duty or politeness to the associates they were entertaining, was a look of benign gratitude.

But this guy – she'd never seen anything like him. He seemed to be looking straight through her, to such a degree that she had to whirl herself around, engaging his face and her arse to see what the attraction behind might be. All that was there was the door to the gents and one of the dicky-bow boys keeping a cool eye on them to make sure nothing untoward happened.

Well, she ground and she jiggled and she slid and she frotted all over him until she might have been done up for indecent assault. Nothing.

When the music stopped, Sandra grabbed her dress and thought to herself, Thank God that's over. Then the big surprise. The Sandy Rock gently grabbed her elbow and said, 'Again.'

Nobody could have been more surprised, but the music started up straight away and Sandra figured she may as well take this chance to see if perhaps it was just Donna Summer and not her that had caused such an acute outburst of indifference in this man.

It wasn't Donna. But Sandra was pretty certain, by the

time her next three minutes were up, that it couldn't possibly be her. She gave him everything she had, eyeballing him with her best seductive glare from beginning to end. She slid up, down, across, behind him and sideways, clipping her long red nails at the edge of her G-string until she thought it was going to snap clean off. The sweat was pouring off her, but still, nothing. This guy was a freak, there was nothing surer than that in this whole wide world and if she was glad when the first dance ended, then she was doubly glad to have the whole thing over and done with now.

Before the last beat was done, and without so much as a 'tip-please' smile, she began to pull the dress on. Imagine then her surprise when, once again Mr Cold as Stone took her arm and said, more firmly this time, 'Again.'

Ah now, this was getting too much.

'Are you sure?' she said, barely able to keep her voice below annoyed hysteria. The dicky bow on guard, attuned to even the slightest tremor in atmosphere in Cupids's private lounge, looked over and said, 'Any trouble?'

Sandra, who had negotiated a bigger cut of her takings than any of the other girls because (a) she wasn't foreign and (b) she was 'worth it', decided that she had better let the show go on rather than have Randy see that there might be a chink in her abilities.

'No problem, Charlie,' she asserted sunnily, and turned, still topless, for what she hoped wouldn't be a hat-trick.

It was.

Sandra licked her lips and tweaked her nips and performed feats of virtual gynaecological guile and cunning. She slithered around the pole until it was sparking with static. Two other men who were being serviced perfectly adequately by their own private dancers craned their heads to see what the sandy-haired bonzo was getting that they weren't.

His body had not moved one iota. You would think out of embarrassment he might have even shifted slightly at this stage. But no. His chiselled features were still just that. That was chiselled as in 'statue' rather than chiselled as in 'conventionally handsome', because Sandra had binned any idea that this blue-eyed long-fingered client was a cut above and had begun to actively loathe him. To whip off her only remaining item of clothing, a G-string, which was well beyond the lemon-freshness it had been not twenty minutes beforehand, and shove it up this arrogant shit-head's nostril was an act that it would be lying to say had only just occurred to her.

When he pitched in again for a fourth time, Sandra was ready to let the on-guard dicky bow at him for some fictional lewd suggestion. Except this time he had the good sense to add the magic word.

'Again – please.'

The last word caught in his throat and Sandra, softening slightly with the notion that perhaps he was a human being after all, indicated to the bouncer not to approach, and sat down next to this strange client on the couch.

'What do you want?' she asked, looking him straight in the eye.

'Another dance,' he said simply.

'No,' she said. 'What do you *really* want?'

He wasn't able to answer that one. Sandra hadn't been entirely sure herself what she meant by it but could see by the confusion and panic that briefly darted across his face that it wasn't entirely fair of her to ask it. He took three chits out of his pocket and apologetically handed them to her. She knew she'd have to go again, but not without a fight.

'Will you concentrate please, this time, and try to give me your full attention. Please.'

To her great surprise, the man nodded like a reprimanded schoolboy and the music started up again.

Sandra didn't dance so hard this time. She'd two more sets at the front bar that night, and she wasn't going to knock herself out. If truth be told, she'd never put so little into a dance before, her hips moving just beyond a gentle sway across his lap. And here's the funny thing. A couple of minutes into the song, she noticed the man holding her gaze. He was staring right into her eyes with the same intensity that he had been looking beyond her before. She turned her attention briefly to the pole beside him, but his eyes kept drawing her back. The harder he looked into her face, the more she wanted to look back at him and the less she felt like moving. Then, to her abject horror and confusion, Sandra began to realize that she was blushing, which all but brought her to a complete standstill. Before the song had even ended she had the dress on, had issued a curt, 'thank you' and was marching across the room to her dressing room relieved to be getting back to the relative comfort of knowing what she was doing.

But it wasn't over then. The man sat back on the couch where she had first seen him and stayed there for the entire night. She saw him looking at her all the way through her following two sets, and could feel his eyes follow her as she walked around chatting to other clients. Once she had coincided with the strange man taking a trip to the men's toilets, the door of which looked out onto the private lounge, and she noticed him hesitate, ever so briefly, as he passed.

Freak.

At two in the morning Sandra left Cupids and began to make the very short walk to the Trinity taxi rank. Instinct made her turn around. And there he was. In ten years Sandra had never been followed or harassed by a punter. Not outside of the heavily guarded confines of a club anyway. Fear scurried through her like scared squirrel. His first words came then as something of a relief.

'I'm not following *you*.'

Something about his intonation made her believe him, although having now reached the rank, Sandra did not engage him with a reply. Lap dancers' code meant you never felt obligated to so much as acknowledge a punter in public. In fact, quite the reverse.

No taxis. Shit.

The streets were eerily empty, Mr Blue-eyed Long Fingers continued pottering about behind her as if looking for somebody, when a group of what could only be described as shell-suited savages came vomiting, literally and metaphorically, out of nearby nightclub in the direction of the rank.

'Oi! Gorgeous! Hey, lads, look what we've got 'ere.'

Cockneys. Probably on a stag. Rule Britannia my arse, thought Sandra, why must English lads always let themselves down abroad?

Torn between two options, one of which, given the high heels and the short coat, surely had 'gang rape' written all over it, she turned to the stranger and asked if he would take her for a nightcap.

He didn't look too happy about the company moving en masse in their direction either, so she took his arm and off they went.

They went to a large, understated but unmistakably expensive hotel nearby.

'This is nice,' she said. Then out of pure awkwardness and because it was a standard lap dancers' line, 'Do you come here often?'

'I live here,' he said.

He didn't expect her to sleep with him. If he had, she certainly wouldn't have. But Sandra hadn't had sex for a while and sometimes, when it's late, taxis are in short supply and conversation is running low, it seems like the only thing left to do.

It was good, but it wasn't a big deal. Sandra had long since given up on the idea of relationships. They were something she could worry about later, after she had seen the world and decided it was time to 'let herself go' and try for a change in career. She thought perhaps one day she might spend some of her savings on doing a college degree.

This guy had a fabulous apartment in an expensive hotel. He was certainly odd, but it was nice making love to him and waking early to find him resting his worried face on the cushion of her breasts. If he had left it at that, Sandra would have been more than happy with a room-service breakfast and a cheery goodbye and never seeing him again.

But he didn't.

The stupid man tried to insult her with money.

She refused in the strongest possible terms. Sandra wasn't a prostitute, and it hurt her deeply when men didn't have the decency to make that distinction.

And when Sandra got hurt, she got mouthy. She threw a string of language at him that would mortify a builder before hurrying out of the door, stopping only to let a man pass into the lift before her. As the lift descended, she took a deep calming breath to push down the reality that it was a mistake any man might make given the circumstances in which they had met.

When she got back to her B&B, unpacked her bag and found that the bastard had somehow placed the money in her bag anyway, she was furious. Disgusted at his complete lack of respect, she didn't even want to dignify his gesture by explaining herself. All she wanted to do was give the creep his money back.

And that was how all the trouble started.

4

Rose looked at her husband in tired despair. He had just come back from Galway and was wearing a T-shirt emblazoned with the logo of his latest campaign, 'KEEP IRELAND IRISH!'

'Snappy, eh?'

He was grinning from ear to ear and held out a crisp new T-shirt, taken from the top of the pile.

'Here,' he said with the humbling generosity of one who is proffering gifts to the barely deserving, 'is one for you.'

'Thanks,' Rose said, privately dreading the knowledge that he would expect her to wear it around the town as advertising.

She was feeling guilty because she had secretly hoped that Brian would overnight again in Galway. Last night, it had been just the three of them: herself, Mary and Davy. Rose had cooked up a special curry and they had sat and watched television without the continuous volley of abuse, 'Dreadful rubbish! They should be strung up and shot, the lot of them!'; that was all that seemed to come out of her husband's mouth these days.

Although perhaps it was just that Rose was noticing it more.

Brian had always had strong opinions. Five years ago he had led a local campaign to prevent a travellers' halting site being built on the outskirts of the town.

'KEEP MOVING ON!' the T-shirts had stated, after Brian had been advised that 'KNACKERS GET OUT!' might have been considered incendiary.

'You're right,' he had said after some consideration. 'The drunken bastards will run riot and wreck the town.'

Some of the more respectable committee members balked at Brian Fitzgerald's particular brand of bigotry, pretending to themselves that there were valid reasons relating to preservation orders and land ownership at play. But in the end, they all wanted the same thing. A homogenous community where the sleepy stability and pecking order enjoyed by Gorrib's business people and professional class wasn't disturbed.

Rose had been disappointed, and not a little upset, to see the five or six traveller families turfed out of the temporary site they had created for themselves on the main road into Gorrib. They had shopped in Cooneys Superstore regularly and she had always found them very quiet. Humble even, as if grateful to be allowed shop there without some manager standing over them to make sure they didn't rob anything. She noticed several of them attending Mass every Sunday. Tiny girls in big hoop earrings clinging fondly to the hems of their father's great coats as they stood at the back. Anxious not to cause outrage or offence in church; always digging deep when the plate went round. They were God-fearing and generous Catholics, and Rose wondered why the local priest never brought that up. Once, her car had broken down on the Dublin road. A passing family of travellers had picked her up and towed her home. Brian had gone ballistic, almost hit her in rage when he found out she had been consorting with 'the other side'. She hadn't even bothered defending them after that. Brian was too strong willed, and she wasn't. It was always the strongest conviction that won through in the end.

And now it was starting up all over again with Gorrib being appointed a refugee allocation town.

'What do those bastards in government know about the country? How *dare* they send a gang of no-good niggers down here because they don't want them themselves? They're the one's going on about Dublin being a cosmopolitan city. Let them take them in and bleed the city dry with their taking up hospital beds and housing so that decent Irish people don't have anywhere to live. It's a disgrace!'

It was falling on deaf ears. Rose knew that these outbursts were only Brian's practice runs for his rallying speeches in the community centre.

'This won't be a community centre for much longer, ladies and gentlemen of Gorrib. Dublin is sending the foreigners down to run our community into the ground. The community we have worked so hard to build up over the years. The community of our parents and our grandparents. The community of generations of honest, decent Irish folk. They are sending them down to us to bleed our resources dry. To profligate, as they do, ladies and gentlemen of Gorrib. To multiply and breed. They are coming down here and they are getting ready to . . .', then in an eerie whisper that put the fear of God into the dozen or so terrified pensioners who were largely in for the free tea and biscuits, '. . . *take over.*'

Rose didn't believe any of that was true, and the funny thing was she didn't believe that Brian thought it was either. First and foremost, her husband was a business-man, and if he didn't want the town filled with refugees, it was because he was afraid they might provide cheap labour for his competitors or, God forbid, open shops themselves and show up his own failings in that depart-ment. Because Brian Fitzgerald, for all his puff and pontificating, was a failure, losing his parents' drapery and stationery businesses, then spending Rose's inherit-ance on a poorly stocked video shop, which had closed last year. After they had got married, they had lived in a town house donated to them by an aunt of Rose's who lived in America and had decided not to come back. Brian had insisted on selling it and moving into a grander four-bedroomed place on the Dublin road, and the small mortgage they had had to take out was paid for by Rose's salary from Cooneys. Rose had managed to hang on to her parents' house on Church Street, opposite the river, but Brian wanted her to sell it to finance his latest scheme; some class of a nightclub. At least while he was concentrating on the refugees, he was off her back on that one. And, at least, she consoled herself, if he busied himself with business and local politics, he would have no time to be running around with other women.

Brian Fitzgerald had always had an eye for the ladies, and they for him. He had been heartbreakingly handsome in his youth. Tall and broad shouldered, his regular features and confident swagger had made him something of a pin-up with the local girls. Rose had never had any real interest in him, or any of his gang. They were the privileged sons of Gorrib's business people, all motorbikes and attitudes – hanging out in the Coffee Bean listening to Horslips records and being 'cool'. She had always been a play-safe girl, placing herself in the middle in whatever she did. At school, she neither excelled nor failed; 'average' the teachers said. Rose's parents were disappointed that she wouldn't be going to college because she was their only child, the centre of their universe. But it was for that very reason that Rose never wanted to draw attention to herself. It was also the reason why she always wanted to stay close to home, and Moses had been 'the boy next door'. While her friends were trawling their electric-blue lined eyes across the local talent struggling to find a Thin Lizzy lookalike to match their 'Purdy' haircuts, a 'good bet' who might whisk them off to the promiscuous freedoms of England or America, Rose had gravitated towards her neighbour with an ease that had surprised everyone. Rose had been a natural beauty. Never taking a chance on the hard fashions of the day, she had kept her hair long and favoured flowing 'hippie' dresses over the hot pants and halters that were scandalizing the modest older generation of 1970s Gorrib. Her limbs were slim and lithe, her breasts plump and round, and in Moses's raw admiration of her, Rose learned to use her body to tempt and tease. She came to appreciate her own beauty through his eyes. Seeing how he looked at her, knowing how much he wanted her, gave Rose a confidence she had never enjoyed before. For the first time, Rose came to understand what it was to have power. But however much he longed for her, Moses was strong. She was too young, he said. It would be best to wait. Rose kept pushing at his boundaries, teasing and touching, edging him towards passion overtaking propriety; eager to cross the line between girl and woman. Although she knew with every part of herself that he wanted to, Moses never budged. Perhaps, after all, it was that safety net that allowed her to play with her own sexual powers as she did.

Losing her virginity had not, in the end, been the intense drama Rose had been hoping for.

She loved Moses, but something overtook her that night in the Coffee Bean that, twenty-seven years later, she was still at a loss to fully understand. The only logical explanation was that she had fallen in love, at first sight, just like they promised in the movies, with Brian Fitzgerald. The alternative, which she dared not think about, was that she was annoyed with Moses for not sleeping with her and went after someone whose brash, bragging manner indicated that he would.

Dympna Glynn had been teasing her about Moses.

'When's the Big Day then, Rose?' she had asked mockingly.

'I don't know. We've not talked about it yet.'

'Yet? You're not *serious*, Rose. If you ask me, you could do a whole lot better than the midget McGreavy. I mean he's all right for the practice wha' but, oh Jesus, Jesus, Brian Fitzgerald's looking over – quick, quick, is my lipstick straight, is it? Is it?'

Dympna was awfully flighty, but for the first time Rose got to thinking maybe she was right. Moses had been getting on her nerves lately, hanging out all the time with that weird friend of his, Iggy, who she could sense disliked her, and who was, for some reason, lurking about creepily in the corner of the Bean that night, which only added to her annoyance with Moses. Her friends all assumed she was sleeping with the publican's son, getting 'practice' in for the Big One. Could that person be Brian Fitzgerald? He was certainly looking over in their direction, and while Dympna minced to the toilets on her cork platforms to redo her lipstick, Rose noticed that he was still looking. Despite herself she flicked back her hair and gave him a sly sideways stare. He came straight over. Dympna was fuming, but Rose was too caught up in her achievement to care, or even to take much heed of the macho brags of her new suitor. Having Brian take an interest in her might certainly put manners on Moses. And he *was* handsome and sophisticated with his own car. As Brian put his arm around her shoulder and led her out of the door, Rose felt excitement rise through her, thinking that she was on the brink of some new adult adventure.

It had come more quickly and more completely than she had expected.

He drove to the woods on the other side of the river, into the clearing where all local lovers parked their cars. She had never been there with Moses. It was too obvious, he said. Unromantic. Everyone knows what goes on there. When Brian kissed her, Rose was flooded with the illicit thrill of kissing someone new, and she ground her body into his. She hadn't intended anything by it. Certainly not there and then. Certainly not before professions of love were made and slow dances were had and flowers picked and hands held and all the things she was used to with Moses. Yet when Brian reached up under her dress and pulled down her pants, she could not object. When he shoved himself into her and held her head still in a tight grip, his eyes pointing up to the roof of his father's Volvo in grotesque, contorted ecstasy, Rose Davitt felt that there was an inevitability about what was happening. As if, for all Moses's professions of love, for all she felt for him as a friend, this was how it was meant to be. Through all of the sore, damaged wetness she felt afterwards, and even though Rose knew what she had done was very wrong, something about it felt right.

And that was how it stayed all along. Telling Moses – hurting him the way she did. Brian marrying her under sufferance, refusing her advances for the nine months she was pregnant with Mary. Meeting Dympna Glynn when she recently returned from London, 'Funny how things turn out,' she had said, and they had both known what she meant. With all that her marriage had been in between, first cruel, then habitual, now dead – there was an inevitability about it all that still felt right. She supposed that to be love. Despite all that she knew Brian would never be to her, Rose knew that she would always stay at his side. No matter what.

As she placed the printed T-shirt on top of the pile of ironing she had just finished, she fingered the paltry gift. It was nothing much but it was, Rose Fitzgerald believed, the very best her husband could do.

5

The thing about a nervous breakdown is that one never sees it coming.

The signs are there: manic working, inability to sleep, loss of libido, paranoia, but it's not until one sees a person suddenly materialize in a public toilet which one could have sworn was empty not a few seconds earlier, does one think to oneself, Hey – I'm having a nervous breakdown, and book into the nearest nursing home. However, such is the nature of this invidious condition that one is more likely to briefly question the reliability of one's eyesight, conclude that it is in working order, then spend the rest of the evening in a state of hunted peculiarity.

And so it was for Gorrib-boy-made-good and erstwhile property tycoon Dermot Leeson.

For he knew himself to be the only customer currently using the men's rest room in Cupids's nightclub – the type of entertainment being provided at the club required a cautious and confining approach to toilet facilities.

'Urinals are my advice to you Mr Mulligan,' the builder in charge of refurbishment had said. 'Keep it all out in the open. With those nudie girls running about, put in more than one box and mark my words but you'll have dirty dogs locking themselves in for a spot of DIY, if you know what I mean.'

And indeed it was in that single cubicle not five minutes before the incident occurred that our hero had been engaging in the very worst kind of self-abuse a man can put himself through. That is to say – the unsuccessful kind.

For Dermot Leeson, entrepreneur, gad-about and part-time playboy, feared he had become impotent. His current effort to raise the drawbridge came at the end of a six-week battle against the flaccid rebellion of the beloved member who had served his boss so loyally over thirty-seven years. Perhaps, Dermot thought, mournfully looking down at the crumpled object he now held in his hand, I have worked you too hard. We all need a break sometimes. But in his heart Dermot knew that the holiday had gone on for long enough, and the boss was getting anxious.

It had started six weeks ago with Tanya Pearson, an astonishingly beautiful creature and just one of a fleet of Dublin fashion models from whom the title 'Ireland's Most Eligible Bachelor' allowed him to pick.

All was going to plan in the penthouse apartment of 'L', Dermot's newly opened hotel in Temple Bar. Champagne on ice, soft music and lights; the usual text-book seduction clichés. Dermot, being in such great demand, found no point in taxing his imagination by providing an 'individual' service for each girl.

He had slept with Tanya a few times before so the subtle, arm-over-shoulder-on-sofa routine was behind them. The six foot blonde beauty had come prepared.

The effect on Dermot, however, was less than nil. Not to put too fine a point on it, if Tanya's efforts that evening had not gone unnoticed, they were certainly wasted. Tanya was not inexperienced, but no matter how hard she, or he, tried, Dermot could not raise a single hormone.

Over the coming days, two other girls had a go, both stunning and both ardent triers. After all, there was always the chance that the right moves might lead this dashing millionaire to thoughts of settling down. He was only three years from forty, and somebody had to get him in the end. 'If you're not in, you can't win' was the overall motto of his self-appointed harem, and sure isn't a shared bottle of Champagne better than a single half of lager?

But Dermot knew how fashion models talked, and after three attempts he decided to call it a day and take a different tack. Hence his opting to go it alone in Cupids. He had not built an empire from nothing (even though thanks to the new hotel most of it was owned by banks) by giving up easy, and no one, not even a little lad who was too shy to take off his coat, was going to stop him. 'I am not leaving here until I have had an erection,' he said to himself as he walked down the red-carpeted stairs to the dimly lit basement. A basic ambition perhaps, but one in which he was resolutely determined and so he headed for the men's to try and help things along.

After failing miserably, Dermot decided to take a best-be-safe-than-sorry pee in one of the urinals before going into the club. He was just shaking himself off when he noticed that his shoes had become infused with a strange white light coming from underneath the adjacent door. He blinked, thinking that perhaps his eyes were still adjusting from the velvety red of the club's bar, but then as he looked up, the cubicle seemed to glow, just for a split second, like a landing tardis. A man then emerged from it, hesitated slightly on seeing Dermot, then said, 'Evening,' and walked out of the door. After a few minutes, Dermot followed him out in a shocked trance. He went to the bar and ordered a whisky to settle his nerves, then sat in a dark corner where he could view the action and concentrate on the business of restoring faith in his own manhood. But he could not get what he had seen, or more to the point, what he *thought* he had seen, out of his mind. The man had been elegantly dressed in tight-fitting cream trousers. Nice looking, Dermot was alarmed to have noticed. The stranger had had that unmistakable air of meticulous effeminacy. How could he explain the white light? Was the floor particularly lit up in that area? Could one of the disco lights that glittered across this girl's body have shot a shard of light across the room? Did the bouncer have a torch in his pocket that he could have flashed momentarily under the toilet door to check for untoward activity? Where was the man now? Was he still here? What was a man like that doing in a place like this? Why had Dermot noticed what kind of a man he was? Was Dermot gay himself?

And so on and so on until three dances had passed without his barely noticing and the girl had sat down next to him and was eyeballing him in a manner that was borderline threatening.

'What do you want?' he remembered her saying.

What I want, he thought to himself, is to know how a grown man can suddenly materialize in a toilet cubic . . .

Then he saw him. The man. Sitting behind the girl to his left with a topless dolly grinding her torso into his lap. He was staring straight at Dermot with a pleading expression that suggested he wasn't enjoying the attention and was only doing it to get a better look at our hero.

Dermot froze. He looked straight at the girl in front of him, asked her for another dance and did not take his eyes off her for one millisecond. He could feel the man's eyes boring into him and was disturbed to notice that the experience of being watched had given him the erection he had come in here for. It was fleeting, but unmistakable. When the dance finished, he sat back in his seat, ordered another whisky and determinedly glued his eyes to the girl as she danced and moved around the room for fear the cream-trousered stranger would approach him. All the time his mind rambling across more mysteries. Why had he had an erection? Was it because your man was watching him or was it because the girl had fabulous breasts? Were they fabulous? Were they as fabulous as Tanya's breasts? Or were they more fabulous? Or was it because a man had been watching them? And why was he watching them? And where was the erection now? Where did erections go when they weren't being erect? Is there another plane where erect penises go when we're not using them? Like souls? Millions of happy erect penises frolicking about heaven, or wherever? Why was he sitting in a lap-dancing club thinking about penises? Was he gay?

After about an hour of this, Dermot thought his head was going to explode. He had to get a grip. Girding himself he decided he needed to find this man and confront him. But first, he needed to go back into the toilets and check out the crime scene. He looked around the toilets, but they looked normal enough. Standard fluorescent strip on ceiling. He came out and checked the private lounge for the man. No sign. He went and sat down, then another thought occurred to him and he went back to the toilets and checked the floor for hidden bulbs. None. The girl was dancing with, or rather over, some old guy. She was nice. Nice tits. As nice as Tanya's. There! He'd had a lewd thought! All by himself! A coherent, fully formed filthy thought with no outside stimulus whatsoever! So why hadn't he had an erection with Tanya? Why could he only have an erection when some strange man was looking at him?

Gaaaah!

Dermot decided to call it a night. He would go home, take a couple of the sleeping tablets the doctor had given him to help alleviate the stress he been living under since the hotel had opened, and wake tomorrow to another peaceful, if erectionless day.

Then, on his way down to the hotel, he saw him. The cream-trousered man walking past the Trinity taxi rank. He chased down the road after him, but as he reached the rank, the man disappeared behind a crowd of English yobs who were coming out of a nearby club.

The girl who had been dancing for him earlier was there, and she looked sort of lost and what with his being all hyped up, he figured this dolly might provide him with some distraction from himself, so he took her back to the hotel and they went upstairs to his penthouse to have sex.

The strange thing was that Dermot had the music on and the champagne ordered before he remembered that he couldn't have sex any more. Then, even more extraordinary was the way that the girl took over and they just sort of had sex before Dermot remembered that he couldn't have sex any more. In fact, Dermot got a full eight hours sleep with no tablet and woke with his face stuffed between a pair of strange, but very-nice-thank-you-very-much breasts.

If truth be told, it wasn't until room service arrived with brunch, for it was nearly midday, that Dermot realized that he had actually done something that he had forgotten that he couldn't do any more. He was so grateful, to God, the girl, whoever, that he did what any decent tycoon worth his salt would do. He opened up his wallet and tried to give the girl some money. He wasn't trying to pay her for sex. God forbid Ireland's Most Eligible would do anything so seedy. It was just a few quid for a new dress or whatever. Girls expected that. Two hundred should do it. Not so much as to raise her expectations, but not so little that she'd think he was a tight bastard and wouldn't come back again for a rematch, now that his fella was back on form. She was no fresh-faced model, but in the morning light she had a dishevelled last-night's-mascara look to her that was kind of sexy.

She threw it back at him, using language that was so unsavoury that junior sprung back into action.

Dermot was so taken aback that he didn't notice the white light slicing across his carpet from under the apartment door.

FIELD REPORT TWO

To: Archangel Gabriel, Director of Conjugal
        Relations, department of R&H, Heaven
From: Christian Donnelly, Officer in Charge of
        Romance, Britain and Republic of Ireland

Case Number: 666
Region: Gorrib, west coast Ireland
Named Parties:
Fitzgerald, Rose (neé Davitt)
McGreavy, Moses
Objectives: To realign a match made bad in
             Year of Our Lord 1975

Arrived Gorrib safely, if day late. Stop. As still awaiting
expenses had two occasions to manifest self without
authorization. Stop. Was not seen. Stop. Job in bar starts
tonight. Stop. Looks v. nice, thank Joseph. Stop. Acquired
additional case in Dublin en route. Stop. Severe case
involving moral ineptitude and impotence. Responded
accordingly but please advise as to where to go from

here. Stop. Named recipient of temporary testosterone treatment: Leeson, Dermot. Ends.

To: Christian Donnelly, OCR, UK&IR
From: Archangel Gabriel, DCR, department of R&H, Heaven

Authorization for manifestation cannot be given retrospectively, and while the department is willing to overlook this occasion in light of the mix-up over your expenses, I need hardly remind you that materializing in a public place on Earth constitutes a serious breech of conduct. Furthermore, Ireland, and specifically the rural region you are now entering, is a Code One zone which, as you know, means it has over-exceeded its quota of visions and miracles this century. Several highly respected saints have already been heavily penalized for moving statues there, so if OHF finds out a lowly angel has been running about with his wings out, there will be big trouble. My neck's on the line here, Christian. I'll cover you this one time, but watch it.

As for Dermot Leeson – we've had our eye on him for a while. He comes from Gorrib originally, so I'll contact Brendan the Voyager and see if he can't arrange for Leeson to be sent down to you there. God works in mysterious ways, huh? However, main priority must remain the McGreavy/Davitt scenario. Good luck!

Gabriel's not the worst, though he's a desperate stickler for the rules. Mind you, I'm no shirker myself when it comes to playing straight, but if I had a plenary indulgence for every time I've sent a memo and it's disappeared off to the wrong department, why, I'd be swanning about upstairs in a white Donna Karan two piece running the show myself. You would think that with every decent dead person in Heaven to pick from, they'd be able to find staff? But, no. The boss is too busy trying to stave off Armageddon. He's taken his eye off the ball and frankly it's a case of too many cooks. Departments? They've one for everything, from your basic whoops-had-an-impure-thought to full scale he-committed-murder-will-we-let-him-in? If you're upstairs, all you have to contend with is cloud-congestion but frankly, they've all the time in the world to be queuing up for forgiveness or whatever. It's us lads down here, on the front line, doing the Lord's Good Work – we're the ones suffering. Expenses don't arrive, so you're supposed to apply for a manifestation permit. So you apply, and they tell you Doubting Thomas is over in Lourdes manipulating pilgrims and can you call back in a fortnight? I mean, is that practical? Have they any idea how it works down here? I wonder myself, I really do, if any of them bother their arses switching on those fancy new monitors and having a look at the real world. Glad to have it all behind them if you ask me. Too busy running around being important. Have you any idea how many *saints* there are up there? And they *all* have to be found jobs. And they won't leave them. Take retirement and enjoy themselves for all eternity? Oh no. Won't let go. Sticking out the same tedious tasks, day in and day out for thousands and *thousands* of years rather than see somebody take their place. Spiritual one-upmanship – it's a terrible thing. So the next lot in gets to form a sub-committee, and then another sub-committee under them, and then next thing you know you've got a Service Operational Implementation Cabinet of Beatific Martyrs debating whether to fork you out fifteen euros to get into a den of ill repute. Newsflash, Gaby! If we cupids all waited for written permission to make ourselves manifest, the job, quite simply, wouldn't get done.

I shouldn't have appeared like I did in the men's toilets at Cupids, but I knew by the cut of your man that it was my God-given duty to follow him in. His aura was a nasty sludge green and my chakras went into overdrive as soon as I came within ten feet of him. I knew that here was a situation I simply could not walk away from.

The dancer I fixed him up with was a sensible, solid enough girl. Nothing fancy in the morality department, but then, you have to work with what's on hand, and I don't think I did too bad a job under the circumstances. Love at first sight is, naturally, always the ideal, but sometimes it's just not practical. This guy wanted an erection, so I gave him an erection. Not exactly the stuff of blessed sacraments, but love's got to start somewhere and for some poor souls, it has to be said, it starts between the legs. And let me tell you, manipulating the human body is not as easy as you might think. You can plant an idea in a mind without too much trouble, but there needs to be some germ already there for you to go on, and nature has set up restrictions of will and the like to stop us overdoing it. Ironically, Lucifer is the only angel who ever had the power to get right in there and take over. I suppose that's why he thought he should be in charge – but that's another day's work. So if you want to elicit body movement, even something small and basic, you'd want to have a bloody good reason, the havoc it plays with your system. On top of that was the unpleasantness of having a topless female writhing all over my nethers while I was engaging in the Lord's Good Work. Most off-putting, especially given my persuasion. Put it like this, by the time they got back to his place and the girl started to take effect, I was flipping exhausted. No rest for the wicked though, as I had to hang about the city all night so I could get back there the following day, manifest myself *again* and plant cash (which I had to make manifest yet *again* from Leeson's wallet – gaah!) in the girl's bag. The cash planting was a bit mischeivous I grant you, but it was the only thing I could think of to make sure she'd be back.

Then, of course, no money so I had to hang about the bus station and somehow find the energy to manifest myself onto an empty bus heading for Gorrib.

Martyrs? They don't know they're alive.

6

It was one of those wet west of Ireland days, Mary noted miserably as she wandered up towards Keegan's to meet Ella. It was also market day, which meant that the farmers were in. While the publicans and the man who sold wellington boots and woollen caps doubtless relied on the trade of their rural neighbours, the young women of Gorrib reserved a very special disdain for the legions of farmers who trooped about their shopping streets every other Wednesday. This latent hatred was born out of years of being 'asked up' to dance by blushing mountains in freshly ironed check shirts and Sunday-best slacks, and having to rebuff them Saturday after Saturday, year after year as the poor sods came hopefully into Gorrib looking for a wife. 'You're a fine help of a woman,' was one of the more flattering compliments Mary had endured over the years. For she, being cursed with the strong, sensible appearance of a young woman who could surely heft a calf out of a kitchen without too much bother, was something of a 'farmer's choice'. How she longed to have the haughty glamour that her friend Ella was blessed with. Fine delicate features that could cock a snoot at a roughneck from fifty yards and put the fear of God into them at the mere thought of approaching her. But no. Mary had the broad rosy face of an eighteenth-century milkmaid; a face that said she was just *dying* to be approached by a man with a couple of acres who'd bathed himself in Old Spice for her edification.

But there was no Old Spice in Gorrib on a working market day. The gentle splash of warm rain on unwashed jumper put the fug of damp silage in the air, reminding Mary that, despite Keegan's recent addition of cappuccino (or 'yuppie coffee') to their menu, Gorrib was still not Notting Hill, London, or indeed anything even slightly resembling the same.

The cappuccino was a disappointment. Frothy white coffee with a few chocolate sprinkles. Not indeed that she knew any different.

'In New York you can order a million kinds of coffee,' Ella said, then threw her head in the air and shouted across to young Liam behind the bar, 'Hi, Bonzo! I'll have a de-caf skinny tall latte – hold the cream!'

'You will in yer shite, yeh daft bitch, yeh,' he called back good-humouredly and she laughed and treated him to a flirty wink.

Ella had spent four months in New York last year, working in her uncle's bar.

'Mid-town – sure the craic was mighty, but I wanted to get back home.'

Mary never failed to be amazed that Ella had come back, although she was glad she had. She had missed her friend terribly, half hoping that Ella would talk her into going over there herself. Jesus, they would have had a great time altogether. But then Ella returned home early saying she'd had enough of big city life, and Mary had to content herself with stories and anecdotes about a place she had only ever seen on television.

'So what are we up to tonight?'

Mary was sick to death of going out in Gorrib. Same old, same old. She wished she could borrow some of Ella's seemingly endless supply of optimism. But then Ella had the advantage of having been 'away' and had chosen their home town as the centre of her universe. Mary didn't feel like she had ever made such a choice.

'Thought we might go to McGreavy's. We haven't done the karaoke for ages, and I believe they have a new barman in. Meant to be a real ride.'

'He's gay,' said Mary. News travelled fast.

'No!' Ella gasped as if she had never heard of such a thing. 'How do you know?'

'Mum's got chummy with him. He's over from London. Grew up here years ago or something.'

'Sure – we'll go down anyway. Do the old Patsy Cline number. Remember, we had great craic there last time.'

'It's soft rock tonight.'

'Jesus, but you're in a miserable mood altogether. C'mon, we'll go out and have a laugh, it'll be—'

'Don't feel like it.'

When Mary got the big morose head on her, they both knew who was behind it.

'Has Theo been skanking about again?'

No surprises there. The only surprise was that Mary still had it in her to give a shit.

'Some girl from out the country. Last Saturday. I saw him go off with her.'

This nonsense had been going on for years. Ella was torn between going along with Mary's delusion and pretending it was terrible and giving her a slap across the head. Ella had been approached by Theo herself, more times than she cared to remember. In truth, she would have loved to have had a go of him herself, just to see what all the fuss was about, what with him having been on the telly and all, but loyalty to Mary had kept her hormones at bay so far.

'Ah sure, it doesn't mean anything to him, Mary. He's only messing. You're his best friend – doesn't that mean a lot more than anything? Look at us.'

'I suppose.'

She hated it when Mary got like this. Resigned and sorry for herself. Her round face went all pale and emotionless and dull. Like the last bread bap in the bakery, left on the shelf to go stale. There was no jizzing her up when she got like this.

'Sure he's mad about you.'

Mary's face lifted slightly.

'Why? Has he said anything?'

Ella's heart sank.

'Well, no – I just know that . . .'

'What? What?'

'Well, you're fantastic. A fantastic friend. He values that. He must do.'

'Yeah, but he doesn't fancy me.'

Twenty-seven. We are twenty-seven and we are still having the same conversation that we were having when we were sixteen, Ella thought. Mary knew it too but she couldn't help herself. She would be having this conversation until they were both dead. That is, if Ella could stick it out.

'Well now . . .'

'Nobody fancies me.'

'Now, Mary, that's not true. Loads of men find you attractive.'

'Yeah, farmers.'

'And so what? Aren't there plenty of perfectly nice-looking farmer—'

'Oh Ella – why? *Why-hi-hi-hi* am I still going on like this?' Mary sobbed.

The ice was broken and they talked then about how it really was. Mary was obsessed and Theo had no interest in her. Whatsoever. Done deal. Forget him and move on. It was not a conversation they had had for the first time, but it was infinitely preferable to the teenage 'Loves me loves me not' nonsense.

An hour later, Ella, exhausted from talking her round, said, 'So. McGreavy's tonight. Glad rags on, see you there at eight – first in gets the drinks and grabs a table.'

Mary, her face streaked with tears, nodded, then suddenly remembered.

'Shit, Ella, I said I'd help Theo sort out his stock tonight at the shop. I'm sorry.'

Two hours talking her around and all for nothing. Ella

was raging. She picked up her bag, threw a few coins down on the table and stormed out.

Ella was all Mary had left in this town, and fucking Theo Malone was adding her to a list that already included her self-confidence, dignity, and hopes of ever snapping her cherry, never mind getting married.

And yet still, *still*, she could not let go.

What in the name of God was the matter with her?

7

'Well now I was coming back from Mass on Thursday. (Pause) No, I tell a lie, it was on a Wednesday. At about ten in the a.m. – no I tell a lie. (Pause) It was earlier. It must have been nearer eight because Wednesdays I go to seven o'clock Mass. But sure what am I saying? (Pause) I remember clearly now it was Thursday after all because wasn't young Father Donlan taking Mass? (Pause) I remember that now because he always—'

'Oh for God's sake get on with it, woman!'

Margaret McGreavy had the 'girls' in. Meena Murray and Breda Fitzgerald and she were all sitting in the bar for their weekly check-in on the local gossip. They had known each other some sixty-odd years but, at seventy-nine years of age, Meena was still considered the baby of the group. She had a tediously slow way of talking, but could occasionally be relied upon for a good story. The other two were glued to her every word, sticking it out in the hope that when she reached the point it would be worth it.

'Anyway, who did I see coming over the bridge but

Matty Durcan and the daughter – was it the eldest was with him? (Pause) Sinead? (Pause) No, I tell a lie, *Siobhan*. That's it now, I have it. Siobhan.'

She looked at the other two significantly, seeking approval for this startling revelation before continuing, and they nodded impatiently.

'Anyway. (Pause) Wasn't she wearing a lovely blue coat with some class of a fur collar. (Pause) And I thought to myself, isn't that a lovely coat she has on her. It put me in mind of the coat I was wearing the day Paddy and I met the great Bridie Gallagher above in Galway.'

False alarm. The bloody Bridie Gallagher story *again*. Would the silly aul fool ever get over meeting the 50s housewives' choice Donegal songstress, and more to the point would she ever tire of bragging about it?

For if there was one thing that hitting eighty had taught the elder two, it was that dwelling too much in the past was the surest way to your grave. The only thing, Margaret and Breda knew, that was keeping them alive at all was being abreast of the here and now. Listening to Meena Murray and her dawdling reminiscences was wasting what precious time they had left.

'She was always a silly girl,' Breda said when she left to prepare dinner for 'Paud-geen', the sing-song pet name she gave to her husband, whom, as her two friends were widowed, she apologetically doted on.

'Wizened 'aul bollocks,' Margaret said, somewhat uncharitably, after she was gone, 'and her gammy-eyed over him still, it's disgusting.'

They always attested that they missed their husbands

terribly. Although widowed for ten and twenty years respectively, Margaret and Breda were secretly glad of the break from the sock darning and spud peeling which forty years of marriage come to.

'Imagine now, having to go home and bother your arse cooking a dinner for some wiry 'aul flute like Paddy Murray. Eurgh!'

'What's for tea, Mam?'

Moses walked in just as Margaret was about to tell Breda that her son waited on her hand and foot. Breda's son, that vile anathema of humanity, Brian Fitzgerald, had taken away her son's only hope of marriage to that lovely Rose Davitt. It had been well over twenty years ago, but she still felt defensive that she'd reared a bachelor, although Moses wasn't fifty yet – there was still time. She'd known older men get married. Everyone in the town knew that Brian had made Breda sell the big house and move into a small terraced cottage in the centre of town – the greedy shit. But you'd pull a mother's toenails off round these parts before you'd hear them complain about their sons. And besides, bad and all as he was, Brian had 'produced'. As Margaret had no daughter-in-law or grandchildren to brag about, she liked to rub it in now and again that Moses was a saint.

His request for the tea menu was blowing her cover somewhat.

'Don't you know well you're cooking one of them special lasagnes for your mammy tonight?' she said, hoping he would take the hint.

'Ah right so,' he said abstractedly, before going behind

the bar to tidy up and check a beer tap that had been leaking the night before.

Breda tore her lips back against the hard downward lines that were etched into her long face. The baring of dentures was her version of a smile. 'That face is a funeral waiting to happen,' Margaret was fond of saying behind her back.

'I'd best be off myself,' Breda said, and the hostess fussed her out of the bar.

'Remember now, the three of us are meeting here again Tuesday to make plans for the finals. We'll win it this year if it kills us.'

The county karaoke competition was coming up and, although Margaret owned the pub where they were being held, she was still fiercely competitive about winning.

'Please God it won't come to that,' replied Breda, and treated Margaret to another one of her terrifying 'smiles'.

'The poor woman off back home now to that bollocks of a son of hers. I don't know why she let him sell the house although you can be sure if it wasn't for Rose she'd be living in a caravan or above with the nuns.'

She shuddered at her own mention of Gorrib's Our Lady of the Sacred Heart of Jesus nursing home. It was a loud, deliberate shudder infused with hidden meaning.

Even though he was a grown man, Moses was still capable of being charmed by his mother. He'd never put her in a home and she knew it. But once in a while, she liked him to say it. It was their version of a flirtation that had always existed between them.

'I'll tell you what now, Mam, you get the dinner on, and I'll see if I can't find it in me to spare you for another few months.'

'Ah sure I thought all that work was over when your father died. You're an old woman's penance, Moses McGreavy. You'll have me killed.'

Moses would have gladly waited on his mother but he knew Margaret needed to look after him. She was a bright woman, and had been called to teacher training before she met Johnny McGreavy and had to give it all up. There was no such thing as working mothers in those days, so she cooked and cleaned and crocheted and waited for the hoard of kids the unrequited schoolmistress in her longed to rear. She had waited ten years for Moses, then it was ten years again before she finally realized that he was to be the one and only. Margaret taught Moses everything. He could read and write before he went to school. He could cook as well as a woman and because he was reared in a pub, drink like a man. He was schooled in everything from Irish history to Latin and had a lovely sensitive nature which, thanks to his mother's peculiar brand of feminism, included a deep and abiding respect for women.

Margaret knew that, despite the mullet, her son was a good catch. It broke her heart that he was still living at home with his mother.

But not so much that she was willing to go and live with the nuns.

So she clattered off upstairs and left Moses to get the bar ready for that night.

The new barman was starting that evening. Christian. He was 'a bit queer' Margaret had commented without any particular malice. The McGreavys never had any bother with people who were a little out of the ordinary. In her day, Margaret had endured being the subject of snide gossip for being a 'slow breeder', and Moses had been teased mercilessly as a teenager for his lack of height. It made them both keep an open mind about other people's peculiarities. In any case, Moses was happier to have someone from out of town working the bar than a local. 'Blow-ins' were casual labour. They came and went and that suited him. He didn't do enough business to accommodate full-time staff or fork out for pensions, and this Christian fellow had a bright and breezy way about him that was a breath of fresh air. Looked like the sort of chap who would shake things up, and might even get up for a song once he got the hang of things.

And Rose liked him.

Moses had come across the two of them recently having coffee in Keegan's. He'd been in having the bit of dinner (they did lovely soup and sandwiches) and had seen Rose sitting with this blondy haired fellow across the bar.

'There's Moses now. Moses!' She called him over, and he blanched slightly at her use of his name. Years living in close proximity had made him adjust to seeing her. Clothes and hair fashions change and time can alter a face so that you have to look harder to see what it once was; but a voice never ages.

'This is Christian. He was just asking me where McGreavy's was and then you walked in!'

Rose had found a new friend. He could see by the way she was lifting herself forward in the seat, all ears and smiles. She had tried to confide in him over the years, but Moses had always put her off. She'd surely talk to him about Brian, and for all that he felt he had got over her, Moses didn't want to tempt fate. So he kept up a level of warm but polite neighbourliness until Rose backed down into believing that he didn't care for her any more.

He asked the young man (although he was strangely ageless) if he had worked in a bar before, and he said he had, although it was a long time ago in America. He was vague about his connection with Gorrib, but neither Moses or Rose cared much about that. There was a mysterious glamour in not knowing everything there was to know about somebody, especially in this town where what the neighbours were having for dinner was front-page news.

Christian arrived early that evening and Moses showed him around behind the bar.

'The baby minerals are on the top shelf here, in easy reach, then we've Cokes and oranges under them. Stuff we hardly use goes on the bottom so we don't have to be bending down all the time. Dirty glasses go in here. Watch now for lipstick smears, especially on the pint glasses. The clientele is offended enough at the idea of women drinking pints, never mind leaving bits of evidence behind them, and the ice banks are down here – watch now for the lines,' he said, grabbing one of a series of medical-looking plastic tubes emanating from two huge steel boxes. 'A couple of them are trailing and if you trip there'll be an awful explosion altogether. The stereo is up on this shelf here and I'll give you the wink to turn it down when the karaoke starts. Now, what else? Oh yes, this tap here is leaking, very important this, so if anyone asks tonight, it's off. The brewery will be down Monday, which reminds me, empty barrels go outside at the front and I'll need you here to help haul in the new ones. If that's OK?'

Moses looked at his new staff member, and could see from the terrified cut of his face that he had never worked in a bar before in his life.

'You've done this before you said?'

'Eh? A long time ago.'

'Ah right, well sure you'll pick it up again. How long ago was it?'

'Well put it like this, everything was in bottles and jugs and there wasn't the, eh, selection you have here.'

Moses was flattered that this chap thought his bar more complex than any American bar, but at the same time he was puzzled by Christian's obvious confusion.

'What was it, a wine bar?'

'Kind of,' Christian said, remembering the spit-and-sawdust speakeasy he had worked in during the Prohibition era in Boston.

'Ah, you'll be grand. I'll be here anyhow, and we have Margaret,' (he never called her Mammy in front of other people) 'and sure you'll pick it up in no time.' Then realizing it was only six o'clock and the first customer was at least two hours away Moses said, 'Come on and we'll head upstairs for the tea.'

Margaret was sitting in her chair by the side window. The two front windows looked straight out onto the river, but her favourite spot was the side one which looked right down the length of Church Street. From this bird's eye position Mrs McGreavy enjoyed the advantage of seeing the neighbours as they walked along, thus enabling her to assess from their choice of wardrobe a destination, such as Muscles' Gym (runners and tracksuit) or coat and courtshoes for Mass. It saddened her sometimes to note that the former mode of dress appeared more and more often these latter days. From their gait she deducted their state of health (Grainne Duffy's hip is playing up again). She was able to see who was calling on whom and occasionally she was witness to a doorstep dispute for her trouble. But there were no such delights today.

'The spuds are on and bacon's on the boil,' she said without turning her head, 'Ah, here he comes. Hemlock, the poor old soul. Who could ever have known he would come to that, he was such a lovely young man.'

She was referring to the aptly named local alcoholic who was wheeling himself up towards town and the only pub he wasn't currently barred from.

Margaret turned towards her guest, for in truth, she could hardly bare to look at this sorry example of humanity.

'You brought him up for the dinner then?' she said, referring to Christian in the third person.

'I've eaten already, thanks,' he said.

Typical, thought Margaret.

'Well, now you're here you might as well sit down and not be wearing a hole in my good carpet.'

Christian sat on the sill-seat next to Mrs McGreavy's chair and looked out of the window while Moses busied himself in the kitchen.

'Will he not end up in the middle of the road?' he said, seeing the wheelchair zigzagging carelessly across the pavement.

'Not at all, he's too cute is Hemlock. He's survived this long and sure it's the same every day.'

'What happened to him?'

Margaret was delighted to have a new pair of ears to fill. She drew herself up in the chair and pursed her lips in preparation for a full story.

'He fell off a building, although *some* say he jumped. It was in the year of—'

'Ah, Mam, leave it eh?' Moses called over as he was setting the table.

She whispered conspiratorially, 'Moses is a little *sensitive*. They used to be friends, although he wasn't called—'

'Mam!'

'Right then we'll leave it for another day,' she said,

throwing her son a poisonous face shot through with disappointment.

'Nip over to that cabinet, Christian, there's a good boy, and pull out the sherry. We'll have an aperitif.'

8

Sandra couldn't help but feel a frisson of excitement as she settled back into her train seat with her cup of tea and soggy sausage roll.

This, she decided, as she bit greedily into the greasy patty, was an excellent idea.

Not just the sausage roll (although it was delicious in a forbidden so-bad-it's-good way) but the whole trip thing.

Dublin had turned out to be a bit of a plague. She hadn't earned nearly as much money as she had hoped, what with the currency having changed, and that whole heart attack incident with the handsome punter had put something of a damper on the rest of her time there. When she had gone back with his money and found the apartment door open, she had just sneaked in, with the intention of putting the money back. As she was looking around for somewhere appropriately visible to place it, she had heard somebody come in and done what anyone familiar with the reactions of sit-com actors would do – she popped herself into the nearest wardrobe. Except it wasn't a wardrobe, it was the bathroom. So she sat down on the toilet seat and waited. A few seconds passed, then the man came in and proceeded to unzip his fly and take a pee in the handbasin, less than a foot away from where she was sitting. He could not see her in the mirror because Sandra was sitting down, but she knew she wouldn't get away with remaining unnoticed for long so she said Hello. He obviously got a fright because he screamed then collapsed, peeing in a magnificent arch over himself and banging his head on the edge of the bath as he fell. Sandra went straight to the phone and rang Emergency. When the ambulance men arrived she made a hurried excuse and left. Two days later she rang the hotel and they told her Dermot was fine and seemed confused by her enquiry after his health. Nonetheless, the whole thing had cast a shadow over her remaining time in Dublin.

Sandra had two weeks until her next booking and so she decided that rather than get on another plane and 'do' Italy as she had originally planned, she would take a trip down to her mother's birthplace on the west coast and revisit some of her old hunting grounds.

Growing up in London, Sandra had never thought of herself as anything other than Irish. Her vast extended family drank Irish stout in Irish pubs, went to Irish clubs after Mass where the men discussed Gaelic football and the children drank red lemonade and clutched packets of Tayto crisps. They broke Lent on St Patrick's Day, stuffing their faces with sweets and wearing corsages of limp shamrock bought from a shop in Willesden.

Mothers competed over first Holy Communion gowns and complained about English sausages, privately hoping that their cockney daughters would excel at Irish dancing and fill their suburban-semi mantelpieces with trophies and medals. They all talked of 'going home' one day; when they could afford it; when there were jobs to go back to; when the children had finished school. But in truth they were having too good a time being Irish in London, organizing Christmas ceilidhs in the parish hall and watching GAA on satellite widescreen in the Claddagh Ring in Hendon, then going home to the polite anonymity of their Indian and Jewish neighbours knowing that their every move wasn't being discussed and judged from behind twitching net curtains.

'More Irish than the Irish, your bairns,' her mother's brother Johnny used to say every summer that they went back to the west to stay with him. Her father would wince at the disguised criticism, always hearing accusations of betrayal, especially after he had had a few drinks. In any case, he didn't like staying in another man's house. It didn't feel natural, and he was proud like that. So by the time she was fourteen, her parents having discovered that it was cheaper and less painful to holiday in Spain, Sandra was going over to Gorrib on her own. Her parents were secretly grateful to have a break from their wayward daughter, and Johnny, not having a daughter of his own, adored the pretty blonde girl, with her hee-haw London accent and her 'mad gear'.

Sandra had loved every minute of it. There was a freedom there for her that her mother, ruled by priests and nuns and gossip, had never enjoyed, because nothing was expected of her. She was, by local definition 'English' and so the basic rules of behaviour expected of respectable young women did not apply. As a sophisticated and promiscuous teenager, certainly by small-town Ireland standards, she had found the locals' reactions to her absolutely hilarious. Torturing the local lads with low-cut tops and Lycra hot pants, there was one of them in love with her at every turn. Her Aunt Maggie was scandalized by the London teenager's outrageous behaviour but couldn't say a damn thing because Sandra always made a show of being the very epitome of innocent charm in front of her genial old uncle. Some days Johnny would take an afternoon off from the pub, bundle his niece into his Ford Escort and take her for a drive to the old homestead, a derelict grey house that might once have been grand, standing in the middle of an overgrown field in the middle of nowhere. He would tell her about her grandparents, and her great grandparents and her aunts and uncles and how they had all died, or left for America or England and that there was no one left here now and wasn't that terrible. Sandra would nod, then plan her wardrobe for that night and not care a jot about any of it. Except that she was fond of this whiskery old boy and glad, for some reason she could not identify, to be out there with him in that still wilderness listening to him reminisce.

Johnny was dead now – she remembered her mother going to the funeral. She wondered how many more things would have changed in Gorrib in the ten or so years since she had been back to the place she had been reared to call 'home'.

As the train moved across the county border, Sandra noticed the black mountain that shadowed Gorrib and its outlying townlands. 'Less than an hour away now,' she remembered her father saying when she had taken this same journey sitting in the back of the family car. She had stared out of the window then, as she was now, but she had dreamed then of lipgloss and discos and black-haired boys with wide blue eyes; the smell of musty jumpers and soap as they held you close and told you they loved you. She'd never noticed the way the watery sky sent funnels of light across the mountain so you could see hidden fields hemming its broad base, stone tracks leading to nowhere etched along its side. She'd never noticed the rich colours spreading across the bogs in confident clumps; the yellow gorse, swaying bronze grasses, purple heathers; the way the sharp, leafless trees looked velvety and soft in the distance. But it was as if this untamed landscape, for all its roughness, had somehow entered her as a child and lay sleeping inside her all this time, for it felt as familiar to Sandra as her own name.

This was the Ireland she knew, the place where her people were from. Not Dublin, with its English chain-stores and cosmopolitan clubs. She had sat on trains and looked out on landscapes all over the world. Landscapes more bleak, more exotic, more magnificent than this. But none had ever moved her as these black peat bogs were doing now. It was as if she knew them, owned them. As if they belonged to her, or rather she to them. Sandra had never felt that she belonged anywhere in particular. Home was a notion that she had let go of long ago. She enjoyed her life, but knew that was because she always kept moving. Everything was transient. Men, money, friends she made in clubs along the way, keeping in touch for a few months by phone, before they disappeared into the ether of her past. She didn't think about the past, or her future beyond the next booking. Her home was a suitcase, and a handful of trinkets was all that grounded her: the framed wedding photograph of her parents, a holder for scented candles, two brushed cotton pillowcases she had used since she was a child. She was happy with the way things were. She spent her money on travelling, saved some and sent the rest home. And now here was this place that looked as if it had been waiting, unchanged, for her return, whispering to her across continents, appealing to a part of her she hadn't known was there.

As the train moved clumsily past the bogs and boureens a desperate déjà-vu overwhelmed her and she began to cry.

Pressing her head to the window so that the other passengers wouldn't see her, Sandra didn't notice a sandy-haired man passing her on his way to the buffet car.

9

Two weeks on and Dermot was dreaming about the days when not being able to have an erection was his biggest problem. Or rather, he would have dreamt of it, were he able to enjoy the luxury of a single night's sleep.

It had all gone: the hotel, the penthouse apartment. He had managed to hang on to a few rental properties and was not exactly at the tin-cup-and-coat-tied-with-baling-twine stage, but Dermot's fortune was nonetheless greatly reduced and so was his ever-dwindling supply of self-confidence. And he could trace it *all* back to that night in Cupids.

Sex, he decided, had been his undoing. The lack of it, then the search for it, but most of all, the consummation of it. If he had left well alone, none of this would have happened. Perhaps his lack of performance had been a sign from God to knock it on the head altogether. No man had the right to everything. The more he followed that line of thinking, the more sense it made. That English girl had surely been in the employ of some dark force, throwing him off track as she did. She was a lap dancer – obviously no job for a nice respectable girl, and moreover, she was English.

He should have listened to his instincts that night, although instincts are always so much stronger in retrospect. The way she had bullied him into four dances – *four* – when one would have surely done the trick. Then followed him home, seduced him and, here was the crunch, *refused* his money. Like he was insulting her when he was only trying to do the decent thing. Then, *then*, when he had gone to his wallet later and found that the money was gone – she had obviously stolen it – did he have his locks changed? No. Like the stupid innocent eejit he was, he hadn't thought. He might have known she'd be back.

Dermot's Merc had broken down in Athlone. He had forgotten to get it serviced (he was forgetting a lot of things these days) and the garage said it would be an overnight job. The option of spending the night in this strange town was not one he relished, so he decided to take a train the rest of the way and come back for the car in a few days.

Unprepared, with neither book nor newspaper, Dermot stared out of the window and went back through that terrible twenty-four hours looking for clues as to how he might have done things differently.

After the night spent with Satan's daughter, he had rushed out of the door remembering he had a lunchtime meeting downstairs. It was with three members of the consortium of backers for the hotel, and they were not in good form. The building had gone over budget by nearly two million, and the projected bookings for the next six months were not as healthy as they had hoped. Dermot knew that if they held their nerve and gave it some time, the investment would pay off, but as he tried to convince them he began to feel queasy. He ate nothing, then tried to settle his stomach with a small brandy, which burned back up his gullet almost as soon as it went down. As he ran retching to the toilet he heard one of them say nastily, 'Hasn't got the stomach for it, poor lad.' The others laughed although Dermot knew that it wasn't a joke. He had one of his dizzy 'turns' in the bathroom, then splashed his face and went back out. After he gave them some lad-chat about a 'heavy night last night', they seemed vaguely reassured, but by the end of the lunch no promises had been made. On the way back through reception, the concierge held out his keys telling him he had dropped them on his way to the lunch. Dermot then remembered that he hadn't locked the door upstairs and he needed a pee and the lift door was open, so up he went. Sure enough, the door to the apartment was wide open. He tutted at himself and headed for the bathroom, and with the contents of his meeting still banging about in his brain, he absent-mindedly unzipped his fly and stood over the sink. Surely not a crime in your own home? Surely not so grave an offence against nature that he deserved what happened next?

A disembodied voice, a female voice, a voice tinged with the unmistakable slant of Lucifer said, 'Hello.' The turn that overcame him was worse than any of the minor dizzy fits that he had been experiencing over the past few weeks. They were, the doctor had told him, merely stress. This one was accompanied by heart palpitations that he felt certain (in the dramatic way that men believe a head cold is Hong Kong flu) were heralding his imminent death. In a grommety voice he managed to stutter, 'Heart attack.' That put manners on the girl, as she dropped the cash she had evidently come back for, and ran to the other room to call for an ambulance. By the time it arrived, Dermot was feeling the bump on his head all right, although the palpitations had passed. But he stayed where he was, partly because the girl was still pacing about next door and he was worried about what else she might do to him. Also, in a perverse way, he was slightly disappointed that he hadn't had a heart attack after all and was worried that the ambulance men would be annoyed at his wasting their time. Indeed, when two burly men did finally belt into his bathroom with their drips and their breathing apparatus and found a man who was, effectively, pretending to be asleep on his own bathroom floor, they were not overly impressed. Fortunately, it was not Dezzie and Anto's first day on the job, and they had their own way of rousing embarrassed false-alarmers into action.

'Oh dear, I think this calls for an emergency anusocotomy. Anto, pass me the tube there while I flip him over and see if I can find an opening.'

A hand administered to the underside of Dermot's supine body was all it took to get him sitting upright of his own volition.

'It's a miracle!' Dezzie exclaimed, not without a hint of sarcasm. But they decided that Dermot looked pale and shaken enough to warrant giving him a lift to the hospital for a checkout all the same.

How mortified was Dermot sitting alone in the back of an ambulance? Especially when Anto cheerily announced, 'Was tha' your mot that called us?'

'No – just a friend,' he answered primly.

'Ah yeah. Wouldn't be the first time we've been called out on a case like tha' now is it, Anto?'

'No indeed, Dez. And might I say that little lady would put the heart cross-ways in any man, myself included. Howz about you, Dezzie?'

'Oh yes a very nice bit of stuff indeed. I wouldn't blame you for . . .'

Before Dermot was added to the hospital canteen list of anecdotes entitled 'Sexual Mishaps Warranting Emergency Medical Attention' he announced, 'We weren't having sex.'

In the ten minutes of formal silence that continued for the duration of their journey, Dermot assumed that they believed him, which actually worried him more.

⬭

By the time they got to the hospital, Dermot was starting to feel the palpitations coming back again and Dezzie and Anto had to earn their keep by helping him into casualty.

Almost immediately after sitting down, a tall and impossibly good-looking doctor walked into the waiting room and called, 'Is there a Dermot Leeson here?' in an unmistakably effeminate tone. Everyone looked around at Dermot as he stood up. Most of them had been waiting for hours and this chap hadn't even been up to the desk and signed in. This passed Dermot's notice as, being an important kind of a guy, he was used to first-class treatment.

Dermot followed the doctor to what he had assumed was a consulting room. In the event, shelving weighed down with gowns and cleaning paraphernalia indicated that they were, in fact, in a supplies closet.

'I'm a private patient,' Dermot said just in case the doctor had taken a wrong turn.

'Well, I'm a very private doctor, and we're very short on space so I thought we could consult in here without being disturbed,' he replied somewhat dismissively.

Despite his millionaire status, Dermot had an unthinking respect for doctors. Anyone who had endured an education that qualifies you to fiddle around with people's innards was entitled to conduct business in a broom cupboard if they so wished.

Dermot started to unbutton his shirt.

'No – no!' the doctor said so sharply that Dermot began to quickly button himself up again.

'I mean no – there'll be no need for *that*. Just tell me what the trouble seems to be.'

'Well, I've been having dizzy fits and just now I thought I was having a heart attack. I got these terrible palpitations and—'

'Stress. What you need is a long holiday.'

Either this guy was very good, or he was fobbing him off. Dermot decided on the latter.

'Fine,' he said, and put his hand to the door.

What happened next was vaguely disturbing and made Dermot suspect later that perhaps this guy hadn't been a doctor at all. Either way, it didn't matter because Dermot quite inexplicably and without warning passed out.

He remembered the doctor putting his hand over Dermot's and saying something along the lines of 'you are going to sleep', then nothing until he woke up alone in the closet what must have been some hours later. Despite the fact that Dermot had been assaulted twice in one day, once by a lap dancer and once by what he now knew to be a nancy boy masquerading as a doctor, he felt strangely calm. He got up, left the hospital and decided to walk home. Along the way, he noticed, as if for the first time, how lovely the plants and flowers were, and found himself almost skipping through Stephen's Green, where he said hello to several trees. Near the gates, he saw a tall birch that he quite fancied giving a hug to, and that put him in mind of the beautiful place he had grown up in. Why, he hadn't been back there for years. Not since his poor mother had died. There were lots of trees in Gorrib. Lots of lovely huggable trees. In fact, it struck him with sudden clarity, the trees and flowers in Gorrib were surely lovelier than these mani- cured specimens, which had obviously been manipulated by the hand of man. The trees and flowers in the country were free and wild, and they needed him. He would go there right now and make friends with the trees and the flowers. But he couldn't. Why? Oh, because of the hotel. Well, he would call every one of his partners instantly and tell them he was selling his shares, call the bank, whatever. It didn't matter any more. What mattered was talking to lovely flowers and trees. So he did. And then there was no turning back.

The following day Dermot woke up, relieved to be back to his old stressed-out self until he remembered what he'd done and made a desperate grab for the phone.

But it was too late. Dublin is small and rumours spread fast. By the end of the previous day deals had been done and Dermot's reputation was in tatters. It was official. He had finally lost it. They had all seen it coming. The dizzy fits, the forgetfulness, the 'other' – even the models had talked.

Two weeks later, Dermot was on his way down to Gorrib. Not to hug trees and talk to flowers any more but because he wanted to get the hell out of Dublin and thought that perhaps he might find something of his past there, something he could cling on to. Something to ground him. At least if he were going mad, it was better to do it where nobody could see him. For sentimental reasons, Dermot had kept on his old family home, employing a neighbouring farmer to keep an eye on it – although God only knew what state it was in now. Still, as the train headed through the flat midlands, it was with some small sense of relief that he found himself having nothing more to worry about than whether to purchase a Twix bar or a hot sausage roll to accompany his cup of Iarnród Éireann tea.

He was making the journey down the carriage next to his when he saw her. The evil lap dancer, sitting staring out of the window. He recognized the back of her head, her coat – everything. It was her, her, her! Following him! Stalking him! Back for more!

Dermot walked in a trance back to his seat and sat, his sausage roll untouched, shaking all the way home to Gorrib.

10

Rose didn't have many friends, and certainly no one she could call a confidant. Brian had the unhappy knack of falling out with most people eventually. He was tolerated in the town but not generally liked, a definite reason as to why he hadn't managed to keep a business up and running for any length of time. His wife lived, oblivious, with the fallout of her husband's social failings. Old friendships were subject to the avoidance tactics in which inhabitants of small towns are very skilled. A cheery but brief wave across the supermarket aisle; 'Up to my eyes!' excuses and a promise to 'get together' before the year's end. When, after enormous effort on Rose's part, a group had finally been pulled together, the consensus in the car home was always, 'How the hell does she put up with him?' accompanied by a resolution from the women to try and meet up with Rose on her own. But Mrs Fitzgerald was nothing if not loyal and, knowing how her husband loved pontificating to an audience of his peers, always took great pains to include him. He became viciously jealous when Rose went out on her own, openly failing to understand why *anyone* would prefer the company of his dull wife when he was brimming with entertaining anecdotes. So it was that she invited Christian around for supper.

She had so enjoyed meeting Gorrib's newest resident for afternoon coffee and chats. There was just something about him that she liked and, in truth, she was flattered that somebody so interesting and, by her standards at least, glamorous, should have sought out her friendship in the way that he had. They had met when he had come into Cooneys Superstore to ask for directions to McGreavy's Bar. She knew at once that he was an outsider because he had bleached-blonde hair and was wearing cream trousers, not a favoured shade for day-wear in this part of the world, where incessant rain and springy soil were enemies of the pristine hemline. She had been taken aback when her friendly questioning was rewarded with a request that she might show him around the town when she had finished work. He was from near here originally, he'd said, but hadn't been back for a long time and things sure looked like they had changed since his day. He didn't look that old, she thought, and his handsome looks and the way he peered into her eyes when she was talking made her blurt out, 'I'm married,' then she blushed, embarrassed by her presumptuousness.

'I know,' he said, pointing at her left hand – and she giggled and he smiled, a very nice kind smile, and she'd thought, What the heck, and arranged to meet him in Keegan's at five.

There was no getting around it, Christian *was* odd. He

didn't want any coffee, and when Rose, assuming his reluctance to order was due to lack of money, bought him one, he didn't touch it. He was cagey about giving out any information about himself, but asked Rose loads of questions, many of them very personal. The strange thing was that, although discretion was her middle name, Rose found that she was happy to answer all of them. In fact that first afternoon she talked and talked in a way that she had never talked to anyone before. There was just something about this new friend that made her feel safe and comfortable. She chatted to him about her family, her kids, about how she had wanted to have two because she had been an only child herself. She even gave away some of the circumstances behind her marriage. Everyone in the town knew her history, and even friends she had known all of her life were careful to avoid it in conversation. She knew that the way she had fallen pregnant and the press-ganging of Brian on her behalf was a local scandal and a personal disgrace. She explained to Christian that that was probably part of the problem in her marriage; the fact that Brian had been held back from fulfilling his potential as a young man because he'd had to marry her. Brian was misunderstood, she said. He was a lovely gentle man, really he was. Underneath it all.

'So you're not happy in your marriage?' Christian asked bluntly, with a peculiar look, almost like he might be glad of the fact, which made her feel suddenly uncomfortable.

'Oh no!' she exclaimed. 'I love my husband very

much, it's just that he's not, well, perfect, you know. But then who is?'

And then, almost to prove the point, she invited Christian over to meet him.

'I'll have eaten beforehand,' Christian insisted, which Rose thought was strange, but then he was probably just being polite.

The evening did not go well.

It started with Brian excusing himself from the table and heading for the kitchen, where Rose was preparing a smoked salmon starter, and hissing, within clear earshot, 'He's a fucking *poof*,' as if the infiltration of a homosexual into his castle was such a serious indictment of his own status that he didn't know quite what to do with it.

Christian did not appear to have heard him and when Rose came in, ashen-faced from the kitchen with Brian following behind her as if using her body as a shield from the airborne homo-germs that had surely already infected his dining room, he was sitting quite happily in the company of Davy and Mary, neither of whom looked especially pleased to be involved in another one of their mother's optimistic attempts at playing Happy Families.

Davy had heard his father and launched into an incendiary conversation about homosexuality and the church.

'Are you a Catholic, Christian?' Mary asked merrily.

'Let's just say I have a very close relationship with God,' was his mysterious reply.

'Not too close I hope!' Brian bashed out to the intense mortification of everyone but himself.

The evening went downhill from there.

True to his word, Christian did not touch a bite. He gave excuses such as he had already eaten, he was on a diet (Brian huffed loudly in fake amusement at that one) and was allergic to fish, meat, potatoes, pastry and basically everything on offer. He made a small inroad on a bread roll, which Rose, to her horror, later discovered he had spat into his napkin.

He would not even have a cup of tea.

Naturally enough, Rose took this affront on her cooking as an indication of how much he thought of her. But as he was leaving, Christian had embraced her warmly and suggested they meet up again the following day for a 'chinwag'.

Rose went to sleep that night thinking how sad it was that a woman of her age had so little life of her own that she was excited by the idea of a new friendship with such a strange person as Christian surely was. As she turned her back on the farting, grunting pile of blubber that was her husband she could not help hoping Christian *wasn't* gay. Almost at once she put the silly notion to the back of her mind. She was a married woman, after all.

PART TWO

mysterious ways

FIELD REPORT THREE

To: Archangel Gabriel, director of Conjugal
           Relations, department of R&H, Heaven.
From: Christian Donnelly, officer in Charge of
           Romance, Britain and Republic of Ireland.

Re: Gorrib update

In situ. Stop. Am staying on site with McGreavy family so please ask Technology & Information not to light portable handset monitor when sending messages as will look suspicious. Stop. Have made contact with relevant parties, both very stuck, tough job ahead. Stop. Fitzgerald daughter also showing symptoms of romantic distress. Will report further but may need help down the road. Stop. In light of this extra work, might be an idea to put Leeson case on hold? Stop. Also, any chance of exceptional intervention on my ability to ingest food? Keep getting invited for 'tea' and my inability to consume wedges of apple pie is causing daily offence. Need to concentrate on work in hand but find am expending excessive emotional energy disposing of tea in plant pots. Please advise. Ends.

P.S. Still no sign of expenses.

To: Christian Donnelly, OCR, UK&IR
From: Archangel Gabriel, DCR, department of R&H, Heaven

I am saddened to inform you that you are currently under investigation by the department of Manifestation, Visions and Miracles in contravention of Rule 179 that clearly states: *'Angels must not manifest themselves on Earth without first seeking a valid permit.'* As you know, failure to declare unauthorized manifestations within a twenty-four hour period can result in a suspension of your Miraculous Licence for up to one hundred years. I need not remind you what a serious matter this is, Christian, and frankly, I am disappointed that you failed to inform me in advance of two very high-risk manifestations undertaken in a Dublin nightclub and hotel, and that I had to hear it from a low-ranking Trainee Blessed who witnessed you on a monitoring unit from up here. I have pulled the stops out for you this one more time, but only, *only* because the task you have been given is so very important. I have asked Doubting Thomas to pass the case straight through to James the Less in Forgiveness. But I warn you, Christian, another slip-up and your promotion will be put in the 'undeserving' box for another five hundred years. I will also be obliged to inform J. Escariot in Retribution. That aside, I'm afraid Leeson is already on his way down to Gorrib. After your last report, a ground-force paratrooper from the Spiritual Awakenings unit was sent in posing as a doctor and I have been assured that our man has been softened up considerably. He should be open to any suggestion you might want to throw at him. See attached file.

As regards Mary Fitzgerald, you are right to be keeping an eye on her. File shows a surprising lack of sexual activity, especially given the century we are in. I'll ask V. Mary if she can't fix you up with a spare seraphim if there's a 'deflowerment' on the cards, but I'm not promising anything.

Will pass on info re glow-signal to Technology but do be careful with your handset monitor, Christian. Not being able to eat will be the least of your worries if some mortal gets hold of one of these babies and decides to patent it off to the Japanese. We've enough trouble keeping ahead of them as it is!

Mind yourself and God Bless (you'll need it!).

Gabriel

Ooooher, Gabs, I'm quaking in my sandals! Actually, I am a bit. I don't think I could go another decade in dreary England and, Lord knows, the hell this damp air is playing on my wing joints is punishment enough for anybody – even a heavenly one. I've to get this crowd sorted if Paris is to be a goer and I'll be honest with you, it's working out harder than I thought.

Since the whole New Age clause was put in allowing us to take note of details like auras, I don't mind telling you I've become somewhat unnerved. Time was if a punter was glowing like a beacon and had chakras like an unsolved Rubik's cube, it didn't matter. You just pulled their files and it was all what religion are they or is he a layabout and is she the type of woman to knock him into shape? In other words – can they live together, produce offspring and run the forty-year endurance test that is marriage without putting one another into the ground before their allotted time has come? Now there's all this politically correct nonsense about locating their inner angst, colours and karmas and all sorts of unquantifiable nonsense. Soul Mates. It's a noble concept, but by God it's hard work.

Example: woman walks out on marriage and three grown-up kids, telling her quietly devoted and very confused husband that she 'needs space'. 'All right,' he says, 'I'll build that new kitchen extension for you.'

I mean what do you do with a situation like that? Frankly, I'm with the husband – but the airy-fairy lobby is always going to win in the end because we all like to think that love is a mysterious thing. Even God.

The McGreavy/Davitt case was different though. They really *are* meant to be together. I mean, really, really *obviously*. They live in close proximity and like the same things and are both capable of love, so that's three of the boxes ticked already. So he's no oil painting, but he's a thoroughly decent specimen, and she's gentle and warm, and lovely really, if a tad misguided. That last bit most certainly being the biggest understatement of my career because here is the thing: lovely people marry vile people all the time. They can even choose to stay with them for long periods of time (although less and less so these days). But rarely, dare I say never, certainly in my own (vast) experience of such things, do they not know, underneath it all, deep down, that they have married the wrong person. They might stay out of fear, or that hideous PC concept 'low self-worth', or because they think they might upset Himself (as if!) or just out of sheer fundamentalist bloody-mindedness. But for a woman like that to continue to love and, worse, *cherish* a man as patently repulsive as Brian Fitzgerald, well let's just say it's *extremely* unusual. But then I suppose if the job were going to be easy, they wouldn't have sent me in. Then there's the daughter, Mary. Aura the colour of green sludge. It just screamed stuck, stuck, stuck! There, you see. In the days before the New Age Policy, I'd have been off the hook. But in all conscience I just couldn't let it go, and you can be sure that there is some odious toad lurking around in the background of her life, and she'll be in great danger of following in her Mammy's footsteps if I don't step in to save the day.

And then on top of that there's Leeson to contend with. His file describes him as 'consummate womanizer of currently nervous disposition. Time he settled. Quality genes not to be wasted.' And on the top of the report? Why – 'PRIORITY GRADE ONE'. Department code for fail at your peril.

Nice. Gee thanks, Gabs.

On top of all this, do you think Finance and Penance could stretch to the price of a pair of tweedy trousers and a rain mac? Is the Pope Jewish?

If it weren't for the few bob Moses McGreavy is paying me, my favourite cream slacks would be for the slag heap. And they say *we're* the compassionate ones?

11

Mary Fitzgerald was walking on air. Actually, she was walking on potholed tarmac on her way over to Ella's house, but the way she was feeling her boots might have been weaving through clouds kissed by angels. A car swerved around her on the narrow road, and let off a loud honk which made her jump. Just my luck to get run over, she thought. Just when everything is finally going my way.

Mary had taken a couple of days to get over the shock herself before deciding to tell Ella her amazing news. Her friend had reacted with something of the same surprise she had experienced herself not forty-eight hours beforehand, yet she felt affronted that Ella wasn't immediately delighted.

'He asked you *what*?'

'To marry him.'

'Theo Malone?'

'Yes.'

'Asked you?'

'Yes.'

'To marry him?'

'Yes.'

'And he definitely asked you?'

'Yes.'

'It's not something you just dreamt?'

'No.'

Then a thoughtful pause.

'Er . . . *why*?'

Mary was starting to feel hurt now. She had been so elated since it happened and now here was her best friend, a person who purported to care about her, pissing all over her parade. She hadn't told her family yet, deciding to save it until she had tested it out on Ella. This was not a good start, so Mary launched her defence.

'Well – perhaps because he loves me and wants to spend the rest of his life with me?'

Ella was not biting, and let it be known with a cynical, 'humff.'

Mary started to cry.

Ella took a deep breath. This whole Theo thing was getting sillier by the minute. But *marriage*? Mary was certainly obsessed, but surely she wasn't unhinged enough to think that Theo had asked her to marry him when he hadn't? Although one thing was clear to Ella. If the creep did want to marry her friend then he had some ghastly ulterior motive. However, Mary was unlikely to see that, and Ella was never going to convince her of anything other than true love finally coming her way, certainly not if they fell out.

'I-I-I-was coming to ask you to be my bridesmaid.

I-I-I thought you'd be ha-a-a-ppy for me,' Mary wailed pathetically.

'I am, *I am*, it's just, ah now, stop crying, Mary. It's brilliant news. Here.' Ella handed her a tissue then said, more as an attempt to look for clues, 'Tell me all about it.'

Mary wiped her tears expansively with her sleeve then, her plump face lit up with girlish smiles, launched into an euphoric recall.

She had popped into TM Sounds with some labels that she had printed up at work for Theo. A gorgeous blonde she vaguely recognized had brushed past her on the way in and she had felt a sense of dread, as she always did when she saw pretty women in Theo's vicinity. But it hadn't been what she had thought at all! As soon as Mary walked in Theo had said, straight out, 'I think we should get married.' Just like that. She'd got such a fright that the legs nearly went from under her. She had thought he'd gone mad at first. Of course she had. She wasn't daft. But then when she questioned him he said that she was his best friend and wasn't that a good enough motivation for any man. Not exactly romantic, she knew, but then it was true wasn't it? Then he'd said he thought they should 'get on with it' as soon as possible.

'Did he have a ring?' Ella asked out of badness.

'No,' Mary said undeterred, 'but I've seen a few I like in Keavany's window, will you come and help me pick one out?'

Ella left it at that. Mary was too happy, and Theo was

117

too awful and the whole thing was so dreadfully doomed that she would need a while to let it sink in before trying to sort out what was really going on.

The visit ended well with the promise of a trip to Galway to look at dresses, but Mary still felt Ella's cynicism. As she walked across the gold, glittering bogs that separated Ella's house from her own, Mary's mind began to mash through Theo's proposal, looking for a place to bury the scrap of common sense that was niggling away at her saying the whole thing was a sham, that it couldn't possibly be happening after all this time.

It was good that Theo had said what he had about friendship. And why wouldn't he? She was a good friend to him and wasn't that the perfect basis for a marriage? She was still a virgin and that was good. Wasn't it lovely and old-fashioned and very right that she should lose her virginity to her husband on their wedding night. Nothing wrong with that at all. And didn't it make sense of the fact that she had hung on all these years waiting for Mr Right? And Theo was Mr Right. Surely he was.

She knew he didn't love her. Couldn't love her. He was a sophisticated heart-throb and she was a plump, ordinary girl who'd hardly been outside Gorrib. But she would change. She'd lose weight. She'd get her hair done. Ella would sort her out. She'd make herself over good and proper and when the time came she would melt Theo's heart when she glided up the aisle like a swan. It was what she had always wanted, and now it was what he wanted too. How it came to be, well that didn't matter now as long as it was.

Mary shot through her own front gate before she realized that she had covered one mile and a half in almost as many minutes, such had been the determined speed of her stride. Moving forward was the key now. Not looking back. She'd go up to her room and start working on schedules and plans. Dresses, guest lists, budgets, hotels and the like. Get on with it Theo had said, and that was exactly what she was going to do.

12

'There he is now, one hour later, is it?' Mags McGreavy moved her gaze from the side window and flicked it across to the mantle-clock. 'One hour exactly. I know what you're at you filthy dog, and that slut living right next door to the Bishop's Palace.' Margaret tutted quietly then, for in all truth, despite her avid watch over her neighbours' comings and goings, sometimes she witnessed something that genuinely saddened her.

It was the third time this week she had seen Brian Fitzgerald furtively inch his Volvo from behind the thick hedge that hid Regina Malone's drive from the road. Each time, he had pulled it up on the pavement one hour beforehand and waited for the traffic to clear before swerving it in speedily so as he wouldn't be seen. Such seedy tactics were surely hiding something, and Mrs McGreavy had no doubt what that was. Brian thought he was getting away with it but then, as Mags explained to her new protégé and gossip conspirator, Christian, 'He was always a very stupid, *stupid* man.'

This belief had been recently strengthened when the

old woman had attended an event in Gorrib's community centre advertised as an 'Information Evening (refreshments provided)' about the incoming refugees. The locals, McGreavys included, being naturally suspicious of outsiders, were anxious to learn about their new, exotic neighbours, who were to reside in an old youth hostel on the edge of the town. The evening had provided precious little in the way of information consisting largely, as it did, of Brian Fitzgerald's red-faced rants about 'niggers'. Anyone who owned a television in the town, which was everyone, knew this to be an outdated and offensive term. It was embarrassing, not least when Brian's son (an enlightened young man) publicly reminded his father that the refugees were from Eastern Europe and were therefore unlikely to be of African origin and that 'nigger' was a term popularized by the Ku Klux Clan so perhaps Brian (he actually called him 'Brian') might think of ditching the T-shirt, which was no doubt produced in a South American sweatshop by four-year-old slaves, for a white pointy hat. Brian did not like that at all. Neither did he like when his 'open question time' was taken over by retired home-economics teacher Maidie Ward's complaint that the refreshments – as advertised – were frankly below par. 'Stale digestives and lukewarm tea?' she said, egged into a standing position by a couple of outraged pensioners who'd been expecting at least a sniff of sherry for their trouble, 'Is this what Gorrib has come to? Time was when that table would have been groaning with warm scones and smoked salmon pâté and *rhubarb* tarts. *Home-made* mind.'

The evening ended with the setting up of an official Gorrib Catering Committee to help organize a welcoming party for the refugees.

In the event the party never happened. The refugees arrived without fanfare and numbered some twenty or so young men and women and a smattering of children – hardly the invasion of Brian Fitzgerald's nightmares. They kept to themselves for the first while, no doubt unnerved by the 'NO REFUGEES' posters, which Brian had strapped to every available lamp post. But after a couple of weeks the posters faded and fell, and the newcomers had become part of the human landscape, attracting neither undue comment nor criticism.

'Have you seen what they've done to the youth hostel gardens?' Margaret asked Christian, who had taken up her place at the window in a relay motion while she had regaled him with the story of the community centre debacle whilst putting the tea on. 'Dug the whole thing up already and making a fine job of it. I'll tell you, them 'fugees can work, they can surely. You'd want to mind your step young man or we'll have them below in the bar and you'll be out of a job!'

Christian was watching a young woman walk, or rather writhe sexily up the street in a manner that was more Marilyn Monroe than Mary Mulligan. She was wearing high-heeled boots, a low-slung top and a pair of outsized sunglasses that, being an avid reader of *Vogue*, Christian recognized as being in the style of Gucci circa spring/summer 2000. She did not, in any case, look local and Christian called out, 'Who's this?'

Mags wriggled him out of her seat, taking up the challenge of knowing every last person in this town.

'Well now,' she said, puzzled, 'I don't know and that's the truth although . . .' then, peering more closely so that her nose was almost pressed to the glass, 'no, surely, it couldn't be?' She was silent for a few seconds, watching intently as the girl drew closer, then, her voice shaking with shock and emotion, exclaimed, 'Well sacred heart of Jesus. Moses – MOSEZZ!' she shouted down to the bar, 'MOSES, THAT MAD ENGLISH GIRL IS BACK IN TOWN!'

Moses hadn't seen Sandra for years, since she was about eighteen. He'd have said that she'd grown except that she always had been a very well-developed girl. He liked her. She had been full of mischief and not a touch of badness, always an attractive quality in a young woman. Although when your first cousin is trawling around your house seductively in barely more than lipgloss and leggings, it can be a discombobulating state of affairs. Moses always treated Sandra like a sister because they were related and she was younger than him and he was a nice person and already had a girlfriend in Rose. But when the lights were off, prayers said and the mind feels free to meander off into those dark corners where your Bad Thoughts hide, Moses often wondered what it would be like to call young Sandra out on her flirtations, and what she would do if he did what she seemed to be asking him, and indeed every man in the town, to do to her.

'Well, how's it going, Sandra? You're very welcome,' he said just as his mother was shouting her warning down to him.

She laughed and said, 'Aunt Maggie hasn't changed then?'

'Indeed no,' he said, not as embarrassed as perhaps he should have been. 'Nothing much changes around here.'

'Including your hair,' Sandra quipped.

'No indeed,' he said, touching it a tad self-consciously. 'Come in, come in,' he added, although she was already inside the pub. 'Will you have a drink?'

'Suppose I'd better,' Sandra said, 'before I face your mother.'

'Oh don't mind her,' Moses said, lifting the hatch. 'What'll it be?'

'Bacardi and Coke thanks. Is it just the two of you here? I was sorry to hear about Johnny.'

'Ah yeah,' he said and they fell into a few seconds silence out of deference to his father's memory. 'Will you be staying?'

'Ah no.' Sandra was surprised to hear her words had suddenly become accented with the local singsong.

'There's plenty of room upstairs. We've a guest at the moment but there's another room. We had an en suite put in since you were last here. You're more than welc—'

'IS SHE GONE YET MOSES? MOSES?'

'YES, MAM, I HEARD YOU!' He turned back to Sandra. 'I'm sorry. You know Mam she's . . .' he trailed off, unable to put words on what his mother was.

'I've rented a house down the road. It's grand,' (there was that colloquial stuff again!) 'Small holiday cottage, you know. Nice.'

'So you're staying around?'

'For a few weeks anyway.'

'MOSES! DID YE HEAR ME? IS SHE GONE PAST YET?'

'Ah here,' he said, coming out from behind the counter. 'Get that drink into you and we might as well go up and get Mam over and done with.'

Sandra laughed heartily as Moses somehow knew she would, even after all this time. People's disapproval never phased her. After all, she took her clothes off for a living and Margaret McGreavy was a small challenge for a woman like that.

13

Dermot was pleasantly surprised when he arrived at his mother's house. Actually, he was astonished. The neighbouring farmer, who had been keeping an eye on the place since his mother's death, had kept the house in perfect condition. The windows of the old schoolhouse had been given a fresh lick of gloss and even in his nervously diminished state, Dermot noted that several roof tiles had been recently replaced and the chimney repointed. A bag of turf was standing at the front door under the porch awning and poking out of the top of it was a damp note on which was scrawled: Please find key under coal bucket in shed.

Lord knows how long the note had been there but then the likelihood of the house being ransacked for a few ornaments and his mother's old clothes was slim in these parts.

Dermot had been unnerved by seeing the lap dancer on the train, but had managed to allay another panic attack by talking himself down from his initial stalking theory. After all, Ireland was a small country, and those kinds of coincidences happened all the time. There were plenty of other places she could have been going to along the way and the train terminated in Galway – so there was his answer. All the same he had to stop himself looking around to check she didn't get off the train after him, and it was with his paranoia firmly in check that he marched determinedly towards the lone taxi that sat expectantly in the station forecourt.

Accustomed to flopping into the back of Dublin cabs and disengaging himself from the rantings of city drivers with a stony silence, the five-mile journey from the town centre had been something of an ordeal.

'Yore down from Dublin, is it?'

Dermot responded with silence, but for the honour of being a paid passenger in this 1993 Ford Estate, information was required.

'Is it Dublin yore down from then?'

'Yes.'

'On your holidays, is it?'

'Yes.'

'You'll have rented one of them holiday cottages so above at Kinvinra – I believe they're beautiful but an awful price?'

'No.'

'Yore staying with people then?'

'No.'

The car had speeded up to over thirty miles an hour to pass a chasing dog, but then slowed back down to a virtual halt. As the car lumbered back into second gear, Dermot could feel the tyranny of the driver's curiosity and knew if he didn't offer something, they'd be unlikely to make the five-mile journey before nightfall.

'I've a house there.'

The driver launched back into third but kept the car at a steady twenty.

'Yore from round here?'

'Yes.'

'A grand spot.'

'Yes.'

'And have you any people round here still?'

'No.'

'And are you . . .'

Dermot couldn't hack it any longer.

'Listen,' he said, 'I don't mean to be rude but I've had a long journey and I'd just as soon get there, if you don't mind.'

The driver evidently did, as he put his foot down flat to the floor causing Dermot borderline whiplash as he sped the cab along the one-car countryside roads, narrowly missing a tractor, an old man on a bicycle and a sheep that had wandered through a gap in the hedgerow. More alarming than this, by far, was the way he pulled up with a sudden halt outside the Leeson homestead before Dermot had got his own bearings.

'That'll be twelve euros,' he said curtly, barely giving Dermot a chance to absorb the fact that, despite the interrogation, this complete stranger obviously knew where his house was, which was more than he knew himself.

Dermot should have known the ways of the people

around here better than he did. He was, by everyone's definition but his own, a native of the area. A member of their tribe. Not just a member but a treasured son, given the public appraisal of his success in business and his regular appearances in Sunday social columns.

Inside, the house was cold and smelt faintly of damp. Otherwise, it was exactly as it had always been. After his mother's funeral, Dermot had simply walked away leaving everything as it was. He had no sisters to tearfully sort through her personal belongings and put them in bags for the Vincent de Paul. No brothers to take over the house and breathe new life into it with another generation of family. No father to be sitting lonely now by the fire, regretting things he had never said to his wife when she was alive.

Dermot had never known his father. Had not even known who his father was. His mother had fallen pregnant by a local man whose identity she had never been prepared to reveal. She was ashamed. Dermot understood that. Despite her insistence that she was not ashamed of him, Dermot never quite believed that was true. And if it wasn't, well he understood that too. His mother had suffered from depression all of his life but it was as if giving birth to him had sucked all the joy out of her. That was what he had picked up from visiting aunts and neighbours who had called in a constant stream to help 'poor Anne' and mind her 'poor child' when the laconic melancholy with which she performed her daily duties descended into breakdown.

'She was so full of life – remember? The best school-teacher around here and that's a fact.'

'Terrible what a child out of wedlock can do to a woman.'

'She made her bed. It's God's punishment surely.'

'And pretty? There wasn't a man between here and Galway wouldn't have taken her on.'

'Still would if she'd only pull herself together.'

'And the child? Poor wee mite, look at him.'

'You'd think she'd make a go of it – for his sake.'

Discussions held openly as if they weren't there. His mother certainly wasn't. Staring into the fire, her blank face occasionally flickering in recognition of some devil she imagined dancing across the flames.

When he was thirteen, Anne was persuaded to send her son to board with the Christian brothers in Maynooth.

'He'll be better off.'

'The boy is too fond of his own company. He'll grow up lacking.'

That was where Dermot had learned the trick that popularity was the key to success. The brothers were kind and encouraging, and he threw himself into the centre of their male world. At home he had never felt like anything more than the product of a disastrous liaison, the author of the pain he saw etched into his mother's face. Now he was whatever he wanted to be, and the selfishness of youth drove him forward to reinvent himself in the eyes of his peers. He presented himself as a lively fun-loving young man and in discovering that people believed what they saw, he gained confidence and freedom. Excelling at both sports and academia, by sixteen, Dermot was king of his year. He didn't go home because some part of him knew that this new personality was not built on a solid foundation and he was afraid it might crumble if he went back. He regularly wrote his mother letters; cheerful tomes full of news and good results. In return he got small cheques accompanied by short notes leaden with effort and never enquiring when he was coming home. So he chose to spend his summer holidays with the brothers. When he was eighteen and starting college, his mother sent him her savings to put towards a flat to live in while he was at college studying business. He used the money as a deposit on a falling down house in Rathmines and filled it with fellow students to help pay the mortgage, earning extra cash as a builder's labourer during weekends and holidays. By the time he graduated in 1986, Dermot had numerous contacts and was skilled enough himself to convert the house into bedsits. He paid off the mortgage within a few years and bought another house, then another. By the mid nineties, when property prices started to soar, Dermot was a wealthy man. He didn't go home now because he was too busy, there wasn't time. He sent hired drivers down to Gorrib to collect his mother and bring her up to Dublin for shopping trips. The two of them would sit opposite each other in some new restaurant or bar he had opened. She would say 'This is lovely,' but her face would be pained and worn and Dermot would sit on his guilt with anger. He would walk it off trawling his mother around Brown Thomas, buying her coats and cosmetics, urgently trying to infuse her with pleasure. 'Would you like *this*, Mam?' he'd say, holding up some exotic scarf. Anne would shrug joylessly and he would know that the only thing that could lift her out of this laconic state was if he had never been born.

After she went, Dermot would ring old college friends and take them out on the beer. He never spent those nights alone, making sure he picked up some feisty girl in a nightclub so that in the morning he would wake up in the breeze of her sleeping breath and be reminded he was alive.

But there was no girl here now to lift him out of this place. To help him recreate his mother's mausoleum; invent some myth he knew he would need to provide a reason for being here.

'Dermot is down the west renovating his country seat.'

'Well – it's more of a retreat for him. Nothing fancy, just somewhere he goes to get away from it all.'

'A modest schoolhouse – the house he grew up in actually.'

Instead he was standing in the place where it all began – trying to stop the truth from seeping through the fabric of his expensive clothes.

If he had a woman with him, it would be different. Someone to march through the house with clicky-heeled pragmatism. Tearing down curtains and flying around with paint swatches. Taking the contents of his humble beginnings and flinging them mercilessly into a skip in the interests of interior design. He had never thought of having a woman like that before now. A wife, he supposed he meant. Someone bossy and energetic who could fill the one gap he had been unable to fill himself. Someone to stop him turning right around and running the distance between here and Athlone to catch the next train up to Dublin. To tell him to pull himself together, then maybe tenderly assert that everything would be all right. More as an exercise, Dermot ran though a list of women he knew, but none fitted. They were all young and expected great things from him. At least as great as he expected from himself. This, this situation, this house with its yellowed nets and its brown linoleum floor tiles, the worn chair where she had sat by the fire; a silver-framed photograph he sent her when he won the 'Young Businessman' award, the garish shine on it glaring out against the dinge of the flocked walls, opened up in front of him like a gaping wound. Why had he come? Was he mad? He could have booked into a hotel. Still could. But he had left the mobile in his car, and his car was in Althone, and in any case he had no cash, and the nearest cash point was where? In Gorrib town, and that was miles away, and it was getting dark and . . . Dermot felt trapped. As if the air in the house were clotting, closing in around him. Dizzy and short of breath, he staggered backwards out of the room and nearly lost his life altogether when he turned and saw a man standing at the front door with a bucket of coal.

14

Brian had taken the failure of his refugee campaign with more grace than Rose had expected. In fact, he was in better form than he had been for a long time and was full of excitement for his new nightclub project which, he assured his wife, would be coming to fruition very soon.

'What kind of a nightclub is it, Brian?' she asked, remembering the certainty with which he had opened the doomed video-rental business.

'No need to worry your pretty wee head about that, darlin'. You'll see soon enough,' he replied, kissing her gently on the head as he left the kitchen.

Rose closed her eyes to soak in the pleasure of a tender moment and said, 'I called Regina Malone and asked her around for dinner on Thursday.'

Brian halted at the door. His back stiffened and, with a gnawing sense of dread, Rose sensed his mood change. He stood for a few seconds, then without turning around asked, 'Why?'

'Well, with Mary and Theo getting engaged and with

you and her going into business together I just thought—'

'I explained to you, Rose, that Regina is a *silent* partner. She's only put up the money – that's all.' Then he turned around, a nasty looked sliced across his face, 'At least *somebody* believes in me.'

It was a dig at Rose's reluctance to sell her parents' house to raise money for a project Brian was not willing to confide in her about.

'Have you no *respect* for me, woman? Inviting a business associate of mine around without consulting me? Going behind my back?'

'I wasn't going behind your back, Bri—'

'I mean – how the *fuck* do you think that makes me look? Did you think about that? My *wife*,' his face screwed up over the word as if he had swallowed a turd, 'calling up a woman like that without asking me first?'

'I thought you'd be pleased.' Even as she said it, Rose knew she shouldn't have.

'Pleased? *Pleased?*' He marched over to the sink, picked up a crumpled tea towel from the draining board and flung it down at his feet. Rose flinched as if it were a cup. She knew what was coming.

'Look at the state of this place. It's a fucking mess. God knows I tried to give you a nice house and what do you do? Turn it into a dump! What makes you think you can entertain the likes of Regina Malone anyway? She's used to better than the slop you serve up, Miss High-and-Mighty Davitt with your smoked salmon pâté and that fucking chicken crap you always do when you're trying to impress people. You're a fucking joke, Rose. A pathetic joke. What are you?' He wanted to frighten her into saying it, like he'd done in the past. '*I'm a pathetic joke, Brian.*'

'*What? I can't hear you?*'

But she didn't want to think about that now. Twenty-odd years later she knew it only made things worse when she conceded.

He was angry with himself. Scared. Frightened that this new venture wouldn't work out. He'd lost a lot over the years. Had a lot of disappointments. When he got like this, Rose knew she was a disappointment too. That couldn't be helped though. Considering how it had all began. Perhaps too, Brian was nervous that Mary was getting married and they wouldn't be able to afford a big wedding and he'd be shown up in front of the town. Rose should have thought of that before she went ringing the groom's mother and inviting her over. At the same time, it was done now and there was no use her getting upset over it. Getting upset solved nothing. She'd learned that. Pointless crying. Pointless.

Rose took a deep breath and tried to insert an assertive tone into her voice, like the one she heard other women use when they talked to their husbands.

'Well it's done now and she's coming and that's that.'

He looked at her and shook his head, as if he could not even begin to imagine the misfortune that had caused him to marry her. He went to leave, then turned as an afterthought and said in a soft pleading tone, 'And, Rose?'

'Yes Brian?'

'Try and smarten yourself up on the night will you?'

⬯

Regina Malone arrived half an hour late. Divorced from a wealthy Limerick man, who, in the gospel according to Mags McGreavy, had made a run for it as soon as the children were a respectable age, Regina had done very nicely in her settlement and returned to Gorrib, buying a grand house with the longest drive, up which she lured 'any man daft enough' to unhinge the vast engineering of her custom-made brassieres. However, as daughter of the local dentist, Regina had stayed close to her roots by adhering to the parochial ideal that snobbery was a virtue. Brian Fitzgerald had also been born to great things, and she thought it a terrible shame that the son of her father's friend had fallen on unfortunate times. Married to a woman reared in a terraced house. Who worked in a corner shop. One car. Last week she had been whipping the jeep out of Dunnes car park and seen Rose Fitzgerald struggling through the rain, pulling a plaid shopping trolley behind her. Now really! Was it any wonder Brian could not make a go of anything with a wife like that showing him up around the town? It was one thing only having a single car, but quite another using the fact to make a public spectacle of one's circumstances.

In truth, however, Regina Malone didn't give a shit one way or another. It was merely an argument she used to justify the fact that she was humping Rose's husband. Brian was no Adonis, not any more. But she had frightened off enough window cleaners to know a genuine opportunity when it came along. And if Brian Fitzgerald was willing to recreate her underwear-as-upholstery efforts as a Benny Hill moment, then stringing him along by pretending she was backing him in business was a small price to pay.

The chance to flirt mercilessly with Brian in front of his own wife was just an added bonus. A sexy game. As for the whole Theo marrying Mary angle? Well, that was just simply not going to happen. For much of the time, Regina remained in denial about her son, most particularly in relation to his age. She had set him up nicely, buying him the shop, above which he lived, after he had blown all his acting fortune lording it in Dublin. They kept out of each other's way mostly. If her son was going to marry, it was not going to be to that plump nobody daughter from a one-car family. She wanted a high-bred fashion model taking over the flower arrangements at Hyannis-Port or nobody at all. Preferably the latter. Anyway, after their last conversation she felt confident it would not go ahead.

'Mary Fitzgerald? What were you *thinking*?'

'I know, Mam.' Theo spluttered. 'It just came out.'

'Jesus, now we've been invited over for the whole mother of the groom thing to their ghastly house. Haven't I told you to be careful about that? This family has a *reputation* to uphold. We are respected in this town.'

'An ex-girlfriend came into the shop and I got freaked out and I kind of told her I was getting married to Mary. I don't know why. Then Mary came in and I thought . . .'

'Jesus Christ, Theo, you haven't the brains you were born with. Well, you've gone too far this time so just get it sorted will you?'

'Yes, Mam. What about the dinner?'

'I'll go by myself and make an excuse, but this is the last time I'm bailing you out, son. The last time. Do you hear?'

Every now and again Regina could to do the whole Do What Your Mammy Says thing, but she didn't like it. It had beige cardigan wardrobe implications. But she was damned if such restrictions would be in operation tonight; instead she shook out the full-length fur and shoe-horned herself into a black cocktail dress.

Davy Fitzgerald took one look at the coat and left the house, wisely deciding that Regina Malone was simply not worth wasting his breath on.

Mary was not so lucky and the disappointment was doubled when she learned that Theo wasn't coming. When Regina spotted the crushed look on the chubby frump's face she decided against her 'twenty-four hour bug' excuse and got the ball rolling by mysteriously announcing that Theo had to 'rush up to Dublin' on 'business'.

'What business?' Mary asked.

'Why I've no idea, dear,' Regina said. 'He never tells

me anything.' Then as a perky aside to Rose, 'Isn't that the way with your children, Rose? They never tell you anything.'

Rose agreed, 'Oh that's right. Mary fairly kept her romance a secret, now didn't you, honey? But sure, we're all delighted here. Theo is such a lovely lad. Such a shame he couldn't make it tonight.'

Actually, she had always found Theo Malone to be rather remote, even as a young boy. She had been surprised at Mary's announcement, assuming the two to be just friends. If Mary was happy, though, which she seemed to be, well then that was good enough for her.

'And didn't he get her a beautiful ring?'

'A *ring*?'

Regina could not keep the shock out of her voice.

'He got you a *ring*?'

'Yes,' said Rose, placing a delicate tower of smoked salmon down in front of Regina.

'It's lovely. Mary, lean over there now and show your mother-in-law your engagement ring.'

Regina flinched on both counts. The ring wasn't bad. A simple gold band with a medium-sized stone. Obviously the common gremlin hadn't chosen it.

'Theo always had very good taste,' she managed to force out between tight lips, but gave Mary a look that let her know the comment did not extend to *her*, 'and he's *such* a generous boy.'

'Actually,' Mary said, 'I chose it myself.'

'Oh and my son paid for it. How charmingly *traditional* of you both.'

Regina was nearing boiling point.

'No . . . well I paid for it myself to start off with. There's such a lot to do with the wedding and all, well, I thought it fair we both chip in.'

'Things are so different nowadays, aren't they, Regina? The young women are so independent. Not like in our day,' Rose added.

'Oh – I've always been something of a freewheeler myself, Rose,' she said, looking directly at Brian, 'and I don't know about you, but *my* best days are yet to come.'

Rose thought the evening went very well. Regina had regarded each plate of food with initial suspicion, but wolfed it all back just the same. Brian had been surprisingly subdued throughout the evening, but her fears that he was still angry at her subsided when he merrily offered to drive Regina home. She was sorry that Theo hadn't come, for Mary's sake. But they were young and, presumably, in love so she felt sure they'd work it all out.

As she readied herself for bed that night, Rose looked at herself in the dressing-table mirror and wondered about what Regina had said about their best days being ahead of them. Forty-five. Maybe it wasn't that old after all. She knew Regina was older than her; she'd been a few years ahead of her in the convent. When Rose commented on her new highlights, Regina said that she had them done in Galway and that they 'cost a fortune'. Rose pulled her own hair out of the barrette she used to hold it back during the day. Still long, it fell down around her shoulders and she wondered if perhaps she shouldn't get it cut into a more modern style. Maybe she could even chance one of those home hair colour kits? It was rather mousy looking. Regina had inspired her tonight with all that glamour going on. Perhaps she could do with some of it herself. Make more of an effort, like Brian was always telling her to do. She'd go up town tomorrow and see if she couldn't pick herself up a new dress. Have a chat with that nice girl behind the make-up counter in Collins chemist. She was always offering to do her up. 'You've great eyes, Rose, you should make the most of them,' she'd said only last week. Rose looked into them now and wondered what miracle might trans-form them from the sad pools that regarded her own reflection to something capable of seducing her husband. For some reason tonight, though, Rose got into bed hopeful and waited for her Brian to come home.

15

Vinny Rouse peeled back the hood of his protective paper suit and noticed the black disc of an escaped tick clinging to its sleeve. Tenacious bastards these. It had dug in clear through the paper and was looking for some skin to grip on to. No use to me now, thought Vinny, but more accustomed as he was to breeding insects than killing them, he gently picked it off and placed the offending parasite outside the door of his lab.

Farmer and Mrs Rouse had taken the unusual step of leaving the farm to their youngest son. Their other six sons had all gone abroad, America, Canada, even Australia, as far away as ever they could from the boggy, stony fields in which their parents had struggled to keep their smallholding going. Loyal Vinny had been left behind to collude in his parents' fantasy that they would leave behind them a legacy of land that would feed their grandchildren. Almost a generation older than his peers' parents, Stanley and Kathleen Rouse had been slaves to those ten acres all of their lives and Vincent could not bear to tell them that the days of living off less than a dozen heads of cattle and a few sheep were over in Ireland. That, in all probability, the fields once owned by their parents would be sold off in half-acre plots to various building contractors and swallow their rural heritage into a suburb of nearby Gorrib.

After their deaths, Vinny kept the land. Earning a small living doing odd building jobs, he had kept things going as long as he could. But after two years he had to sell the last of the cattle to pay for a new roof. Then his small flock of sheep had been all but wiped out with an infestation of bluebottles.

'I'll tell you one thing,' said the local vet through the haze of buzzing carnage that raged around the poor sheep's anus, 'you're obviously one hell of a lot better at breeding parasites than you are sheep.'

The last of the flock had to be put down and the veterinary had walked back to the house asking Dermot if he had any whisky within. The vet had a routine for breaking this kind of news to small farmers in these parts, which generally involved a drop of the hard stuff and a counselling-type chat about what the future might hold. He could well afford the time, as experience had taught him that, in all likelihood, this would be his last visit to the Rouse farm.

They got talking and it came out that he himself was involved in veterinary field trials, which were starting up in the next county, to develop antidotes for the parasite problem. Would Vinny mind if he took some of the sheep away for examination, although he didn't know how much use they would be because it was the parasites themselves that they were interested in. Vinny listened intently as he was grateful to be provided with immediate distraction from the terrible truth that he had finally run his parents' dream into the ground. When the whisky ran dry, a bottle of his mother's cooking sherry was dusted off so that the company might continue. They talked about his parents and how farming had changed and about how spaying a pet cat was no match for being called out at 3 a.m. to deliver a breech calf. One conversation led to another and before the night was ended Vet Smith and Vinny Rouse had come to a sort of an agreement. The doctor would investigate regulations pertaining to conditions for breeding parasites for experimentation and get back to him.

Five years on and Vincent was running a small lab out of his renovated cattle sheds supplying ticks, fleas and flies for veterinary trails and entomology studies all over Ireland. With business building fast and at three euros a tick, Vinny found that he had enough money to completely refurbish the house and have his dinner served up to him every night at the bar in Keaveney's. His bank statements had begun to contain numbers that, frankly, he was a loss as to how he might spend. In an effort to make some sort of an inroad into the six-figure sum, Vinny had booked his first foreign holiday. An all-inclusive 'sunshine' holiday to Spain. But it had been a lonely enough week and Vinny had felt self-conscious and foolish sitting alone by the pool in his new swimming togs and embarrassed by the attentions of skinny English girls in minuscule bikinis, who several times had approached him with shocking forward talk that had made him blush down to his knees.

Despite his best efforts to spend money on fancy umbrella-decorated cocktails and an 'authentic' Spanish sombrero, the holiday appeared to have had made little or no impact on his bank account. So he gave up worrying, seeing the balance as an abstract number that wasn't anything to do with him at all. When the numbers got too frightening, he simply began to hide the envelopes away without opening them.

However, Vinny never forgot when times had been harder. He had been too proud to approach his brothers for help, especially as they resented the fact that he would not sell off their parents' land for the few hundred pounds that might have helped each of them upgrade their car or buy a new television. They had chosen to interpret their younger brother's refusal as greed rather than the sentimentality it was. In those first few dry years, a regular cheque from their neighbour for keeping an eye on his house while he was in Dublin had come as all too welcome relief, so when he heard through Dermot's solicitor that Mr Leeson was coming back soon for a few days, Vinny kept an eye out for his arrival.

They had been at the local primary together, but when Vinny literally bumped into the smartly dressed businessman on his own front door, he hardly recognized him. He had turned into one of those nervy city types whom Vinny had seen sitting around in the restaurant of the Holiday Costa Hotel, clutching their mobile phones and smoking fags, even thought they were supposed to be on holiday.

In the event, Dermot turned out to be all right. He had come down woefully unprepared, and Vinny was glad to be able to help him settle in. He took him over to his for the cup of tea and, as it happened, he had a nice loaf and a few slices of ham left over from the lunch, so they had sandwiches for their tea. Vinny offered to drive him into Gorrib and buy him bar-bites in Keaveney's ('They do a lovely lasagne – it's Italian, but you can have chips with it.') but Dermot said he'd rather not. He was in strange form right enough, but Vinny took it on the chin and offered to put him up for the night. He knew what it was like going to bed for the first time in your parents' house after they were gone, and said that Leeson's house would probably be damp after the winter and need airing. In any case, he was proud of the work he had done on his own place, and it was the first time the 'guest bedroom' with its flowery curtains and matching bedspread had ever been used. For the want of anything better to talk about, Vinny told Dermot all about the renovations he had undertaken on the place since his parents' death. 'D'ye see these presses here now in the kitchen? Well, you wouldn't think it now but they're not real wood at all. Mammy would turn in her grave if she seen I had blinds up, but sure the old curtains weren't fit to dress a dog and, well there's a time to let things go.'

When he said that, Vinny noticed a look pass across

his guest's face; a cloud from the past. He knew it only too well. You put it behind you, then at intervals it wanders through you unannounced.

Vinny knew of only one way to keep such haunting at bay, keeping busy, so he said, 'I expect you're down to do some work yourself on the house?'

'I suppose,' Dermot said, as if he had only just thought of it himself.

'Right enough, well I've tools in the shed and a load of leftover paint,' and remembering all the money Dermot had sent down over the years, he would not take no for an answer.

'I'll be down tomorrow between eight and nine.'

And Dermot did not object.

his green face, cloud from the part. He like it out no well. You put it behind you, then at forward, with enough you unregistered.

PART THREE

hallowed be thy game

FIELD REPORT FOUR

To: Christian Donnelly, OCR, UK&IR
From: Archangel Gabriel – DCR, department of R&H,
        Heaven

What am I? An endless source of forgiveness and light? I simply cannot believe that you are looking for an invisibility and flight permit after the whole unauthorized manifestation debacle. You really are something else, Christian. On a simple job like this why on Earth (pardon the pun) is all this miraculous activity necessary? However, like I said before, this mission is very important to the department so I have managed to grant you one for the date and time specified but please, *please*, Christian, make sure you are not seen. Or rather, not seen to be not seen.

Dermot Leeson is in place and his report is attached. He's a tricky biscuit and his soul is in a wobbly state. We expect a report by return.

I've had Mary Fitzgerald monitored and put on Red Alert. Her engagement (which I *assume* you know about) is a disaster that we had hoped you might have been able to avoid. Given that you missed the boat on that one, Emergency Services have had to be called, so you'll get your wish, help is on its way – you know what to look for.

I am disappointed thus far, Christian. Things are going more slowly than we have come to expect from you.

I cannot stress the importance of this mission. Try to pull the finger out and don't let me down.

G.

There is something fishy going on here. On the one hand it's all threats and 'pull the finger out'. On the other, Gabs is granting me all sorts of permits post-haste, which frankly, I wasn't expecting. It takes weeks – months sometimes – for an invisibility and flight permit to come through and yet, despite all the huffing and puffing, here it is less than a few hours after I requested it. It just doesn't make sense. I mean, making sense of things is supposed to be our job. Collectively, that's what being a Deity is all about. If we can't add up, then what hope is there for the mere mortals?

And what's the rush? I've been doing the requisite information gathering. Leeson's going nowhere; the Fitzgerald girl's engagement, OK, I took my eye off the ball on that one – but there's plenty of time.

Anyway, as far as I'm concerned moving in with the McGreavys was a stroke of genius on my part. Old Mags is a *fantastic* source of information, some of which is even useful. The great thing about some of these devout old souls is that sometimes you get the strangest feeling that they know what you're about. Nothing said, of course. But like, here I am, this odd queen who doesn't eat, who arrives up at her house without so much as a suitcase, and even though she's obsessed with everybody else's business she never asks me any questions. I even heard her defend me last week to one of her cronies.

'Mind you own bloody business,' she snapped as they started quizzing her about what I was doing there and the like.

Odd.

And here's something odder. This story she told me about that local unfortunate I saw the first day I arrived in Gorrib. The one in the wheelchair. The fella Moses was all funny talking about. And no wonder! He's a contemporary of his, Hemlock they call him, although his real name, before he took to the drink was Ignatius (or Iggy). Seemingly they were chums in their late teens/ early twenties. Inseparable, although Maggie always thought there was something a 'bit queer' about him. 'Like you,' she said. 'If you know what I mean.' I did. Reading between the lines, Iggy got a passion on for Moses. (A challenge in itself I can tell you – all hair and flares, I've seen the pictures.) Moses, as is the wont of straight men, didn't have a clue until one night, Iggy (and I really *did* have to read between the lines on this one) dropped the hand and Moses got the land of his life, rejecting his friend's attentions in the strongest possible terms. Iggy then went mad altogether and became very creepy. Took to the bottle big time and started hanging about the bar saying he was going to put a spell on Moses and his girlfriend at the time, who was Rose of course. The legs went when he climbed up onto the roof of McGreavy's one night saying he could fly and *smack!* landed straight on the pavement. Apparently, it was all downhill from there (pardon the pun), wheelchair, filthy overcoat with a quarter bottle of Jameson in the pocket – your standard issue, sad small-town drunk. Looks seventy if he's a day, which is sadder still, as Moses hasn't aged too badly, despite the mullet. An example of the Liz Taylor school of growing old gratefully. Stick to your hey-day look and no one will be any the wiser.

I don't know why that story stuck to me like it did, but the hypnotic way Mags related it too me, all googly eyed and full of significance, fairly freaked me out until we copped on to Brian's affair and Sandra arrived to liven things up a bit.

There's a complication as well. I think Moses might be falling for Sandra. I can't blame him. She is, even by my standards, a dish – but she could tone down the faghag routine and be subtler about my status, especially in front of Margaret, and especially in the light of Moses's past experiences, although I expect she doesn't know anything about that. And can you believe her turning up like that, out of the blue, with Leeson down here as well? Of course, it makes my job one million times easier, but say nothing to upstairs. I'll let on it was all my doing. Shouldn't be too hard given that they have already 'met' so to speak.

No, my toughest job is going to be letting Rose find

out about Brian. How I'm going to bring myself to do it I do not know as she is quite a peach. I know all that simple naivety can be irritating in this day and age, but sometimes you just have to operate on another level when you're an angel. And being thick when it comes to love isn't a crime. She's letting herself down. Nobody else. Oh, and Moses. But with Sandra's underwear acrobatics, he doesn't look any too bothered. That will have to come later. In the meantime, I've just got to focus. Take all this one step at a time and not get bogged down with any more of Margaret's mysterious stories or let officious memos put me off track.

It'll all sort itself out in the end. It always does. Somehow.

16

'Bugger and feck.'

Sandra had melted her acrylic nails trying to get the fire of newspaper scraps and a damp log going in her rented bungalow. She had asked the travel agent to find her a traditional cottage and they had come up with a vast four-bedroom bungalow complete with fitted kitchen, garishly patterned carpet and scalloped blinds. The central heating panel, when she eventually located it, looked like Nassau pilot training equipment and the landlord was currently sunning himself in Marbella – no doubt on the proceeds of the astronomical rent he was charging her. The woman in the local garage, where she went to get her milk, had told her that her nearest neighbour had worked on the house and was a very approachable, helpful young man. She'd have sent her own husband down to take a look, only for this English tourist had pink painted toenails poking out of her high-heeled sandals. Exposure to that class of glamour might give him notions, and he'd surely come home looking for a rummage about in the bedroom, an activity which she'd had quite enough of, thank you very much, after twenty-five years of marriage.

Sandra didn't know much about lighting fires, but she knew enough to know that she was getting nowhere with the log. Turf was your only man. The first thing she had noticed when she got off the train in Gorrib was the smell of turf smoke. She had always loved that about McGreavy's. Curled up in a blanket by the kitchen stove watching her Aunt Maggie lever open the hot disc upon which the teapot lived and throw sod after sod of furry turf into the greedy hole of fire that fed heat around the whole building. The pub and its upstairs flat were centrally heated now. Just a small gas fireplace in the bar 'for atmosphere', Moses said, although he said he wished he hadn't bothered sometimes as he was forever picking fag butts out of its 'genuine coal effect' nuggets, where customers had mistaken it for the real thing.

Sandra had enjoyed spending time with the Mc-Greavys since she arrived, and had been both surprised and delighted at how they had welcomed her. Her Aunt Mags had been horrified at first – but then that had always been part of the fun. Despite the old lady being thoroughly 'scandalized' by everything to do with Johnny's English niece, she displayed a ghoulish curiosity in Sandra's line of work.

'It's disgraceful taking your clothes off for a living – and tell me, how much do you get paid for showing yourself off like that?'

'You've brought despair and disgrace on your family – and what percentage of that would the club owner take?'

'It's an offence against God's Holy Kingdom and the Blessed Virgin in particular – and there's five clubs operating in Dublin at the moment you say?'

Sandra suspected that Maggie's feigned dislike of her was merely the cute old bat keeping her bread buttered on both sides. The truth was Mags rather liked having her around, but she had to make a show of pious disapproval in case Him Upstairs was tuning in. It was the same with that queen they had staying with them at the moment. Whenever he was out of the room she would mutter conspiratorially, 'I don't know about that fella, he's very *odd*,' but when he was in her company there was this extraordinary synergy in the way they spoke and moved around each other. A sort of seamless shorthand, like an old married couple – in a bizarre way it was like they were meant for each other.

Then there was Moses. Sandra knew if she asked he'd be round in a shot to fix the fire and central heating for her. Yet she didn't call him. She liked Moses; in fact Sandra was slightly troubled by how very fondly she felt towards him. She had certainly never missed him over the years; hadn't thought about him at all except for the vague curiosity that had led her to walk into his pub that afternoon a couple of weeks previously. Yet from that first moment they had linked back into some old familial intimacy she had forgotten was there. They had always got on. Or rather, as a boisterous and promiscuous teenager she had enjoyed his protection on the rare occasions she had requested it, and his alliance in dealing with Aunt Maggie trying to restrict her holiday socializing and her somewhat colourful Mass wardrobe. He had been like an older brother, without the 'touch my sister and I'll kill you' hang-ups her own brothers had.

But things were different now. They were both older, and Moses was lonely. Sandra didn't even know if he knew that himself. In fact, she was certain that he didn't. The male ego required them to cover their tracks pretty thoroughly on that one, but there wasn't much that could get past the seasoned eye of an experienced lap dancer. A barely discernible softening in their smile; eyelids flickering slightly over a pause in conversation. Lonely men were her best and worst customers. Best because they tipped well and came back for more. Worst because the attention of a lonely man could chip a corner off her porcelain armour and make her feel naked. Not feeling naked whilst actually *being* naked was an essential part of her success to date. Vulnerability was not in the job description and other people's vulnerabilities had a way of tapping into her own so she avoided them. Moses coming out here to play house, under whatever practical circumstances, was something worth being cautious about.

The sun had somehow managed to muscle its way through the grey sky, and Sandra decided to take a stroll over to this alleged nearest neighbour's house and see if he would be able to help. In any case, Sandra had been trying to broaden her circle in Gorrib beyond Mc-Greavy's. It was nothing so definite as a decision to set down roots, but she had already stayed beyond her original two-week holiday and when she finally remembered to check the messages on her all but redundant mobile, Sandra found she was remarkably calm about the news that she had been let go from the Manchester agency on account of her being uncontactable for three weeks. Perhaps it was something to do with the fact that she had recently had a conversation with a local businessman who was setting something up locally. A guy who was married to Moses's ex, Rose, who she half remembered through her teenage haze of Babycham and late nights as being a nice woman. Anyway Rose had hooked up, years ago, with this bloke Brian who was thinking about opening a lap-dancing club in Gorrib and, hearing she was an expert in that area, had approached her about a job. Not just dancing either. He had lined up a few foreign girls, who it seemed were living locally, and was keen for her to train them in. They hadn't talked money or anything like that, and actually, he had left his wallet at home and Sandra had ended up picking up the tab for lunch, but he seemed serious enough. He was a fat, sleazy, shallow prick. But then, in her line of work, that was generally a good enough recipe for success. Although, poor Rose. But then, as Sandra firmly believed, that's where falling in love and getting married got you. Men were all very well and good up to a point, but at the end of the day their cocks and their egos turned them into flabby know-it-alls. Good job for her, but bad news for those women daft enough to expect everlasting romance. Moses was a gem for sure, but then Sandra knew she'd only have to flick a G-string in his direction and he'd collapse in his shining armour like the rest of them. He was just too nice a guy to test the theory out on. Besides – they were first cousins. What was she thinking! She'd already had a close enough encounter with her past when she had walked into that guy's record shop.

'Sandra!' he'd said as soon as she walked in. She had tried not to look too vague. Gorrib was a small town and if she was going to be hanging about for a while, she couldn't afford to piss anyone off. Everyone knew everyone here, and her Babycham-fuelled youth and the many thousands of men she had encountered since put her at a distinct disadvantage when it came to reminiscing.

'It's me. Theo. Theo Malone.'

'Ah, hi . . .' was the best she could manage, having no memory of him whatsoever. He'd blabbed on for a bit about how he was engaged to some girl called Mary, who she also had no memory of but subsequently discovered was Brian and Rose Fitzgerald's daughter.

'Do you remember the night we kissed out in the field? I wrote a stupid poem about you afterwards. Foolish youth, eh?'

He was all boyish smiles, like it had happened yesterday. Jesus, what a stupid slut she must have been back then. He caught her on the hop bringing it up casually like that. For the rest of the day she had felt stupid, wondering how many more of the local men she had slept with. Was that friendly nod from a passer-by genuinely neighbourly or sleazy secret code? That man pushing the double buggy, his dumpy wife following close behind, did he deliberately look away when he saw her or was his attention genuinely diverted? Paranoia and neurosis were not traits in Sandra's emotional make-up, but somehow, she wanted to feel as if she belonged here. She was never going to be a Mass-at-dawn die-hard but, at the same time, if she were going to be able to justify her frisky years, it would be an advantage to be able to remember them.

Sandra's 'sensible' brown boots were not holding up in the mucky field she had decided to short cut through to her neighbour's house. Mr Gucci had clearly not designed them to commune with nature. Or rather, they were currently communing with rather more nature than they were designed for. Three inches is reasonably low for Paris pavement pounding, but it sure feels like a long way down when they're sinking into a fresh cowpat. Sandra rummaged about in her clutch bag for a packet of Wet Ones and dabbed hopelessly at the soft leather of one before noticing that the other had sunk into the soft ground up to the ankle. Reluctant to subject the semi-rescued boot to the same she balanced there on one foot for the nano-second it took for her 32DD chest to surrender to the laws of gravity and send her plummeting to the ground. One boot lost for ever to the grasping blackness of a Mayo boghole, the beaded flimsy, which only deserved the description 'cardigan' in the most urban of surroundings, ruined, Sandra promptly learnt that the inner hardiness she had built up in matters pertaining to people cut no mustard when dealing head on with Mother Nature. Bootless and bruised she began to cry, as the sun abruptly changed its mind and it began to rain down on top of her.

'Are you all right there, missy?'

'Graaaaaah!'

For the figure that stood above her was some sort of an alien, looming massively over her, and shrouded entirely in white.

'Sorry if I gave you a fright, Miss,' it said as it removed its helmet and revealed a kind, if rather large and ruffle-haired human head. Human male, she was relieved to note.

'I seen you from the laboratory. You know, you really ought not to be walking across the fields at this time of year. Not without wellingtons, and even then—'

'Would you ever shut the fuck up and . . .'

Vinny didn't go in for cursing, and tried to interrupt if he could. Which he did now by scooping this dishevelled female up into his arms, flinging her over his shoulder and carrying her sturdily across the field to his house and, unbeknownst to the wriggling objections of Sandra, safety.

Scantily clad, in the middle of nowhere and being carried to a laboratory by an ape. Not exactly an advertisement for Mayo tourism.

As it turned out, Vinny was very nice. He made her tea and buttery ham sandwiches and had a grand fire sparking in the grate in no time. He scored her an enormous sweater which smelt old fashioned, like dust and Imperial Leather soap, and said he would come down and give her a hand with the house – no problem. They chatted nicely about his family and her family, and both sagely avoided talking about their respective lines of work. He asked how she was settling into the area, and she said she knew the McGreavys and he said he knew the pub well and it was lovely and she said indeed it was, and he said he went down for the country and western karaoke sometimes and she said she'd be sure to look out for him. And that would have been that, except that Vinny didn't meet many women and seeing how this one had literally fallen out of the sky and into his field, he decided to push the boat out. He had more or less given up on the whole looking for a wife thing. Any of the local girls he fancied when he was younger thought he was a bit of a gom and while he'd seen a girl in Gorrib he liked, very much, he was too terrified to approach her and any time he tried to make that long journey across the disco dance floor, she looked at him as if he was something swept up off the cattle shed floor. This one was scrawnier than he liked, but she was English, so it didn't count if she turned him down so he said, 'I'm going to Bosanova on Saturday with my friend if you fancy coming down.'

'That would be lovely,' she said.

It was that easy.

17

Mary could not believe her luck.

Dear Mary,

Romantic Moments magazine, Britain's premier lonely hearts magazine is delighted to inform you that you, (yes, YOU!) are the lucky winner of this month's holiday prize draw for a romantic holiday for two on the sun-drenched island of Lanzarote. The prize includes flights and accommodation for two weeks, all meals and subsidies, and free use of the hotel's many sports and leisure facilities.

The only catch is that you have to be available to have your photograph taken in the next fortnight for our Lucky Prizewinner page – and, of course, find that special someone to take with you on what we're sure will be the trip of a lifetime!

Yours in the spirit of romance,

Mr M. Matthews

She read the letter over a few times, checking and rechecking the address and her name. (A holiday! Free!

To Lanzarote!) She had rung the number at the top of the letter and spoken to Mr Matthews, who was very friendly and assured her it was no hoax. She could take up the offer any time she wanted and take whomever she chose. While she could not ever remember having ever seen a copy of *Romantic Moments* specifically, Mary was a prolific magazine consumer and filler in of Find Your Ideal Man/Job/Dress Size quizzes in general, and she wasn't going to sift through her mind looking for reasons to argue this opportunity away.

Wait until she told Theo! The honeymoon was sorted!

And yet, here was the strange thing. While a few weeks ago Mary would only need the slightest excuse to pop into Theo's shop and loiter in his general vicinity, now with this fantastic news, she did not feel in any particular hurry to rush over there. It was nothing as specific as not wanting to tell him. It was more just an overall feeling of indolence that seemed to be seeping in where matters concerning the marriage were concerned. She had started with this huge burst of energy, buying the ring, telling everyone, trawling through wedding magazines and cutting out dresses, going on a diet. However, in the past few days her enthusiasm seemed to be tapering off. Men, she knew from magazine articles, were hopeless at wedding arrangements – and she gained some comfort from that with regard to Theo's apparent lack of interest. It was easy for her to find excuses for him. The pragmatic way he proposed; his reluctance to contribute financially; his not turning up to meet her family, she could always find a reason to justify his indifference in her mental catalogues filed under denial. But this feeling that had been creeping over her was less to do with him than her. Reluctant though she was to admit it, there was some germ of an idea forming in her gut that perhaps she didn't want to marry Theo Malone after all. The truth was, if she didn't want to marry him, then perhaps that meant she didn't love him. And if she didn't love Theo Malone any more then, well, what was left?

She had a shite boring job, a shite boring family, a shite boring life. For most of these twenty-seven years she had been that fat boring bitch who was in love with Theo Malone. Now she was that fat lucky bitch who was in love with Theo Malone. Except she wasn't. Not really. Not now that it really came down to it. Because loving the unavailable Theo had made Mary's life easy. She didn't have to worry about a career, about moving away from home, being chubby, getting dressed up, losing her virginity, or getting a life in general. That's not to say these things didn't bother her. They did, in a low-grade whingy sort of way – but she didn't have to worry about them on a level where she might have to do anything about them. Her obsession with Theo was an excuse to sit in her bedroom eating crisps and feeling miserable instead of hauling her fat arse out into the world and joining in. Now, these two worlds were colliding. Reality was setting in, and she was finding that losing weight was a lot more manageable as a good intention than the actuality of Weight Watchers Healthy Options Breakfast when every extra inch of her was craving a bacon butty.

Wedding dresses looked like the stuff of fairy tales in magazine pictures, but they were a whole other kettle of fish when you had to lever yourself into metres of polyester lace and ended up looking like your grandmother's sofa, all cream bulges and doilies.

Then there was the sex thing.

Ella, who had been wonderfully supportive given how much she hated Theo, had made a good point.

'You can't marry him a virgin, Mary. It's too weird.'

Mary had pretended to be scandalized at the notion that she should 'get a bit of practise in' before the wedding night. But, in truth, she was absolutely terrified at the idea of having sex with Theo. Of course, she had thought about it. But thinking about things and actually *doing* them were very different things – as she was discovering with her Weight Watchers meals. They looked delicious, substantial even, on the packet, but once you took them out of the microwave they were wobbly and shrunken and didn't fill you up at all.

Ella had half-talked her into going to Bosanova this coming Saturday to see if they couldn't pick out a suitable 'stunt groom' to unwittingly take Mary through some moves beforehand. This chatting was all very well and good when it remained just that, but Ella seemed determined that the time for talking was through and Mary could feel herself being wheeled into action despite herself. That was the trouble with habitual inertia. Once someone decides to get you moving, you are powerless to resist.

So while winning this holiday was, undoubtedly, thrilling, Mary could not help but in part feel slightly exhausted at the prospect. First, she had to tell Theo and prepare herself for him being not quite as excited as she would like him to be. Then, the magazine editor was coming over to take her picture. She had to go out this weekend and have sex for the first time, lose another half a stone in a number of weeks, organize her hair, the dress – it just seemed like an awful lot of stuff when all she felt like doing was disappearing up to her room with a bucket of crisps.

It was nine thirty now, Theo would be setting up shop and she had to be in work at ten. Joylessly, Mary closed the fridge door and stopped cruising the sausages.

In the hall mirror she applied some lipgloss and, clutching the letter, gave her chubby reflection a big chirpy smile, like she genuinely meant it, before heading out of the door.

18

Regina's Merc was parked in the forecourt of the all-night garage where she had just scored her first packet of cigarettes in over five years. She had given them up to preserve the youthful glow of her complexion, an achievement obvious to no one but herself.

Her shaking hands tore eagerly at the packet until she had the cellophane pulled aside and a tube of weed stuck firmly in her gob.

'Come on, come on,' she shouted at the lighter until finally it clicked and she snatched it greedily out of the dashboard and lit the fag. She dragged deeply as if it were her last breath, and indeed Regina was not entirely sure that it wasn't.

Nicotine was small comfort against the mighty ordeal she had just been through, but it was the best she could do until she got home and steadied herself with the more medicinal properties of her drinks cabinet.

The evening had started well enough. Brian had called to say the kids were out and Rose was above at the church taking a gang of infirm pensioners round the

Stations. The house would be empty for at least two hours and did Regina fancy popping over to his for a quickie as Rose had taken the car and he wasn't mobile? It was late afternoon, Regina's friskiest period and an hour noted by local window cleaners as the time most likely to endure a terrifying encounter with the Duchess of Church Street in a see-through negligee.

She threw her mink on over the same, put the foot down and was pulling into the Fitzgeralds' drive in a matter of minutes. 'Quickie' pertained largely to the early stages of their relations and consisted of little more than Regina dropping the mink. Now things had slowed down a bit and Brian's age and build meant he could be banging away there for a good forty-five minutes before there was a result and, once there was, there was no hope of a repeat performance. On the up side, his enthused shoving meant that while there was little actual physical pleasure on Regina's part, at least she was getting value for money from her Italian catalogue underwear and, in this instance at least, it gave her time to look around and mentally criticize Rose's bedroom decor. She was assessing the price of the curtains when, from under Brian's armpit, she thought she saw something in the en suite. A small, sharp movement, like a camera flash.

'Brian,' she whispered, 'I think there's someone in the bathroom.'

His coitus interrupted, Brian leapt off and turned around.

That's when the madness started.

'What the fuck are you doing?' Brian yelled. 'GET OUT! Get out of my house! Now!'

Regina pulled the sheet over her head and peeked out, terrified at who it might be. She could not see the intruder, only Brian's buttocks wobbling fiercely as he waved his arms in the air at the bathroom doorway.

'Who is it?' she asked, raising her voice to a higher pitch so it wouldn't be recognized.

'Put that fucking camera down. Give me that fucking camera, you perverted fucker. GIVE ME THAT CAMERA now!'

By this stage, Brian was standing in the centre of the bedroom, naked and shaking with rage.

Regina tentatively looked out from behind the sheet (Dunnes Stores, polyester mix – honestly, some people) and asked again, 'Who is it?'

'What do you mean, who is it, woman?' Brian, now facing her screamed. 'He's standing right next to you! It's that dirty queer who works for McGreavy. GIVE ME BACK THAT FUCKING CAMERA!'

Regina looked behind her. Nobody. She stuck her head out from under the sheet and looked all around the room. There was no one there.

Only Brian. Going stark raving mad.

'You filthy homosexualist bastard. Stop fucking laughing at me. I'll give you something to laugh about, you perverted bollocks . . .' and he lunged towards this invisible foe, flinging himself onto the floor by the bed.

Regina was getting scared now.

'Brian – calm down, there's no one there.'

'No one there? No one there? Are you fucking blind, woman? He's here, HERE! LOOK!'

And he raised his arm aloft in a Hitler salute, clearly under the delusion that he was holding a substantial three-dimensional object.

'Calm down, Brian. Please, calm down.'

If there is one expression that is designed to further infuriate a man already in an infuriated state, it is the words 'calm' and 'down' used in conjunction with one another.

'CALM DOWN! CALM DOWN! A man breaks into my house, into *my* bedroom, takes pictures of me and starts dancing about the place ... STOP DANCING about ... STOP ... STOP OR I'LL ...'

Then, the most frightening thing of all. Quite suddenly Brian stopped and, as if he had gone into a kind of trance, he stood staring open-mouthed at the window.

'F-f-f-f-flying,' he said, pointing feebly at the (unlined, cheap fabric) curtains, his incoherent mumbling trailing off in astonishment.

'He f-f-f-f-flew out the window ... d-d-d-did you see that, Regina?'

But Regina had already flown herself.

Brian was a bit slow in the scratcher and no genius in business, but she had never had him down as an unstable head-the-ball.

And that was strange because usually, Regina some-how managed to convince herself, she was very, *very* careful about who she slept with.

She stubbed out her fag and lit another, sucking and

chewing it voraciously as she drove on home. Still shaken, she was standing by her drinks cabinet pouring herself a Waterford crystal tumbler of brandy before she realized she had left her coat on Brian's bedpost.

In Tuffy's garage, young Anne was stuck to the mobile telling all who would listen that Regina Malone was after coming in and buying a packet of twenty Major in nothing more than a see-through nightie.

19

Dermot clicked off the immersion and threw in the final load of boiling water. The old tank could heat just enough for half a bath, and it took three kettles to get the water hot enough to comfort his aching muscles.

He stripped off and sank quickly into the tub before the chill of the damp room set in, dipping his head under until he could feel the water fill the insides of his ears. The bath was not big enough for his long limbs, so he sat up and stretched his calves, dipping them in and out of the water, noting with a vague satisfaction the defined muscles that had been developing over the past few weeks since he had started work on the house.

Used to the luxury of the life in the hotel, no shower and having to boil kettles for a bath should have irritated Dermot, but he had come to quite enjoy the domestic details of his everyday life – creating out of them a daily routine that was almost monastic. He rose at seven, cleaned out the fire grate and walked half a mile to collect fresh spring water from the stream that ran in from the mountain. Carrying the four-litre container back to the house, he washed and prepared himself a breakfast of porridge, brown bread and tea, using just enough of the spring water to half fill the kettle. The rest he would save for drinking throughout the day while he sweated buckets working on the long list of building chores he and Dermot had compiled. Each room in the house had to be stripped back to brick, dry lined and plastered; a central heating system installed; the back kitchen knocked down and rebuilt. There were trees to be felled, lawns to be laid, a drive to be tarmaced, sheds to be cleared, roof tiles to be replaced, floors to be laid. Man's work that meant Dermot hardly thought about why he was bothering except that the heavy labour of it all seemed to be taking his mind off everything and serving as some sort of therapy. Since Vinny had started him off with the idea of renovating the house, Dermot had thrown himself into this new country life with the vigour of a fugitive being offered a second chance at freedom. He hadn't even gone back to Athlone to pick up his car, preferring to drive Vinny's tractor up as far as the local garage, where he could purchase a pint of milk and whatever meagre groceries he needed. Dermot knew that one day soon, on a date he was not prepared to specify just yet, he would have to collect the car and go about the business of checking his mobile messages and taking back control of his interests in Dublin. But he knew that the longer he left it, the more things he would have to deal with, and as each day passed he felt less and less inclined to think about anything other than perhaps throwing down a few spuds or pushing the boat out altogether and purchasing a hen so he might add the boiling of a freshly laid egg to his morning routine. Sometimes, late at night, if the moon glowered mercilessly in through his curtainless window and Dermot couldn't sleep, he would sense the sword of Damocles hanging over the bed. Was the hotel sold yet? Were his tenants trying to contact him? Was the junior mechanic having sex with the boss's wife in the back of his Mercedes in Athlone? Would he ever have sex again himself? Most nights he was too tired to care. And when he wasn't, Dermot would get out of bed, throw on a pair of wellingtons, grab a torch and wander out across Vinny's front field to see if his neighbour was still up for a chat. Sometimes he would be halfway down the path when he'd see Vinny's bedroom light click off, and he would switch off his torch and just stand there for a few moments, letting the night envelop him, wrapping up his thoughts in a cloak of silence. Reminding him that everything around here was asleep, cows and birds and Vinny. It was that simple. And in that moment, Dermot would find an oasis in the vast complicated mess of his mind, where his life was that simple also, and he would trot back to the schoolhouse anxious for nothing else but to rummage his feet back under the warm patch of hot-water bottle.

Tonight was an experiment in edging himself out into the world again. He had been reluctant about the idea of the big Saturday night out in Gorrib, but then he was doing it for Vinny sake, and his new friend had been so generous in his time and labour, that he was helpless to refuse.

While Vincent Rouse was the undoubted champion of all things manly and rural around here, knowing as he did one end of a cow from the other and the intricacies of retiling a roof, he was something of a bumpkin when it came to matters concerning women. A conversation they had had earlier that week over their by now regular consumption of cocoa and fig rolls at the end of their working days had confirmed the same.

'You never married?' Dermot asked, suddenly noticing his new friend's liking for check shirts, bringing to mind the cowboy from Village People.

Vincent's immediate answer was coloured by his nervous realization that Dermot had maintained the sharp cut of his sideburns despite the fact that Vinny was the only living soul this city boy had encountered in coming up for three weeks.

'No, but I like girls very much. Very much indeed.'

'I don't,' Dermot said automatically, then realizing how bad that sounded added, 'that is to say, I *did*, up until a few weeks ago actually. Until I came here.'

For a few seconds the two men pointedly disregarded each other until Dermot realized that the dreamy way he was staring out of the window could be construed as fey, and Vinny caught himself fingering the paper doily that sat under the biscuits and said, with unnecessary apology, 'It saves me washing the plate.' Then in a flurry of awkwardness he blurted out, 'I can't find a woman. None of them round here like me.'

'Why? What's wrong with you. You're a good-looking man.'

That didn't come out too well either and so somewhat frantically Dermot found himself offering to take Vincent out that weekend to the local disco to find a woman, an undertaking that he assured him he was a expert in, and Vincent agreed with more enthusiasm than he actually felt. They nearly tore each other's arms off with firm handshakes at the door and both sighed with relief when crawling alone into their own beds that night, hopeful that the female quota in Bosanova that coming weekend would put pay to any unsavoury notions that the other might be entertaining.

Dermot shaved and checked himself in the mirror. He could do with a haircut, but the few curls waving around the nape of his neck were quite dashing, actually. He stood at his mother's full-length dressing-table mirror and eased on the white shirt he had not worn since his first day here, feeling the fresh cotton crisp against his skin. And there they were. Brown biceps. Real men's arms. Working men's arms. Why, he'd be straining out of the shirt, they were getting that big. What a hunk! Maybe tonight was not such a bad idea. After all, it would surely be criminal to keep all this suave surety blended with solid manliness to himself.

And so it was, refreshed and temporarily infatuated with his own gorgeousness, that Dermot Leeson, his smart shoes polished and placed in his jacket pocket, made the wellington-clad journey across his neighbour's field to Vincent's house from where they would journey together to Bosanova's disco in Gorrib to launch their onslaught on the hearts and hormones of the unsuspecting females therein.

20

It was funny the way time changed things.

The last time that Moses had seen Sandra, he had been involved with Rose. His English cousin wasn't somebody he had thought about during the intervening years and, let's face it, aside from being a blood relation she wasn't exactly his type. Although, in truth, Moses knew he was not the sort of man who could ever enjoy the luxury of having a type. Rather, as his first, Rose was the benchmark by which all other women were judged. Beautiful and innocent and full of love. It was the element of her love that had drawn him so tightly to her, and its betrayal that had pushed him so far back inside himself.

Moses was nearing middle age and it wasn't as if he hadn't tried to form another relationship. Albeit half-heartedly, in the early years after Rose, when he felt that he only had half a heart. He had dated girls and women who were beautiful and innocent. Some of them both. But the love was always missing, and although he knew that some of them had been keen enough to marry him, he wasn't prepared to enter into a sturdy practical coupling for the sake of not being alone, or take a chance that love would dribble down the years over rocky patches and shared habits until there was a small pond to draw from. Not after he had come so close to bathing in the warm pool of Rose's passion. He had slept with half a dozen women or so in his life. There was relief and gratitude always, but never completion. If he had slept with Rose back then perhaps the circle would have been completed, but Moses was done cursing his own higher judgement. It was time to move on.

Sandra was different from the other women he had met. She was hard and brassy for sure although beautiful in that confident city way, but there was something kind about her. There was a gentleness underneath the high heels and the low-cut tops, that he felt certain of. The fact that he saw it when she went to such pains to hide it was surely a type of love? Perhaps she was giving him clues in her readiness to flirt and her easy laugh?

Margaret had spotted what was going on. She knew enough to realize that her disdain would only drive her son into Sandra's arms, so the old woman tried to dilute her disapproval the only way she knew how.

'Deirdre Nolan's on her way up to Mass. I see Sandra stayed late again last night – third time this week, good girl Deirdre.'

Moses said nothing.

'Would you look at that dirty Kenny dog fouling the footpath – the two of ye seem to be getting on very well altogether – you mark my words someone'll step in that now and drag muck in over the bar carpet.'

He continued gathering up the breakfast things.

'We've to order in oil from Tom Fahy this week – I expect she'll be off back to London, or wherever it is she lives now, soon enough – he says he's out the door with orders.'

'She thinking of staying around for a while,' Moses said, putting the last of the plates in the dishwasher. 'I'm off out now.'

It was spiteful leaving that bombshell in the air and then walking away, but he didn't have the energy for Margaret today. A clot of irritation was building in him while she was rattling on, and Moses knew that if he didn't leave the house he might say something hurtful. His mother's generation did not go in for open confrontation. If you said something critical, they just went tight-lipped and silent putting your judgement of them away into their bank of Catholic guilt, to process privately with God in their final hour. The slate could never be wiped clean with apologies. That was the rule.

Much of the time, he and Margaret lived in relative harmony, but today Moses felt tired of his own moral code. Tired of being respectful and good-natured and dutiful. He felt sad and sorry for himself that his primary relationship was with his mother. As he walked along the river towards the town statue of his mother's precious Virgin Mary, it seemed that the very pavement under him was part of some plot to secure him to this square mile of town land where he had spent his whole life. This cosy safe existence where nothing ever changed. An extension to the pub, a few new tracks on the karaoke, switching from solid fuel to oil heating, minor alterations made to try and convince himself that life was somehow moving on. Pathetic attempts to keep busy in a life that had become stagnant, one year moving into the other until Moses would become a man of sixty with a grey mullet sitting in an empty pub.

Of the four people who had ever truly loved him, one was dead, one was an unbalanced homosexual, one had married another man, and the other was his mother. It was hardly a reference for Ireland's Most Lovable. Hardly enough, surely, to have kept him welded, as he was, to this place.

He should have left Gorrib after Rose did what she did. He saw that now. Gone to England or America. Pursued his music. Joined a band. He'd be living now in Liverpool or Boston, married to some girl with Irish roots who was impressed by his heritage and his lyricism. Spending Saturday afternoons in shopping malls on the outskirts of some big city, with a rake of kids tugging at his jacket looking for money for an ice-cream or a new pair of runners. Like the dozens of boys he had been to school with who had turned their place of birth into a personal myth. Coming home once a year to coo over the Guinness and lament the changes. Small-town Ireland was better when you carried it around in your heart as memories. Living here was a different story. The past spilled into the present in the ageing faces of old schoolteachers, the bells for Benediction, the river coming and going on its circular journey to the sea – a new generation of swans dipping and gliding as they had done twenty years ago when he had watched them with Rose.

Moses stood for a few minutes beyond the statue and watched the swans in that blank way of a man who has long since immunized himself against the dangers of romantic recollection. He was vaguely aware of a woman walking down from the town in his general direction and as he turned with the automatic curiosity that was inherent in every Gorrib inhabitant regardless of their emotional state, he saw it was Rose.

She looked terrible. Even from this distance, he could see by the thoughtless swaying of her gait that she was in a distressed state. As she moved closer and saw him, Moses knew that she was going to come over. That whatever it was that was the matter with her, she was going to come and tell him about it. She was wearing an old tracksuit and a pair of flat flip-flop sandals which, while not quite slippers, were not outdoor wear. She wasn't carrying a handbag and it was pretty obvious that she had probably just run out of the house. She must have had a row with Brian. A row with the scheming shit that she had married, and now she wanted to come and tell Moses all about it. Nice, good-natured, understanding Moses. The man she had dumped in favour of the bastard who was clearly making her life a misery now. That she married another man was forgivable, but somehow, the fact that she was unhappy in her choice was the ultimate insult. Moses could cope with her loving

Brian. He had got used to that idea. That he was still alone himself, well, that was his own lookout. But the thought of her suffering was too much for him. Making shit of all the years he had half waited and fully wanted in between. The mountain of grief he had climbed just to reach this flat plateau that was his bachelor life. Her misery mocked him, and today, Moses was having none of it.

He turned towards her and started walking in a hurry. He saw her hesitate as he passed her out, nodding, 'Morning, Rose,' and walked back towards the bar.

If he felt bad, Moses put it to the back of his mind in the box marked 'Do Not Open'. Seeing Rose had pushed him into a kind of epiphany. Sandra coming back into his life was the most exciting thing that had happened for years. She was different and sexy and she was full of life. Rose was a part of his life that had been swallowed by the deadening chug of every day passing unnoticed into the next.

Sandra was going to save him from a future as uneventful and predictable as his past.

And if he had to shave off the beloved mullet and upset his mother in the process, well then, so be it.

FIELD REPORT FIVE

Extract from *The Cupid's Handbook*. 1957 Edition.

THE SOULLESS

The confiscation of a mortal soul is not a task that can be taken lightly, which is why only God Himself can undertake it. The eternal facility of OHF means that He is the only Deity who is omnipresent and therefore He, and only He, is in a position to judge which individuals are no longer deserving of this most basic human right. It is spiritual law that everyone, no matter what crime against fellow or God they have committed in their lifetime, has the right to redeem themselves right up until their death and thus stand a chance of entering the kingdom of Heaven. However, from time to time God may come across an act so heinous that He deems it only fit He exercise His right to declare a human beyond His forgiveness and expel them from His kingdom. These people are known as The Soulless, and being no longer possessed of their spiritual facility, they are impossible to monitor from our heavenly dimension or any department within it. Angels who may have to visit Earth (and especially cupids who live there) must at all times be careful if appearing through such dramatic means as flight or cloud surfing as The Soulless will be undetectable by our Clear Coast Monitors and may be watching you from an airborne vehicle. It has been known for an angel to appear to a chosen party for a standard dream advice session and find a Soulless partner in the bed next to them staring at said angel in terror. (Some might argue that such individuals deserve a fright from time to time, but making one's identity known to any human is against the rules and disciplinary proceedings may nonetheless be considered necessary.) However, the risk of this happening is slight as there are never more than a handful of The Soulless on Earth at any one time.

Note: A list of the current Soulless can be acquired from the department of Mortal and Deadly Sin, Purgatory.

Well firstly, what angel in their right mind is going to voluntarily enter Purgatory just to pick up a list and secondly, 'handful' my arse. Everyone knows that there are literally thousands of Soulless on Earth at any given time. Sure, even mortals know that. They have an expression for it. It's called 'being soulless'. I sometimes wonder who writes these bloody manuals, honest I do.

When it comes to big G deciding which souls to confiscate, normal rules and regs do not apply. It always just comes down to whether He likes you or not. It's His job, of course, to like most people. Or at least love them, which as we all know is not the same thing. So when He does decide to knock somebody off the books, there is usually a reason although it is rarely as grave a crime as people imagine. To be fair to God, there is not one of us working in any department who would swap places with Him. It's a tough job. Omnipresence? Don't be talking! To be everywhere at the same time – monitoring all those millions of souls – keeping an eye on world events? I mean try to take it in. It would be like watching every TV station in the world simultaneously and playing PlayStation with your feet. Having the eyes pinned on CNN whilst keeping up with a Delia Smith soufflé. Only worse times a million again.

So what really fascinates God (and who can blame Him) is that people are complex. OK, so he murdered someone – but he loves his mother and has an interest in landscape painting. You'd want to check in with a guy like that in another few years to see if he'll come around. Dictators are another case in point. So they do horrible, horrible things, but you know, sometimes they are acting in the misguided belief that God is driving them. And religious wars? Where do you start sorting that one out? God's a clever guy. He's all seeing, all knowing – that kind of intelligence needs a challenge. Something to get His teeth into. So while there are the big guys down here being bad, it is often those minor sins that will get you excommunicated from His kingdom. Imagine now being Himself and it's a busy Monday morning and He has better things to do than check in on some nobody in the suburbs for no other reason than He said He would in the scriptures. Guy's been given everything. Nice wife, couple of kids, house, car, blah, blah – all your basic Western civilization amenities. And there he is, pissing on the toilet seat, again, just like he was last time G checked him out. Knowing that his wife has to clean up after him. After she's been pleading with him not to every day for fifteen years. Deliberately. Because he can. Because he knows she's a soft touch and will never leave him. Now that's just mean. God's got East Africa running at the same time, a place where people are having real problems, dying of starvation and disease. People are not pissing on toilet seats just to annoy their wives because they are too busy trying to find food. They are grateful for every mouthful, every drop of rain. Well, you'd lose patience, wouldn't you? You'd say, 'I don't give a shite about you petty bollix. Sink or swim, why don't you, I'm not wasting my precious time on you any more.' It's the bores, the ingrates, the bigots. Those endless, complaining monologues that, despite Love Thy Neighbour being shoved down humans' throats now for centuries, remind God that He is losing all those mini-battles every day. Racist jokes. Hold me down or I'll die laughing. Patronizing your neighbours because you've got a better car than they have. Well of course you have, a reward for going to Mass on Sunday and looking down your nose at other people's coats. It's those people who have missed the point. Who think they're off the hook because they haven't murdered anyone, or were fortunate enough to be born into the 'right' religion. It's the smug, self-satisfied creatures – the 2.4 with an Audi in the drive – who say their prayers at night, as if butter wouldn't melt and it's always 'God bless Us Four, no more, for ever and ever, amen.' They're the ones He targets.

My guess is Brian Fitzgerald wasn't made Soulless because he was riding Regina Malone on the sly or planning to exploit refugees in his lap-dancing club. He just said the word 'nigger' once too often.

Did I know he was Soulless before I decided to cash in the invisibility and flight permit and have a wander round the house looking for something I could use to discredit him with his wife? Answer no – but it was no great surprise to me and honestly, while torturing a Soulless by dancing around the place going ner-ner-ner-ner-ner could not perhaps be strictly defined as being in the direct service of the Almighty Father, I can't say I didn't thoroughly enjoy it. Especially when I took flight. How his ticker didn't give out and floor the bastard, I swear I'll never know. Never mind. Maybe next time. That would put an easy end to this sorry business, God forgive me (and I'm pretty sure He will).

So where am I now? And more importantly – who cares? Certainly not the lads upstairs. There is an eerie silence from the department. It's been a couple of weeks since Gaby's last huffy memo, and yet I'm not daft. I know they're up there watching. I was fully expecting hailstone and thunder over the whole Brian incident, but there's not been a word from them and, like the book says, I went to the trouble of checking, they should have been down on my head over my flagrant abuse of the invisibility and flight permit. Yet there's not been a sausage out of them. And Dermot Leeson? Well, frankly, who he? I've virtually forgotten all about the poor bastard, though I've plans afoot – but *they* don't know that. They could not wait to get me down here, then there's some blah-blah get on with it, then – nothing. Well, it's like I don't exist. Have they stopped caring, I wonder? I don't think so. Am I just so fantastic that they've decided to put the rule book aside and apply some sort of amnesty on yours truly? *Au contraire* is my bet. I suspect, not to put too fine a point on it, fishiness of the highest order and I'm not talking loaves. I've heard of one or two cases over the years of we innocent field workers being lured into nasty situations outside of our normal domain. If you want A to marry B I'll do my level best. But if there's something else on the agenda, you better let me know about it early so I can be prepared, because frankly, if you're going to swarm my patch with pestilence all of a sudden, I don't know if I could cope.

Anyway, the job in hand isn't going too badly. Over coffee a few days ago I popped the camera film into poor Rose's bag so part one is more or less accomplished. She got the film back, saw the photos and was upset. In the end of course, I needn't have bothered because Her Royal Lardy Arse Regina had left her coat on the bedpost and Rose's suspicions had already been severely aroused before she got the pictures developed. Then there was the whole messy business of *who* had taken the pictures seeing as how the two culprits featured. I had to allay the beginnings of a whole Gorb sex-ring theory in poor Rose's mind by bluffing my way through a limited knowledge of 'cameras these days', automatic timers and the like. I don't know that I'd have got away with it except that Rose was so distressed that she wasn't thinking straight. Not pretty to watch, but then you've got to be cruel, etc. She moved back into her parents' house and I'm working away on the next stage. Managed to get my contact in Probable Futures to cross-reference Gorrib and a few names and, what do you know, it looks like the key players are going to be at Bosanova's disco this Saturday. Hopefully I'll be able to throw a few shapes around and make some – whoops – excuse I – the monitor's flashing up 'MAIL'.

Help is en route. Not long now. Keep the faith. Gabriel.

Help? What's not long? What, in the name of God, and you can be sure He's behind this somewhere, are they up to?

I do not – and I mean *do not* like the sound of this.

The sooner I get those matches made and get the hell out of here the better!

21

Rose had not walked on this beach for years. She used to come here all the time as a child. As soon as there was a glimpse of sun in the weekend sky, her mother would throw together a few sandwiches and her father would then hurry the three of them into the car, impatiently revving the old Cortina, anxious that the clement weather mightn't last the twenty-minute journey to Killa Strand. Once the rain had held off for the duration of their hurried picnic lunch, Mrs Davitt would pack the basket back into the car and wait on the Foxford rug while Rose and her father walked the length of the strand. Frank Davitt made magic out of sand; 'Millions of tiny diamonds,' he told his five-year-old daughter when she asked why the ground glittered in the sun. Then he would lift her up and carry her on his shoulders as the young girl put her tiny hands under his chin, delighted that she and no other could use her father as a carriage. As she grew older, Rose walked with him, begrudging the fact that she didn't have a sister to swap bikinis with or a brother to introduce her to his friends.

She would think of her father's sand diamonds and of how one day a man would buy her one for real and make her as happy and safe as she had been when she was small enough to rest her cheek on her father's tweed cap. When he would raise her up so she was close to the clouds and say, 'Blow them away, Rosie. Blow those rain clouds away until we're safe back in the car.' And she believed him. Believed she had just enough wind in her to keep the clouds at bay. It would rain. It would always rain. Rose couldn't stop that, but somehow they would always make the car before the first drop pelted the white sand, turning the world grey again.

Rose knew she didn't have power in her life. Not real power. The kind that made her able to stand up to her husband or inspire her children to respect her as an individual. But she had always managed to keep trouble at bay. Keep the clouds that sometimes threatened to engulf her in their shadows from pissing down all over her life. And now here it was – the big storm. She had always known, somewhere in her heart, that her husband didn't love her. Now she had the pictures to prove it. She could huff and she could puff but as sure as the world keeps turning, Rose could not turn this storm back. It was too late.

She sat in the car and looked out over the bay. The white houses of the seaside resort on the other side of the coast were as small as buttons; she could just make out the matchstick figures playing on the tourist beach. Killa Strand was empty. The first sunny day this year and everyone was over there having fun while she was here, on her empty beach.

Rose was devastated and, while she knew there were people around her, she felt utterly alone. Davy was disgusted, and had chosen punishing his father over supporting his mother. He had turned the house into a twenty-four-hour rave-a-thon and filled it with every scrap of unsuitable local gutty and layabout he could muster. Mary was caught up in doing her own thing, and had said rather insensitively, 'He's a complete bastard. You should have done this years ago. Why did you stay with him so long?' Challenging statements that Rose had neither the energy nor the inclination to answer, even to herself. She had moved back into her parents' house on Church Street and while she felt grateful that she still had a place she could call home to go to, and was glad that neither of them were still alive to see the mess her marriage had become, her parents' absence nonetheless made Rose feel more alone. The only person she had properly spoken to since it had happened was Christian.

'I feel partly responsible,' he said.

Rose had thought that was strange and asked, 'Why?'

'Well, I went to the chemists with you to put the photos in. I mean, if I hadn't found your camera when it fell out of your bag in Keegan's, and if I hadn't suggested you get the pictures processed that day, well . . .'

'I'd never have known? It's better that I know, Christian. It's always best to know the truth.'

But even as she said it, Rose knew that she didn't believe it. It was better not to know. Better for women like her who were happier plodding along in the half light of a loveless marriage than being alone. That was all she had ever wanted. To not be alone. As an only child, she feared the day her parents would die and leave her with no one to care for. When her parents finally did die she had Brian, and the kids were still small enough to need her. But now they were adults and Brian was what? He hadn't left her. She was the one who had walked out. The greater part of her wished now that she hadn't. In truth, it wasn't that he had slept with Regina that bothered her as much as the fact that she had found out about it. She had set this chain of events in motion and she did not feel entirely in control. She could have, she thought now, *should* have stayed and worked things through. Although she knew deep down that the marriage was dead, if she went back now and stuck this whole thing out, the incident would blow over and life would be back to normal.

She'd said as much to Christian while he was helping her unpack the large suitcase of her things he had insisted she bring down to Church Road.

'What life?' Christian had said to her. 'What on Earth would you want to go back for. You have to move forwards, Rose. Forge a new life for yourself.'

Rose allowed herself a cynical shrug.

'Rose, you're a great woman. You don't need him dragging you down like this. Look, I'm a stranger here and I took to you straight away. I'll help you through this, Rose, and Moses he still has a graw for you. I'll bet now he'll be down any . . .'

Christian trailed off as Rose began to cry. She didn't like dissolving like that in front of him, but Moses had looked clean through her that awful day when she had run out of the house not knowing which way to turn. She had seen him standing along the river and had allowed herself to hope – but he had walked straight past her. If the rejection was deliberately meant to hurt her, Rose didn't know or care. Whatever they had once been, it was a long time ago and she could hardly blame him for not wanting to get involved.

Then Christian did the strangest thing. He put his hands on her shoulders and he said, 'God loves you, Rose. God loves you. Never forget that. Everything will work out fine. I promise you.'

She stopped crying, partly from the genuine warmth in his voice, but also from surprise at his choice of words. She had never put Christian down as a, well, Christian! Rose went to Mass regularly, and while she purported to have great faith, and religion was an everyday feature of life in Gorrib, God was not a name that cropped up in everyday conversation. At least, not in any real sense. Platitudes were two a penny, but actual faith was an essentially private thing that you didn't share with other people. The way this camp new friend of hers brought it up embarrassed Rose and she started to unpack her case.

Sitting now watching the sky boss the sea around with its changeable whims, whipping lines of foam across the horizon where the inlet met the ocean, turning it from deep green to black as the clouds spun over and back in front of the sun, Rose struggled to believe that there was someone up there watching over her. If God was behind those clouds somewhere, he was probably far too busy manipulating this erratic weather to be bothering with the likes of her. Still, the rain was holding off, so she got out of the car and clambered down the wide stones that formed natural stairs from the recently tarmacked 'viewing point' to the beach itself. The heel of her sandals slid across the polished stone, so she took them off and then padded barefoot across the powdery sand facing into the deserted strip. As she walked, the familiarity of Killa Strand, with its tall golden grass whispering into the breeze, shallow waves sniggering across the shoreline making shot silk of the damp sand, calmed her with the knowledge that some things never change. She could still smell the salt and the dead crabs where the wind caught yesterday's abandoned seaweed. The sand still glittered a billion tiny diamonds and despite the holiday villages and activity centres that had swallowed up chunks of the western coastline, this place was still deserted. It still belonged to her. As she walked, Rose began to remember the times she had been here before, with her parents, with Moses. Never with Brian. Not in all the years they were together. This place was the same, and Rose was somehow comforted by the knowledge that some part of the girl who had walked this strand before was still here. There were things that she would never know again. The smell of the backs of her babies' necks; their tiny hands seeking out her breast in the night; her first kiss with Moses. Moments she had treasured that were gone for ever. She struggled to find a treasured memory in which

Brian featured, but couldn't find a single one. Her wedding day had been tainted with morning sickness and . . . she felt suddenly cold. The weather was turning. On a whim Rose threw back her head and she blew. Then she ran, as fast as she could, back in the direction of the car. She made it just before the first drop splashed the windscreen and seconds later it was lashing down in sheets.

Rose joined in, sobbing in that gushing, ugly way she had always feared, even when she was completely on her own.

But even as she did, some part of Rose knew, for the first time since that fateful night when she had met Brian Fitzgerald, that if she had enough wind to hold back the clouds, she was going to be all right.

22

The man from *Romantic Moments* magazine was making himself right at home.

'Any chance of a biscuit, love?' he said when Mary, entranced by the pink plaits topped off with a quirky Boy George-style hat, plonked down a mug of tea rather clumsily beside him on the coffee table.

'I'm afraid we don't have any,' she replied. Mayday Matthews looked her up and down, his face openly wondering how she managed to achieve such a lumpen figure without the aid of biscuits.

'I'm on a diet,' she added somewhat mournfully.

'Well I'm *not*,' Mayday announced, determined to make the most of his temporary food amnesty permit. The London-based cupid, whose undercover role as editor of *Romantic Moments* magazine made him one of the best troubleshooters in the business, hadn't eaten a bite since his last permit had expired in 1972 and he was determined to make the most of it.

'What say we wander into town for a frappacino and a bagel? On me.'

Mayday was no gaw. It was full expenses and permits upfront, or he didn't move an inch. He had two invisibilities, a flight, two months' food amnesty and at least half a dozen manifestations in his armoury. He had been surprised, firstly that the department had acceded to what even he felt to be a somewhat greedy list of requests, and secondly shocked at the expediency at which they were granted. Christian must be on some mother of a mission if even his appointed second in command was getting the royal treatment. And there was the other thing. He knew Christian, of course – he was something of a legend. Bit of a serious character, though. Very committed. None of your hats and handbags and mincing around Soho on his days off. Officially, he was Mayday's line manager, but the lawless lady boy was a law unto himself and had set himself up as a freelance 'emergency service' to take over where other cupids were failing. He had always thought that Christian disapproved of him and was surprised that he had requested his help on this job. But still, here he was, and secretly Mayday Matthews was rather pleased and proud to have been commissioned. Besides, he could eat his head off for the next few months and if there was mischief to be made manifesting oneself in all the wrong places, Mayday was the man to do it.

Mary didn't look like she was going to pose too much of a challenge. Fat virgins were something of a speciality, being among his core readership on *R. Moms*. He'd already nipped into town and had a look at the love interest earlier and frankly – despite her file saying that she was in danger of aligning an 'unsuitable union', as far as Mayday was concerned, the lanky lad-about-town was simply out of her league. She had 'farmer's wife' written all over her and, from what little investigation he had done (mainly cow-counting on the train down) Mayday felt confident that the place was crawling with suitable specimens. Lovelorn farmer with chubby virgin. How hard could it be? Yes, this job was going to be a doddle and he'd be back in Soho chawing down dinner in the Ivy, courtesy of a leftover invisibility permit, in no time.

Winning the competition and then this exotic creature from London arriving on her doorstep was undoubtedly the most exciting thing that had ever happened to Mary Fitzgerald in her entire life. And yet it was just her luck, she thought, *just her luck*, to be so immersed in a miserable bucket of shite that she couldn't enjoy it.

Mary had taken her mother walking out of the house badly, but not in the sense that she thought she would. She was shocked that her father had been having an affair – and with Theo's mother of all people. But when she stopped to think about it, the shock was more that her own father was having sex with her soon-to-be mother-in-law than any surprise that her father had betrayed her mother. The whole thing also brought up two unpalatable realities: how much she genuinely disliked her own father and how much she loved her mother. Facts which she didn't feel she had the energy to deal with as she was still trying to wade through the increasingly confused mire of emotional stress she was developing around her impending marriage to Theo.

Ella had made her write a list of pros and cons, but she became more confused when she realized that the only pro was 'Theo Malone!' and the cons were non-payment of ring, no interest in wedding plans, disinterest in everything to do with Mary in general – including free honeymoon and his mother was a slut. She had to stop herself there before the imbalance became so obvious that sanity might prevail.

Mary had tried to be there for her own mother but, frankly, found the whole thing too painful. There was not a person in the town, her own children included, who did not know that Rose had married the wrong man, and the whole issue of marrying the wrong man was not one that Mary wanted shunted to the top of her own agenda right now. She talked to Ella about her parents' break up, but her perky friend made her feel small by saying, 'Really you should be able to talk to Theo about all this stuff, Mary. You are going to *marry* him after all.'

'But his mother's involved.'

'Even more reason for you to thrash it out with him.'

She sensed that Ella had had enough of all this Theo business, and sometimes wondered if her friend wasn't possibly jealous of her marrying the town hunk. If only she knew! Which of course she *did*, and that just added to Mary's confusion. Life seemed to have gone from being very simple to very complicated in a matter of weeks. Mary had read enough self-help books to know that the problems life threw at you should be viewed as 'learning experiences'. Except that she was beginning to realize that she had never had any problems before, not real ones anyway. She had kept real life at bay for this long and now it was all tumbling down on her like an sack of rats. Squirming and nipping and demanding her attention when, in all fairness, she did no know where to even begin sorting it all out in her head. And now, on top of everything, this mad transexual with his pink plaits and his funny hat and his, surely not, lipgloss was here, looking for a feed of fancy coffee and buns in Gorrib. If only she knew how to say no. But so rarely did anyone ask anything of her that she didn't, so Mary put on her raincoat and walked Mayday up to Keegans.

'Eugh! Who he?'

Mayday was experiencing mild culture shock. It's not that he hadn't travelled. In the hundred or so years he'd been on the job he had seen things far worse than a wheelchair-bound drunk blowing his nose in an open arch onto the pavement. It's just that, as a confirmed urbanite, he felt it behest his position to make a fuss about it. What was glamour, after all, if not a sensitivity (albeit faux) to the crudeness of the uncultured male?

'Hemlock Anam.' said Mary

'Ahhhh.' So now. That was what this gig was all about. He hadn't heard that name used in a long time. Anam – Gaelic for 'soul'. It was the name given to cupids in this part of the world, years ago. He hadn't realized there were any of them left. Although by the cut of the poor sod wheeling himself through the Gorrib lunchtime traffic, spitting obscenities at drivers and pedestrians alike, it didn't look like he was currently gainfully employed in God's Good Service. Must have been expelled, and on his last legs by the look of him, thought Mayday. This is a cover-up job. No wonder they came through pronto with all the permits. Virgin with farmer set-up, my arse. They've sent us in to make sure the resurrection goes off without comment. And if he's a bad bastard (which Mayday felt fairly certain he was judging by his basic manners) Lucifer might decide to step in at the last minute and try to recruit him. Then it'll be a plague of crows and all manner of bedlam if they can't get a priest on board for the last rites. Plus, if the mortals get a load of that going down – well things could get ugly. Exorcisms and satanic things in general were not within Mayday's wardrobe of skills and he felt slightly annoyed that Christian hadn't bothered to mail him and give him the low-down himself. Him Upstairs had a huge gob-on when it came to resurrecting expelled angels. There had only ever been two others in the whole world, that Mayday had heard of in his lifetime anyway. He could have screwed a million more permits out of them for the huge responsibility he was about to deputize. He sure as hell hoped Christian knew what he was doing because, frankly, if they messed this one up they'd be knocking on Lucifer's door begging for a bedsit in Hell.

On the bright side, Mary had said that she was going to the local disco that evening and there was nothing in the whole wide world Mayday liked more than dressing up for a disco. He'd pop into Christian on the way down and surprise him. If he was headed for a stint in Purgatory, Mayday thought he might as well live it up while he still could.

23

In their anxiety to get at the women of Gorrib, Dermot and Vinny arrived at Bosanova early. There was no queue, which relieved Dermot who, on account of his high profile, was accustomed to being ushered past the shuffling Saturday crowds that huddled around the door of Dublin's night spots by compliant bouncers. Dermot felt a tinge of mortification on both their behalfs as Vinny grandly paid their four euros entrance fees to the girl at the front desk, insisting that she keep the change from a ten euro note, then looking at Dermot, seeking approval for what he clearly thought was a gesture of supreme suavity.

The place was empty. Not 'quiet' nor 'not busy' – but empty. Not a sinner, not even bar staff in sight. After all of the trouble the pair of them had been to preparing for this evening, this was not a good start. They sat at a booth overlooking the sunken dance floor like a couple of expectant schoolgirls at their first disco, both too embarrassed to mention to the other the golden rule of the Irish mating etiquette. That is, first you spend four hours in the pub, linger at the bar at closing time, then pretend that the only reason you are going to a disco is for the after-hours drinking. Even though you are going there to pick up women, and privately know you must be absolutely hammered in order to have the courage to do so. A detail that both men had overlooked. After half an hour, Vinny was beginning to shake with fear. The emptiness of the room, the soberness of their state and the close proximity of the dance floor made both men feel more like contestants in some bizarre single-sex dance competition than two lads out on the town. When a barman did eventually appear, Dermot bounded across the room in two steps and ordered a table load of alcoholic beverages, forgetting that Vinny's favourite tipple was Club Orange. There was no way Dermot was going back up to the smirking barman to order a 'mineral', and his look left the teetotal farmer in no doubt whatsoever as to that fact. And thus it was that Vinny had his first drink. A vodka and tonic, then a Bacardi and Coke, followed swiftly by a pint of stout – in his urgency to make up for lost ground, Dermot's selection had been somewhat chaotic. By the time Bosanova started to fill up, swiftly and with much readjusting of waistbands (men) and rushing to the toilets to reapply lipgloss (ladies), Vinny could feel the warm glow of artificially instigated self-confidence flood through him.

'I'm getting up forra dance,' he announced to his companion, although the two square metres of corralled pine floor was still empty of jigging bodies. Dermot grabbed his trouser leg in the nick of time and hissed, 'You'll do no such thing. Sit down.'

'Rightio compadre,' Vinny said far too loudly, almost spilling his full pint down the back of a man who was, impressively, even larger and more ham-fisted than he.

'You're the boss, me bucko – ah now lookaher! Look at that one over there – will I go over and have a go, Dermot? Will I? D'yasee there's two fine things after walking in the door there.' Then, driving the point home by holding his slopping pint aloft in the direction of the entrance, he continued, 'Over there in the pink top with the blondy haired one. Can you see, Dermot? Can you see, there, look at them, sure they're lovely! HERE GIRLS! OVER HERE!'

This was turning into something of an ordeal. Men getting drunk together is fine if it happens at the same rate. Then the pair of you are making gobs of yourselves on the dance floor *together*; clutching each other's arms and swearing eternal friendship *together*; getting lost on the way home *together*. If one of you gets sick in a taxi, that's fine as long as the other party is too drunk to either notice or care. Minding messy drunk friends, especially, it seemed to Dermot, large naive farmers, was simply not on his agenda for a stress-free fun night out. He knew he should try to relax. After all he knew nobody here (although he could feel eyes boring into the back of his head, and suspected he'd been spotted as the prodigal son) and it wasn't as if this was a corporate event where Vinny might screw up some big deal for him, even if Dermot were in a position to have a big deal screwed up. Which reminded Dermot that he shouldn't, by all accounts, be in a disco called Bosanova in the middle of nowhere cruising women when, in actual fact, his life was falling apart at the seams. He should be back up in Dublin trying to sort it all out. Following this line of thought was an increase in his breathing speed accompanied by a sensation of physical panic, and as Vinny, taking advantage of his minder's loosening grip on his trouser leg, decided he could wait no longer and launched himself onto the dance floor, Dermot made a beeline for the men's room. It was a small affair with just two urinals and a cubicle, and as far as Dermot could ascertain, he was the sole occupant. He ran the cold tap and splashed his face with water. As he was drying himself off with the hand towel, Dermot noticed that his shoes had become infused with a strange white light, which seemed to be emanating from underneath the toilet door. The cubicle then seemed to glow, just for a split second, reminding Dermot of Doctor Who's tardis. A man emerged, a right worrying-looking creature with pink plaits and a girl's hat, hesitated slightly at the mirror to apply, surely not lipgloss? and on seeing Dermot casually said, 'Evening,' and walked out of the door. The man did not, Dermot noticed, wash his hands.

Dermot was faced then with a choice. This was clearly an extremely worrying turn of events. Once, such a thing might possibly have happened and there might, if you were prepared to spend a couple of years researching said event, even be some logical explanation. Twice, and you were into the realms of best-case scenario – madness, and worse case – fantastical semi-erotic homosexual day-dream of inexplicable peculiarity. His choice was to go home and spend the rest of the evening, possibly the rest of his life, crouched in a corner of his house drowning in his own drool. The other was to just forget it. He'd had a few drinks, he was in a disco, he looked nice, he smelled good and, yes, after a quick check, Dermot found that he still had all ten digits, both arms and both legs. So a man with pink hair manifested himself out of thin air. Again. What could he do about that? Nothing. What did he do the last time? Nearly have a nervous break-down. What was he going to do about it now? Bloody well go back out there and forget all about it and do what he did the last time, which was get his hands on some lucky female and show her he was in full working order.

Quietly calmed by his mini-epiphany, Dermot all but glided back into the thronging club. He spotted Vinny talking enthusiastically to a couple of girls and decided to just let him get on with it. They all looked happy enough and maybe that was all the guy needed to give him a push – the few drinks. The dance floor was heaving with bodies now, and Smokey's hit song 'Living Next Door to Alice' was belting out. When a natural break in the chorus occurred, everyone in the room, including the DJ and barmen, shouted in unison, 'ALICE! ALICE! WHO THE FUCK IS ALICE?' Everyone except Dermot. He was, he knew, a stranger here. Although this was where he had been born, he was estranged from this tribal voice. That was the way he had always kept it. He always made sure he was where he should be, always joined in; but kept part of himself back; then stood on the periphery and watched for where he could make his next move. He had the mates he went drinking with, and a respectable amount of back-slapping blagardery went on, but he had never witnessed anything like the universal camaraderie that existed in Bosanova that night. It felt like a wedding where everyone knew everyone and, for this evening at least, liked each other. Dermot felt a small twinge of regret that he hadn't grown up here, or rather a child-like sense that he was somehow being left out of the party.

When Smokey was through, the DJ slid on a bang-up-to-date dance track. Dermot's heels started to swivel from side to side, drawing a size ten triangle on the sticky carpet. By anyone's standards, Dermot had always cut a cool dash on the dance floor. None of your amateur shite; he was a smooth foot slider as opposed to a psychiatric arm flinger and it was just as he was contemplating licking his legs into a few sly moves that he saw her.

Not just 'her', as in your reasonably pretty female who you'd be happy to put up for the night. If all truth be known, this wasn't a 'her' with a lower case 'h' at all. This was a 'She'. As in 'She who must be obeyed'. A top-to-toe hot-trotting scorcher. Dermot was heating up just looking at her from across the room. She was just this side of out-and-out tarty in a tightly cut corseted jacket with a high collar and a plunging neckline, from which her tortured tits were struggling to escape. Next down was a long black skirt that a nun might have worn, except it had a side split, which Dermot ascertained was almost certainly crotch height. An undertaking that was helped somewhat by the glimmer of thigh flesh that indicated hold ups were also on the menu tonight. The long, shapely legs (in hold ups!) were rendered all the more delectable by the supports on which they teetered, which was a pair of the highest, pointiest, strappiest most complicatedly tied buckled shoes that Dermot had ever seen. They were pure Parisian porn shop and, as he walked over to her, Dermot wondered where a girl from Gorrib might score herself a pair of shoes of such monumental fetishism. She was standing at a small pine bar on the edge of dance floor looking down on it, and Dermot stood himself next to her, noting that She and her two friends were without drinks. There was the simplest intro. She briefly flicked her gaze in his direction and that was when he nearly lost the run of himself altogether. Black eyes sunk into her face with a mountain of kohl and mascara and glossy scarlet lips. A face that was drawn on in pure fantasy. This woman was sex personified. Sex on legs, legs with hold ups and porn shoes. He doubted if he'd be able to get her as far as his place without tearing into her like a deranged dog. This (and his chum in the Calvin Klein briefs agreed) was more like it.

He had his mouth open and arm outstretched in a gesture of gentlemanly can-I-buy-you-ladies-a-drink? generosity when Vinny, carrying an armful of glasses and a glowing expression of unadultered drink-infused joy suddenly landed on top of them.

'Now girls – here we are then. A lager and lime, a Bacardi and Coke, a gin and tonic and a Cinzano for me. Jesus, Dermot, where'd you come out of? I thought you'd disappeared off into the night.' Then as a jokey aside to the short fat friend, 'Dermot's a *terrible* ladies' man. You look awful empty-handed there altogether. Will I get you a pint?'

Vinny was certainly taking to this whole drinking lark big time, and seemed touchingly impressed by his own ability to go to a bar, purchase drinks and ferry them across a crowded room all by himself.

'No – I'm all right,' Dermot mumbled, put out that Vinny had somehow managed to inveigle himself into the company of the only woman in the room that interested him.

'To my hero, Vincent!' the back of the tight, black jacket announced.

It was the voice he recognized. English. North London. Unmistakable.

'Dermot, this is Sandra,' Vinny said, glowing.

The lap dancer turned and looked at him, through him actually, then turned again to Vinny and addressed her two friends.

'This man is my hero,' she said in the pronounced way of a confident woman about to relate an anecdote. 'He literally saved me from drowning.' Vinny shuffled around modestly, clearly delighted to be basking in all this female glory. 'Scooped me up in those big arms of his and carried me away to safety.'

The two friends looked bored and when Sandra flirtingly declared, 'Big strong farmers – you don't get many of them to the pound where I come from!' Vinny was in his element, an open grin plastered across his chunky face.

Dermot felt . . . Dermot felt . . .? He struggled to define it. Surprised? A little. Disappointed? Very. Confused? Definitely. But more than that he felt, well, tired. It seemed to him that he had been so frightened and so worried for so long that he had just sort of had enough. He didn't want to know how Sandra came to know Vinny, or why she was here and in those few moments since he had walked across the room the overwhelming desire to ride her had just, sort of, dissipated. She wasn't stalking him, he knew that from the way she didn't even recognize him, but far from being happy about that fact he felt slightly crushed. Like a balloon with the wind gone out of it. There was him all puffed up and tight with his sleek city manners and his big ideas, and there was poor 'aul Vinny enjoying the attention of a woman whom Dermot had first assumed was stalking him and was now disappointed that she wasn't. Life was just turning out to be too strange for him to take tonight and all he wanted to do was to go home.

So he did.

24

Mags McGreavy was flaming. She knew that Sandra had stayed over; had seen her scuttle out of the back bar door just after six. Margaret had developed a dawn routine since Johnny had died. She found herself waking automatically at five a.m. each day, and instinctively came to believe that it was her husband looking for some chat from beyond the grave. The old woman's morning reflection, the time she spent in solitude with her first cup of tea wandering across her memories in the company of God and her dead husband, was extremely precious to her. Margaret shared every minute of her day with family and friends and customers. While she loved company, the old woman cherished this secret time above all the gossiping and business that followed when the world rose. Now the spell had been broken. And not just by anyone. It was that brazen English hussy, always a competitor for her husband's affections when he was alive. Margaret felt Sandra had somehow deliberately muscled in on their musing now that he was dead. She was hurt by the intrusion, but Margaret was not reared in a generation that 'gave good hurt'. Hers was the pre-therapy era where punishment could permute to suit every occasion.

'Your new girlfriend stayed over,' she announced to Moses as he had the first spoonful of cornflakes held to his lips. He paused slightly, said nothing and carried on. There now. She had him.

'I told Christian his friend Mr Matthews could stay the couple of days. Save him spending out on the B&B. You don't mind, do you?'

'Not at all.'

Moses swallowed the first mouthful after an inordinate amount of chewing and with deliberate nonchalance lifted the second spoonful to his lips. He was guilty, she could tell. But not guilty enough.

'She's your cousin you know.'

She could tell he was la-la-la-ing her away in his head. This was not good enough. Not by a long shot. Enough of the nicey nicey now. Margaret went in for the kill.

'It's none of my business, I know, and Lord knows, Moses, you've had your share of trouble with women over the years . . .'

It was a cheap shot. He hadn't had nearly enough women over the years to have trouble with, and they both knew it.

'But your *cousin*. We-ell . . .'

Moses had had it now.

'Well *what*?' he said, defiantly eyeballing her, but Margaret could see the fear in his eyes.

'It's illegal.'

She said it matter-of-factly. As if she had long since abandoned all hope for him. As if he were just some stranger she was giving independent advice to.

Moses didn't need this today. Not today, of all days. *Illegal? Illegal? What do you mean illegal, you mad old bitch?*

That was the obvious course for the argument to take but, Moses realized, there was another route. One that would render his mother utterly powerless. Throw her right off, get her off his back and give him time to think.

'What do you mean *"it's* illegal?"'

'It's illegal. Against the law.'

'No I mean the *"it's"*. *What's* illegal?'

He had her now. Backed right into a corner. There was nowhere to go from here.

'It just *is*, that's all.'

Easy. She thought she was scary but she wasn't. Would he go the full way? Scare the living shit out of her? *She* wasn't going to say the word. She'd die first.

'Do you mean *sex*, Mammy? Is that what you mean? Do you mean it's illegal to have *sex* with your cousin?'

Margaret got up from the table. She wasn't having filthy talk like this in her . . .

'I won't have that kind of talk in my . . .'

'Because if you do mean *sex*, Mammy, having *sex* with your cousin, well then that's an interesting one. Because as far as I know, having *sex* with your brother or your sister is illegal, but having *sex* with your cousin is perfectly within the boundaries of the law.'

Margaret was bustling out of the kitchen now, powerless to stop this barrage of filth.

'Unless you're a PRIEST,' he shouted after her. 'IN WHICH CASE YOU CAN HAVE *SEX* WITH ANYONE YOU LIKE!'

He shouldn't have done it, but Moses wasn't in a fit state to tolerate one of his mother's sideways lectures when he was feeling this raw.

Sandra had come into the bar last night at around nine. She'd been done up to the nines and Moses had allowed himself the thought that perhaps the make-up and the fancy outfit was for his benefit. The place was jammed. Saturday nights would often fill up with the pre-disco crowd as McGreavy's was on the edge of town and Bosanova was only a short walk away. It was going to be a busy few hours, so Moses set Sandra up with Rose's daughter, Mary, and her pretty friend Ella in a corner table near the bar where he could keep an eye on her. Throughout the evening, during quieter patches, he would try to sit down with the girls for the bit of chat, but Christian kept calling him back to the bar asking him stupid questions and letting on he couldn't cope on his own. Then that loo-la friend of his from London arrived and all hell broke loose.

Your man with the pink plaits arrived at about half nine, just as the farming regulars were settling in for the night's drinking. He was wearing a skintight T-shirt that could have qualified quite easily for a ladies' top. On the front of it was emblazoned in large lettering 'I'M QUEER, DON'T FEAR . . .' and as he walked through the front bar, Moses could see the locals visibly relax as they saw the back of him announce, '. . . YOU'RE NOT MY TYPE!'

'Did I hear somebody call "Mayday"?' were his opening words to Christian, who stood staring at him for a full five seconds in obvious shock.

'Christian, *darling*,' he continued, to the open delight of the more staid regulars as their worst suspicions of this new barman were finally confirmed. 'What*ever* are you doing in this dull little town? Mine's a vodka and tonic, thanks for asking.'

Christian reddened with, it looked to Moses like, a combination of embarrassment and fury. He was, in his boss's brief experience at least, a very even-tempered, calm sort of chap, despite his odd manner and anorexic habits and as is often the way with this type of person, the threat of Christian deviating from his usual serenity was terrifying in itself. So when he asked if he could leave the bar for a few moments, Moses could only accede. Christian took his friend over to the back door, and the two men waved their hands vastly at each other in obvious dispute. Christian, seeming to lose the fight, came back to the bar after ten or so minutes and remained tight-lipped for the rest of the evening. Mayday, on the other hand, ensconced himself with the three girls and held them entertained in such hysterical rapture that Margaret joined them for a piece of the action. Moses privately despaired at Sandra's obvious delight in the whole scene and felt depressed that he wasn't the centre of her attention.

At eleven they all got up. Margaret headed off for bed and, as the others waited for her at the door, Sandra shouted across the bar to Moses, 'We're off to the disco. I'll see you later.'

'Pop in for a nightcap on your way home,' he called back, trying to sound as casual as he could. 'I've work to do on the karaoke so I'll be up late tonight anyway.'

It was a lie, and after the last punter left at half-past midnight, Moses killed some time by asking Christian about his friend. Even more reluctant to reveal information about himself that usual, Christian eventually admitted that the two of them had worked together in the past and that Mayday was in town on business so he had naturally popped in to see him. End of story, although Moses could clearly see that Christian, for some reason, wasn't telling the whole truth. Eventually he persuaded Christian up to bed, for despite his unwillingness to confide in Moses, he seemed reluctant to leave him alone in the bar. Moses dragged out the clearing up for as long as he could, then paced the bar for a full hour until nearly three before he heard a tap on the front window and leapt to unlock the front bar door.

Sandra was pissed. Not obnoxiously so, but she had the unmistakable tang of somebody who didn't know how late it was or how drunk they were until they hit the fresh air.

'Fought I'd cummin like hugh said. No taxis. Drantoo-mudge Cinzanhole. Feel a bit . . .'

Moses managed to get her to the sink behind the bar, where she threw up heartily, then he made some coffee.

After a few minutes the emptied stomach and the coffee seemed to sober her right up.

'I'm sorry, Moses. I'm sure you're dying to get to bed. Maybe I'll kip down here in the bar for a couple of hours, if that's OK? Sleep it off. I'll be out before you get up.'

'I'm not tired,' said Moses.

It was true. He had been hyped all evening with this feeling that something was going to happen tonight. Sandra turning up this late had allowed him to entertain the notion that he was on a promise, although the sane part of him knew that she was here taking refuge with family – the vomiting and the coffee consumption paid testament to that. At the same time, she was here and it was late. It was now that secret part of the night where, if a man keeps a slightly drunk woman up beyond a certain hour, chemistry and tiredness will surely conspire to make something happen. She had not gone home with anyone else and, the cut of her, she certainly could have. The outfit alone would have had them queuing twenty deep at the bar around these parts. Even with the glossy red lips reduced to a dry stain and the eye make-up no more than an inky, messy blot, she was still alluring. More alluring somehow for the spent, sleepy mood that was washing over her. Moses had to keep her awake somehow. Awake, but still tired enough to be persuaded into the comfort of sleeping with him. He kept talking.

'Was the music good tonight?'

'Sure,' she said, pushing the second cup of coffee aside as a hint she was ready to retire.

'Did you dance?'

OK. Stupid question. But he didn't have to impress her. She had just thrown up in his sink after all.

'Oh yeah, sure. The music was great.'

'I bet you blew them away. Were you off about the room on laps then?'

She looked slightly hurt. Christ. What a fucking eejit.

'I mean like, you weren't able to stop yourself . . . force of habit and all that . . . Ha Ha.'

Worse and worser still.

'It's a joke like.'

Sandra didn't look amused, but she didn't look angry either. She just looked very, very tired.

'I'm sorry, Sandra. That was a stupid thing to say.'

Men apologizing. It happened so rarely, she had to acknowledge it. 'Well, it's a stupid job.'

'No it isn't. I'm sure you bring a lot of pleasure to . . . I mean . . . I'm sure you're . . . Ahra fuckit, I don't know what I mean.'

What had he been thinking of? He wasn't able for this at all. It had been too long, and he was too out of practise and you know what? He was feeling tired himself now and what was the point of carrying on. He was only torturing the two of them.

He stood up and said, 'I'll go and get you a duvet.'

'I know you think I'm cheap, Moses. Everyone thinks I'm cheap.'

'No I don't.'

'Ah you do. I don't mind. I don't blame you. I'm

not ashamed of my job. It's just what I do. It's not who I am.'

'Well I think you provide a valuable service. To society.'

That sounded good. He sat down again.

'That's what they say about prostitutes.'

Time to go and get the duvet again.

'That's not what I mean, although . . .' Ah go on, man, chance it. 'I've got a fifty float change in the till if that would cover me?'

Sandra laughed, and said, 'It'd cover you for a dance anyway.'

Moses relaxed. Slightly. Enough to say, 'Well we've no pole but I think I have a ladder out back? Or a spade. I could drum you up a spade, no problem.'

She was awake now. He could see it in her eyes. They were back to life again in that manic, no sleep way.

'I could dance around a spade if I had to. Will I have a go? Go on, go and get me one.'

Moses laughed and walked towards the back door while Sandra took her jacket off. When he turned around, she was standing in the arch of the back bar taking her skirt off.

By the mother of every saint canonized but the woman was stripping off! Fuck's sake, Moses thought, giving himself a stern talking to, it's not like you've never seen a naked woman before. And if you haven't seen many, certainly not for a good while, and certainly never in the bar, well then you'd better not let on or you'll blow your best chance in years and mortify the poor woman into the bargain! Trying to keep the squeak out of his voice, he closed the back door and said, 'Would you believe I lent the spade to Matty Malone the week before last and he hasn't returned it.' Then he wandered over to her, right up as close as he dared without touching and said, 'Does this mean all bets are off?'

Sandra shoved him down onto the velvet couch. It didn't take much to remove the legs from under him. Then she sashayed her G-stringed butt over to the CD player behind the bar and fiddled around making her selection. Moses's head was flying. Supposing his mother came down. Supposing Christian came down. He forced his eyes away from the Country Scene of Rural Ireland upon which they were resolutely fixed and swivelled his head in the direction of Sandra's bare bottom. If this moment was going to be the climax of his evening, he may as well make the most of it. She snapped in 'Disco Fever' and moved towards him. Slowly. So he could drink it all in. How, Moses thought (knowing he had best keep his thoughts off the main event if he was going to last the course), can she walk in those shoes?

With her long manicured nails, she parted his legs at the thigh and took his hands, which were locked together on his lap in the manner of an old lady protecting her handbag, and gently placed them on the long couch. Then she straddled his left leg and began to grind. Her breasts were close to his lips as she expertly put one hand behind her back and, still moving, slid her bra off and stroked it down his face. It smelt of baby oil and cigarette smoke and he could almost taste the salt of her sweat behind its perfumed disguise. He wasn't able for this at all. He'd explode. She was looking directly at him and her eyes were soft and lost in something that, given these close quarters and her state of undress, Moses took to be desire. He held her gaze and frantically rummaged around in his head for some football results so he could keep himself afloat. He could feel the pressure building as beads of sweat broke out on his forehead. She had her arms behind her head now and her breasts were brushing the side of his face, bobbing like apples. Apples, Moses grabbed the notion and clung onto it. They're only apples, he thought. I can do this. Sure what's sexy about apples? Nothing. I can do this. Apples. Eve in the Garden of Eden. Sin. And they weren't apples. They were breasts. Lovely breasts. Sexy Sandra's breasts. Sexy Sandra who was full of sin. Sandra who was his cousin and who it was a terrible crime against God and his mother to be carrying on with like this. This train of thought was just making things worse. Who scored the winning goal for the World Cup in 1978?

'Lick them.'

'Pardon?'

That was not the correct answer.

'I said, *lick* them.'

Really a woman in Sandra's position should not be required to repeat the request, but surely to God she didn't actually mean it? Just part of the act, surely. Still,

Moses thought, in the bit of him that was desperately trying to retain brainpower under this unholy assault to his hormones, best do as the lady says. If just to be polite.

So he did. And there were no objections filed. In fact, quite the reverse could be said to be true.

From beginning to end the whole thing didn't last more than fifteen minutes on either side. Not that either of them were checking their watches.

When it was over, Moses wrapped his still fully clothed body around Sandra's bare skin and they fell asleep. He woke an hour later to find Sandra dressed and lacing up her jacket. It was still dark.

'You go on up to bed,' she said. 'I've called a taxi. It'll be here shortly.'

She was standing over him. Towering actually, as he lay on the sofa. In charge again. Moses struggled to sort it out in his head. Surely there must be something to sort out. Shouldn't he invite her to join him in bed or something? But despite what they had shared that night, the notion seemed silly. Forward. As if the intimacy of sleep would be so much more intense than sex.

'Moses,' she said with a look of concern so different from the pouting lustful expression of earlier that she seemed like a different person. 'Are you falling in love with me?'

Gaaaah. What was the correct answer to that one? He thought perhaps he was, maybe?

'After a fashion,' he said. Best to keep something back. Safer. And then, in saying it, he realized that it was strangely true. He had been in love before and that was the terrible thing about it. The certainty. Being in love meant there was no get-out clause. No back door of doubt to creep through when it fell apart. This was better. This not being sure.

'I'll take that as a "no" then,' she said, obviously relieved. 'Go on. Up to bed with you!'

That bossy assertive tone again.

The strange thing was, thought Moses as he finished his cornflakes, how similar his mother and Sandra were when it came right down to it. Perhaps that meant something in itself. Perhaps this casual, friendly feeling he had around her was what he needed in his life. The whole thing had been so easy and so, well, *enjoyable*. There was no other word for it. 'Fun' was too light a word for what they did and 'love' was too heavy. And yet, he knew too that it did not deserve heavy-duty analysis, so he'd leave it at that. If Sandra wanted a replay, she knew where to find him and, by God, she certainly knew how to spin things around to her way of doing them.

She'd be in touch and if she wanted him he'd be there, but he wasn't going to torture himself with anticipation either.

As he put his breakfast things in the dishwasher there was a slight tinge of regret as Moses thought again of Sandra's loaded post-coital question and, in his heart of hearts, realized that in all probability he wouldn't be sleeping with his cousin again.

25

Hemlock knew his time was nearly up. Did he mind? In fairness, he was surprised he'd lasted this long. Although he wasn't particularly looking forward to the next leg of the journey; make your mind up time. At least, he consoled himself, whichever choice he made it couldn't be any worse than the living hell of his life for the last twenty-odd years. It didn't get much worse than this, at least not in the eyes of the smug inhabitants of Gorrib. Wheelchair-bound alcoholic squatting in an abandoned traveller's caravan on the edge of town. The priest, of all people, had intervened on his behalf when the council tried to throw him out a few years ago. Arguing that 'the poor unfortunate' had nowhere else to go. Another good deed done in God's name and doubtless driven by fear that the ravaged troublemaker might end up knocking on the presbytery door.

The ramp in front of his caravan was rotting away, but it hardly mattered now. At the same time, as he hauled himself backwards up through the open door, Hemlock thought he hadn't made much of a job being bad. If you were smart about it, evil could bring great rewards, in this life at least. If he had committed himself properly to the Other Side when this whole thing had blown up, he might have been rewarded with all sorts of goodies. He could have been a pornographer or a politician. Lived his life with loads of money and power. Used this badness to take advantage of others instead of punishing himself. Instead he had put the head down, ignored all he had ever learned about life – and death – from working for Him Upstairs all those years, and fallen down the trapdoor of self-destruction. He had come, as these wretched mortals put it, to a 'bad end'. Got his just desserts. Fallen by the wayside of life before he'd even had a crack at it properly.

And all for what?

For the love of a man with a mullet. A man with a kind way about him, which put the young Ignatius Anum on a misunderstood promise that was, in fact, a filthy lie from day one.

Of course it wasn't all Moses's fault. God had had a hand in it too. God, with his pretence of love towards all mankind when He inflicted His own family, not to mention people in His employ, with all kinds of underhand misery. Testing them. Forcing them to endure humiliations in His name to see if they could make the grade. Pregnancy without sex at fourteen – what was that all about? And as for the crucifixion! How could you trust a guy who would do that to His own son? So M & J stuck it out and earned a place in heaven. Big deal. Two thousand years later and they were still in His employ.

The responsibility of it all. Call that paradise? And that was just His nearest and dearest. What about the legions of cupids that He struck, for no apparent reason, with homosexuality? Playing happy families for everyone else and not getting a look in themselves. Of course, that was the plan. If soldiers in God's Heavenly Army started getting in amongst humans and impregnating them, every second person would be a saint or martyr, and Hemlock was no fan of either.

Being born in this small bigoted outpost and growing up gay had not been easy. He hadn't been one of the lucky ones who'd just been spirited down from above. Ignatius had been born mortal and given his calling via a visitation, BVM style, as was the way, back in the seventies. (Of course, New Age Policy had come in since and all cupids were now given the choice to take up vocations, usually via reiki therapy or astrology or some other dingly dangly nonsense – although Himself would always be lurking there somewhere in the background.) Anyway, that pompous bag of white puff, Gabriel, had bollixed the whole thing up by choosing to enunciate while Iggy was on a school field trip to Knock. 'Look – over there! An angel! It's a miracle!' cried the hapless fourteen-year-old, convinced that the other twenty boys could see the nine-foot winged creature floating outside Hannah's Religious Novelties Shop. He sank to his knees and listened intently to Gabriel's instructions, 'You have been chosen, etc.', Meanwhile, his school chums roared their cynical little skulls off until he was found by a Christian brother and dragged by the ears into the basilica to do confession and atone for this public display of blasphemy.

No one had much time for him after that, apart from Moses. The squat, curly-haired publican's son even said he believed him. They were both odd kids and they knew it. Outcasts together. While Iggy never mentioned his work to Moses, he was glad nonetheless to have somebody on his side.

Ignatius was quite the diligent junior angel for a number of years. He was that busy doing God's work as a teenager that the whole issue of his sexuality never came up. Until he was seventeen and Anne Leeson, a schoolteacher who he had been trying to fix up with a travelling salesman from Offaly, had seduced him. She and the salesman had been in Bosanova drinking. Iggy had been sending out love vibes, but he was young, and inexperienced and nothing was happening. Except that Anne, who was an innocent enough woman but near enough thirty for her file to be marked 'priority', got legless drunk and the salesman had an early start to Limerick in the morning and decided to abandon her to the night. Iggy, feeling partly responsible, took her home. And she seduced him. Successfully in terms of your basic biology, but the young cupid was expecting more. Lightening flashes, or at least a few cherubim floating about. Instead he got this horrible empty sick feeling.

Anne got pregnant, but she left him alone, mortified by his age and her own looseness. As far as he knew, he hadn't been 'seen', and he knew he'd be long out of all this before it became apparent that the child might have extended mortality. Some lived to be over hundred, but if they went to one-twenty, the department would know someone had stepped out of line and launch an investigation. Only time would tell, and there was no need to worry about that now. Now that it was nearly all over.

A few days after his encounter with the schoolteacher, he was undressing in the changing rooms of the new swimming pool. Brian Fitzgerald, who was a fine thing in those days, was in the open shower and young Iggy found himself staring. Brian caught him, and although Ignatius wasn't sure what it all meant, the cruel Fitzgerald certainly did. He cocked his wrist at him and said, 'What are you looking at, queer boy?' Then spread the encounter all around the town. Iggy did nothing to confirm or deny accusations. He just kept the head down. Moses, because he remained loyal and didn't seem to mind about the accusations, became a natural target for the sensitive young man's affections.

For four years he kept his feelings for Moses bottled up, and as their friendship grew and matured, Iggy's fantasies grew and he became more and more sure that his feelings would be returned. Moses ran about after girls a bit, like the others, but then that meant nothing. Didn't he himself have a four-year-old son? But when Moses fell for Rose, the insult was doubled by the fact that Iggy was powerless to stop it happening. This was a genuine human coupling. Unusual, but it happened sometimes. The more Iggy tried to put Moses off, the deeper his feelings for Rose seemed to become. The cupid became convinced that there were higher forces at play. That God was intervening to punish and prevent him from creating his own corner of happiness in a place that had already been cruel enough to him. Turning him into a martyr against his will. Well, it wouldn't work.

Because Ignatius, although largely well intentioned and devout, was essentially a weak character, he had already been spotted by Talent Scouts from the Other Side as a possible recruit. Department employees made the most prestigious of conscripts if you could get them to turn. When the thought of buggering up Moses and Rose's union crossed Ignatius's mind it took only a matter of seconds for one of Lucifer's minions to plant the ancient Poison Arrow spell in his head and the obsessed Ignatius never even stopped to think how it got there. He passed Rose in the Coffee Bean that night and jabbed her lightly with a pin, silently saying the dark prayer as he did so.

He could hardly believe when it worked and Rose went off with Brian. Ignatius was so elated that he went straight around to McGreavy's. He was that stupid then. That naive. He didn't know what he thought would happen, but then young Iggy had always thought that putting heart in front of head was the way to do things. But not, seemingly, when God has taken a personal interest. Moses rejected him. Nicely, but firmly. Said he was in love with Rose, that there was nothing wrong with being homosexual it just wasn't his thing blah, blah. The fact that he was nice about it just made Iggy feel worse. Moses offered him a drink that night and, although he knew he wasn't supposed to, being an angel and all, he took it. And took to it. It was his act of defiance. I can drink and get drunk and be miserable and there's not a damn thing you can do about it Mr High-and-Mighty think-you're so-clever *GOD*!

He didn't know he had been made mortal again until the night he jumped off McGreavy's roof. He hadn't risked flying before but this was in the days before permits, when all you needed was faith and practise. He chanced it because he felt certain that, despite everything, God would not let him fall. Then *smack*! The final insult. The ultimate rejection. God loves you. God will always love you. No matter what. Yeah right!

Did he die then like he deserved to? Did Lord God Almighty take young Iggy back for the telling off and a few years in Purgatory? He'd have served his time and be sipping mead cocktails on a cloud by now, or what-ever the hell it is they do in paradise. He didn't know, and was beginning to think he never would. He could atone now, of course, now that the end was near. But then what was on offer? Couple of hundred years in Purgatory, shuffling around with a load of no-hopers under the merciless sympathetic glower of volunteer blesseds, and at the end of it what? He'd never get to paradise the way he'd been carrying on. They might even put him up for training and reincarnate him back here to tread the same path again. Not exactly a thought he relished.

Then there was Lucifer. Iggy'd had his head split sideways with his wretched 'dreams'. The Prince of Darkness had never quite got the hang of manifesting himself on Earth, although occasionally he'd inhabit the body of some poor unfortunate adolescent. But there not being any available in Hemlock's vicinity, he had to 'appear' to him in dreams. Not a pretty sight but, if you could get past the horns and the fright wig, what he was offering wasn't bad. As a fallen angel, Hemlock would be immediately appointed to Executive Office, which meant he wouldn't have to go through the whole hellfire bit and spend the rest of eternity being flagellated by sadistic lunatics. Instead he was promised a nice pad on the borders of Purgatory where he could indulge in gluttonous orgies at his leisure and oversee proceedings from a wide screen. He'd get to hang out with Borgias and bad bishops and he wouldn't even have to enter the pit if he didn't want to; he could just loudspeaker through a few instructions from time to time. ('There's a man masturbating in booth nine. Could we get some testicle tongs over there, please. If it's not *too* much trouble!')

Of course, he knew it wasn't because he was especially talented that Lucifer wanted him. Or indeed especially bad. It was all egos when it got to this level. God *Vs* Prince of Darkness. He was just a pawn. L used to think it was something special to get a high-ranking religious over to his side, but they were ten-a-penny these days. What with all the paedophile scandals, he was out the door with them. Hemlock suspected he didn't know where to put them any more. But a fallen angel? Someone like himself? That would piss G off big time. Worry Him even. And a pissed off, worried God was the Devil's ultimate aim. Put him right off his game.

And Himself was worried. Hemlock knew that. He'd already spotted a field worker, a right dandy, hanging around McGreavy's. He may have been stripped of his power, but he still knew a mole from the department when he saw one. Although he hadn't been approached – yet.

Hemlock peeled back a Special Brew. He had a headache with all he had to think about, but he knew he didn't have to make a decision until the last minute so he'd leave it until then. He'd know what to do when the time came.

He was frightened, but he was more frightened the beer wouldn't make it go away. It hadn't let him down so far, though, but you never knew what might happen when these guys were on your back.

As the first flush of alcohol drained through him, despite all that lay ahead, Hemlock allowed himself a feeling that resembled smugness. For the first and, he knew, last time in his mortal life – he held the cards.

It was nice, alone as he was in this wretched hovel, to feel that he was the centre of attention.

26

Sleazy Brian had been vague about Sandra's role in this lap-dancing club he was opening, and when it came to details like the location, the decor, the opening date and the staffing, he 'wasn't prepared to release the details just yet'. However, his manner wasn't vague when it came to anticipating his new employee taking her clothes off and dancing, but Sandra was well used to the smutty eye-stripping advances of novices to the business.

'You want to keep it as a "surprise" then?' Sandra said, her tone a toxic blend of perky excitement and sarcasm.

'That's it, dear,' he replied, full of admiration for her obvious intelligence. 'I can see we are going to work well together,' and he gave her a leery wink. Honestly. It never failed to astonish Sandra how a certain type of middle-aged man believed these social charm ticks from 1970s television comedians were the very height of sophistication when it came to seduction techniques. You had to pity them really.

Still, she had nothing better to do today, so she decided to follow up on his suggestion that she approach some of the foreign girls who had recently moved to the town to see if any of them were interested in well-paid, cash-in-hand work.

'It might be better coming from a young . . . lady,' he faltered at the last word and Sandra saw the hint of a sneer play around his thin lips.

She'd seen the scary old trout he'd been having an affair with and frankly if that was Brian's definition of 'lady', well then she was quite happy for him to think of her as an untouchable slut. Poor Rose. And her daughter was a dote. In fact, meeting Mary and Ella was the one good thing that had come out of the other night. She needed some more female friends. She'd gone off attracting male attention of late. Maybe it was the whole Moses thing getting in amongst her, or perhaps she was just growing out of it. She was certainly growing out of her wardrobe. And it wasn't just in that big dinnery way. Of late she had begun to crave sensible footwear and, while she wasn't quite at the stage where she was ready to relinquish her addiction to looking glamorous at all times, her own vanity was beginning to irritate her. Her nails were cracked and torn where the acrylic fakes had long since flaked off, and that annoyed her too. But what annoyed her more was that she cared. I mean – what sort of a shallow person was she when the sight of her own stubby fingers could depress her?

Sandra had noticed some of the girls knocking about the town already. East European she guessed by their dark looks, scrunched eighties haircuts and stone-wash denims. Noted too that a couple of them had the lithe figures and distinctive way of walking that, to Sandra's trained eyes, suggested they may have danced before. Sandra wasn't naive enough to imagine that they'd jump at the chance of lap dancing when their families were around but these girls often led double lives and there was certainly no harm in approaching them.

It was around lunchtime and Sandra knew that some of the men from the converted youth hostel would be down in McGreavy's playing cards. Her Aunt Margaret loved them. Aside from the fact that they had doubled her lunchtime trade overnight, the swarthy new cus-tomers gave her something to gossip about with her cronies.

'You'd know they were foreign all the same,' said Margaret.

The three old ladies were studying the men from behind the glass door in the back bar. Between them they had dissected and analysed every person in Gorrib from birth, and they were delighted to have the challenge of new people to get their teeth into.

'It's not like they're a different colour or anything but there's just *something* about them.'

'Is it the way they carry themselves, do you think?'

'Well, it's that surely but there's something else as well. A kind of a . . .?'

'Swarthiness, Breda.'

'There now you have it! A *swarthiness*.'

The three old birds sat and ruminated privately on the

adjective for a few seconds as they looked over at the group of men aged between thirty and seventy smoking their cigarettes and shuffling their cards about, oblivious to their OAP fan club, until Margaret, who as proprietor of the establishment these exotic new creatures had chosen to drink in had claimed part ownership of them, said, 'No. There's more to it than "swarthy", I'm telling you. Look now at the way he's holding that cigarette. Not backwards into the palm like the scruffy Joes around here. Look *there*.' The other two strained to peer. 'Up! He has the cigarette *up* at the tips of his fingers. Do you know what that is, ladies? That's *sophistication*.'

'You're right!' they exclaimed.

'Swarthy *and* sophisticated.'

'*Omar Sharif*.'

'Omar Shaiff,' the other two chorused in hushed awe.

'They're from Bosnia, I bet,' Sandra had butted in as she was passing. 'Muslims.'

The coven glared at her for having the temerity to interrupt their romantic reverie with actual facts. They still had great mileage out of speculating on where they might be from and how they might have got here without some scrap butting in. Why did the young have to rush things? Did they not know that all the fun, the *drama* in life, was in the making of a good story? Once you knew, then it was all over. They could be drug-dealing terrorists from Russia, or deposed Turkish royalty, or Omar Sharif's brothers. 'Muslims from Bosnia'? Where was the glamour in that?

They knew Sandra was a stripper because she had told

them. And that was the crime of it. If she'd have kept it quiet and let them gossip and guess around it for a few weeks, they'd have had much more sympathy for her. They might even have become part of her conspiracy then, and the whole situation of Margaret McGreavy's niece being a fallen, loose woman had enormous potential as a Mary Magdalene-type adventure. She had cheated the old crows by being open about it from the off. Of course, Sandra knew that now. She was only just learning the strange rules of small town social etiquette and was beginning to realize they might take a lifetime to master.

In any case, she arrived at the old youth hostel fairly certain that the women would be alone there at this time. It was a fine day and Sandra could feel the sun on her bare back where her halter-neck top left it exposed. Instinctively she took her cardigan from around her waist and put it on. Best not to give herself away too soon. She was glad she had when she passed through the tall iron gates and saw a couple of old women. One, sitting on the stone steps leading up to the house, held a young baby on her lap in that stern confident way grandmothers have, while the other was pulling weeds from the cracked paving stones and throwing them into a tin bucket. Their headscarves and weathered skin combined with the sunshine, made Sandra feel like she might be in Italy. She approached the lady on the steps and asked, 'Are the girls in?'

The woman closed her eyes, indicating that she either

didn't understand or didn't care to, and waved towards the door that was open. Old women, thought Sandra, are the same the world over. They complain constantly about lack of manners in the young, yet they think their age entitles them to be rude themselves.

Sandra stepped inside, waiting for a moment until her eyes had adjusted.

'Hello?' she called out, as a toddler suddenly appeared from the back of the house and almost took the feet from under her. In hot pursuit was a young woman who grabbed the child by his shoulders and scooped him up, looking at Sandra with a mixture of apology and shyness.

'Are the girls in?' Sandra asked, slightly stupidly as she was addressing one already.

The girl shrugged. 'I done understan'' she said, clearly a much-practised phrase. I don't blame her, thought Sandra. It was certainly the first foreign phrase she learned when she visited a new country.

The girl pointed down the hall to the back kitchen. Sitting at a long table in what used to be the youth hostel canteen were four women in their early twenties. There were a few brightly coloured scarves hanging from the window, and some jam jars with wild flowers in them. Apart from that, the plastic chairs, Formica tabletops and stainless steel catering units gave the place an institutional rather than family feeling.

One of the girls was putting rollers in another's hair, and the other two were manicuring each other's nails. Sandra stood there awkwardly for a few seconds being ignored, until the girl doing the manicure looked at her lazily, then cocked her head in the direction of the hair-roller, indicating that she was the only one who spoke English.

Suddenly, Sandra felt extremely nervous. Face a roomful of lecherous half-drunk men in a G-string? No problem. But four beautiful foreign women in a family environment and she was terrified. Sandra was a loner, and this scene was somehow so intimate, she felt like an interloper. Like she was invading their privacy.

'I'm er . . .'

'You from immigration?' the hairdresser asked.

When she said, 'No,' all four women glared at her in astonishment as if to say, 'Well, who the hell are you then?'

'I'm a . . . em . . . dancer . . . and I'm,' she held her hands out as one of the manicuring girls got up from the table and walked towards her.

'I'm wondering if . . .' The girl took Sandra's hand, but rather than shaking it began to study it, then said something to the others. Pretty soon they were all gathered around looking at Sandra's chipped nails.

The hairdresser spoke. She was smiling now.

'You wan manicure?'

'Well, I don't know, I was . . .'

'Sure, sure,' she said as the four women dragged her over to the table. 'Lana she give you manicure, sit, sit.'

So Sandra did. To her astonishment Lana produced a full beautician's acrylic nail kit from under the table. It was only then that she noticed that all four girls had extraordinarily long and beautiful nails. Twenty-five minutes later, a record in her long years of experience of having this treatment, Sandra's nails were perfect. Better than perfect because they were fake. And better than fake-perfect because they looked utterly real. She felt like crying.

'How much?' she said pulling her purse out of her bag.

The girls shrugged and looked embarrassed, pretending not to understand. They were just doing it for the fun of it. In all likelihood, the old women outside had painted red talons and she hadn't noticed. All this in twenty-five minutes.

'You can all do this?' she asked. They nodded.

Four technicians, charging, Sandra estimated, forty euros every twenty-five minutes, five days a week. She could make over three grand a day. Overheads? Fuck – they could do it here to start with! Why not? They could teach her to do it, then there'd be five of them. They'd clean up. It'd sure beat lap dancing.

And in the very moment that she thought it, Sandra realized that she was right. Maybe this *would* beat lap dancing. She'd never thought about giving it up before now but, you know, maybe her time *was* up. It had become, like she said to Moses, just something that she did. Maybe she could do something else. Or rather, maybe she could be *good* at doing something else.

In her excitement, Sandra found that without thinking she was standing at the sink with a kettle and was filling it, making herself right at home.

FIELD REPORT SIX

Extract from *The Cupid's Handbook*. 1957 Edition.

POISON ARROWS

Due to their constant exposure to the human condition, all cupids will make mistakes from time to
time (*see 'Living Among Mortals', page 556*). Before
spiritual advances in soul reading and manipulation,
all matches were made via the basic bow and arrow.
While such crude methods seem laughable today, bar
the odd cross-wind and angel error, in global terms,
results were often surprisingly accurate.

Then in the early fifteenth century an English king,
Henry VIII, set in motion a chain of events that
seemed beyond the control of even God Himself.
Cleverly wheedling his way through Church rules, he
somehow managed to marry a staggering eight
women – beheading a couple of them along the way
as an excuse to get his hands on the next one. Slaying
Catholics and divorce became the order of the day.
Bar the occasional religious war the Catholic slaying

died down a good deal, but the British took to divorce in a big way and it was matter of grave concern to OHF that such an event could take place without His direct sanction. A major investigation was launched but the powers that be remained mystified. It was not until the king's death in 1547, when the Gatekeeper was alerted because a fat man in a fur hat was causing a commotion at the back of the queue and demanding an audience with OHF, that the truth of these events finally came to light. It turned out that Henry had believed that he was acting on the direct instructions of God Himself. That he was happily tucked up one night with his wife of twenty-four years getting stuck into a roasted suckling pig when it suddenly occurred to him that what he should do was ditch her and marry Anne Boleyn. After that, according to the monarch, his life was hardly his own as he kept becoming, in his own words, 'struck with these mad notions' to chase after women, mowing down Church and Catherines in his urgency to move on. While he had put a brave face on it, poor Henry was beside himself with all the romantic comings and goings he had experienced and had professed himself 'frankly, exhausted'. His only solace was that he was doing God's bidding and would be greeted at the gates with a regal fanfare and open arms. Instead of which he found himself in the possible Purgatory section of the queue next to his old adversary Cromwell. He was not a happy man. Over the coming years, every member of Henry's court was killed off and questioned. It seemed that the cupid appointed to his court had sold out to the the Other Side sometime before all the trouble started. He had found a way of diverting the course of true and proper love with a devilishly concocted potion which, if applied to standard issue cupid ammunition, could make anyone fall in love with anyone, even if their souls were not remotely matched. He decided to make an example of this popular and scrupulous monarch and the rest, they say, is history.

God was furious and passed an act banning all use of poison arrows under pain of expulsion from the Kingdom, and any angels caught using them were made to live the rest of their lives as humans. Rigorous security and training procedures were put in place to ensure that cupids, while still allowed a measure of camp playfulness, were generally incorruptible. However, there have been recorded usages over the centuries, although specific numbers are impossible to gauge.

It was not until Heaven was restructured in 1700 and the department of Conjugal Relations was formed that the problem was finally put to rest. With the abolition of the old system and the implementation of the modern method of Mortal Matchmaking, poison arrows have now become a thing of the past.

Yeah right. Of course, nothing in the literature about what happens when it all goes horribly wrong. Lucifer never gets a look in. Nothing about what happens when one of us does decide to move over. Oh no. Because that would be admitting that there's a problem. That would be admitting that there were certain things beyond even

His control. Young angels get a half-day training in exorcisms, but it only shows them what happens when the Devil is successfully expelled from a human soul. All crosses and triumphant priests. The resurrection of dark angels is an altogether different affair. Best brush it under the carpet. Keep it as a legend, a myth, nothing tangible you need worry about until – bam! – you get put on the spot to deal with it and then you've to pretend you know how to handle it, and by God you'd better not skip a Hail Mary or you're finished.

You know, if He'd contacted me Himself. Put it up to me straight, 'Christian, you're my trusted servant.', 'Christian, we've got a problem.', 'Christian, you have been chosen from my legions of cupids,' etc. etc., I might be more inclined to sort this mess out. There are ways of handling these things; motivating workers into doing things that are above and beyond the call of duty from time to time. It's not as if I haven't proven myself to be devoted to Him over the years. It's not even as if, in principle, I'd object to stretching the boundaries of my skills to negotiate with the Dark Forces. It's not the mission itself that upset me, as I explained to Gabriel in my resignation memo, it was the *way* they went about it. Sending me here under false pretences. It was under-hand. Sneaky. The fact that they didn't trust me enough to tell me. After all these years of honest service. I'd come to expect more than that. And the inefficiency of it all. Sending me on a mission like this without even properly equipping me. No money, delays in getting expenses, no manifestation permits. Insult to injury.

Even that mightn't have been enough in itself to make me take such drastic action, but then there was Mayday. Honestly! Mayday Matthews! What were they thinking, landing him in on me like that? And the jumped up tranny knew *all* about Hemlock Anam. He says he figured it out for himself, but frankly, he's a vicious manipulative queen, the very worst type, and I don't believe him for a moment. He was tipped off and my authority over him, not to mention my two-century struggle to reach middle management, had been completely compromised. And he's got more permits and waivers than I've had in the whole of my working life.

Well that's it. Let them put Mayday Matthews in charge of Europe, the whole bloody world for all I care.

I've resigned. I'm going mortal and that's the end of it.

27

Vinny woke up with a bad head. But he didn't mind the hangover because if it hadn't been for the drink, he would never have had the courage to approach Mary. And if he hadn't approached Mary, she would never have come back with him and stayed the night. And if she hadn't come back and stayed the night he might never have decided that he was in love with her. And if he wasn't in love with her he mightn't have minded her accidentally discovering his breeding lab when she got up before him and went for a wander around the yard. And if he hadn't been drunk he might have woken up before her and impressed her with a big fry instead of being out cold, drooling and snoring in the bed. So perhaps drinking wasn't such a great idea after all.

Life seemed very complicated indeed. And really it was very simple.

He was in love with Mary Fitzgerald. That was her name. Mary, after the Virgin Mother herself. Fitzgerald after, well, her father. Not a very nice man by her own account. Vinny knew that because she had told him.

Here. In his house. In the early hours of the morning. Four thirty-five actually. He knew that because it was just after she had told him about her parents separating that she had said that magical thing.

'You're a nice guy, Vincent. Shall we go to bed?'

He had checked the clock then and said, 'I suppose it's late.'

What kind of a stupid thing was that to say to a girl? *I suppose it's late.* Making out like it was time for cocoa and pyjamas.

'Would you like a cup of cocoa?'

'No thank you.'

Cocoa! What had he been thinking? They weren't children!

'I've some clean pyjamas, not mine, they were my mother's, I mean . . .'

'I think we should just go to bed.'

Pyjamas. His mother's pyjamas. He was useless at this. A hopeless case. Here was this lovely, fresh faced girl asking him to go to bed with her and all he could think of was his mother's pyjamas.

And then they went upstairs to his room, and all he *could* think about was his mother's pyjamas. Not Mary's lovely mauve-coloured hair, sitting on the nape of her neck as she shyly took off her blouse. Not the soft curve of her belly as she removed her skirt and quickly pulled the duvet up over her legs. Not the vulnerable look in her eyes as she lay there stiffly in his bed, clearly mortified and waiting for what would happen next. Not the gentle way he should be kissing her to let her know she wasn't going to be roughly ravaged or taken advantage off. None of the above. Just his mother and her pyjamas. Standing in the corner of the room saying, 'Well, Vinny, this girl must be something special when you haven't had the mug of bedtime cocoa.'

It was no use.

'Are you sure you wouldn't like a cup of something?'

Mary was looking quite terrified now. He had taken his shirt off, but still had his T-shirt on. It was funny how you could stand around a pool in Spain in nothing but a pair of togs but somehow exposing your chest hairs in your own bedroom in front of a girl you liked was different.

'Hot milk then? I'm having one myself.'

'All right then,' she squeaked.

A cup of something would make her feel better. And him. Hopefully.

When he came back with two steaming mugs on a tray, Vinny could hardly believe his eyes. There she was sitting up in his bed, wearing his shirt. *His shirt!* Looking right at home. There was a sparkle in her eyes. Well, less of a sparkle and more of a – glittering?

He handed her a cup and said, 'There you go.'

'Don't you like me?' she said. Right out like that.

'Of course I do,' he said. Then carefully, so as not to frighten her, 'I like you very much.'

'Well then why,' she said, 'haven't you, you know?'

He was genuinely puzzled. By her manner more than anything else. She seemed slightly, well, annoyed.

'Haven't I what?'

'You *know*,' she said.

'No,' he said. 'I don't.'

He kind of did. But he didn't like to say it out loud. Just in case he'd got it wrong.

'Oh for God's Sake, why haven't you dropped the hand? Kissed me or something – and the rest.'

She was as mortified as he was. The colour had risen to her cheeks and she was blushing. Lovely rosy plump cheeks that he longed to . . .

'I didn't like to be, presumptuous.'

'Presumptuous? Presumptuous? I come back to your house in the middle of the night, come up to your bed, take off my clothes, well some of them anyway. What did you think I wanted? Cocoa?'

'Well, I thought that . . .'

Vinny was starting to shuffle. *Stop shuffling, Vincent!* He could hear his mother from the corner of the room, where she stood in her pyjamas.

'SEX! I do *not* want cocoa! I do *not* want to borrow a pair of pyjamas! I want sex!'

Vincent did not have a great deal of experience with women. Actually, he had virtually none. What he did have, though, was a fantasy list of possible scenarios about what might happen in an ideal world.

So far, this situation had been indicative that his wildest dreams were about to come true. He had, in his wanderings in Gorrib, long since earmarked Mary (as he knew her now) as by far the most attractive woman around. He had met her at the disco, been formally introduced to her, so to speak, by that English girl, had bought her drinks and even enjoyed a dance or two. When she asked him to take her home, then suggested they go back to his, he could hardly believe it. They had got on well, talked nicely about this and that, and then – she had suggested bed. So far, so fantastic. What he had planned next was perhaps a few cuddles, see how we go and maybe nature might take its course and if it didn't, well then, what about it? Wasn't there plenty of time, and he'd waited this long for the right girl so surely there was no sense in rushing?

Now, here she was, sitting there in his bed demanding conjugal relations. He hadn't pegged her as loose. It was unexpected and well, upsetting.

'Well?' she said, in a manner that was more matronly than minx. 'Are you going to get on with it or what?'

'Well I . . .'

Vinny didn't know what to say, but he sensed, very strongly, that the offer of a top up of cocoa was not going to get him out of this one. He would have to tell the truth.

'I've not done this before.'

Her reaction was immediate.

'Oh – I don't believe it!'

Vinny, always ready to see the good in people, took her up the wrong way.

'Yes I know it's hard to believe but . . .'

'Oh no,' she said, her voiced edged with a sharpness that contrasted with her soft features. 'I *believe* you. A farmer? Living on his own? Marvellous. Fucking marvellous.' Then she took a slurp of cocoa, grimacing as if she had thought it were gin. 'Just my bloody luck.'

Vinny stood there, not knowing quite what to do next with this young woman inhabiting his bed and not looking much in the mood for company. Still, there was something wifely about her sitting there. All cross and bothered in his shirt, with the cup of cocoa between her soft, chubby hands. It made him want to get in beside her. And why not indeed? It was his bed after all. His house. At least she knew now. Wouldn't surely be expecting much. At least, despite her harsh reaction, she hadn't mocked him. That would have been worse. Although he had never told a woman before that he was a virgin, had never got that far, Vincent often felt somehow mocked by them. He didn't get that feeling with Mary.

So he took off his trousers, left his T-shirt on and got in next to her.

They lay side by side, not touching, and eventually fell asleep.

In the morning when he woke, Mary was gone.

Vinny rolled over to where she had left his shirt in a crumpled mush on the pillow and he buried his face in it to see if he could still smell her.

'Eeeeeeeeeeek!'

A high-pitched scream from outside made him rush to the window.

He saw Mary run from the laboratory and down the drive at lightening speed. He rushed to get dressed and follow her. It was five miles into the town, she'd never walk it. But as he reached the gates he saw her flag down and clamber into a passing car.

It was eight on a Sunday morning and Vinny felt his life had begun and ended in less than twelve hours.

He was in love, and the handsome farmer knew that his life would never be complete without Mary Fitzgerald in it. But if that was going to happen, he would have to do better than this. She had shown herself, for all her vulnerability and innocent looks, to be a modern young woman of the world. With some regret, but more determination, Vincent Rouse decided he'd better get some practise in before approaching her again.

PART FOUR

the resurrection

one month later

28

Say what you like about Mayday Matthews but he didn't muck about. Even Christian had to admit that.

He had taken one look at Rose Fitzgerald and openly pronounced her as, 'A makeover in waiting!'

And there was nothing Mayday liked better than a good makeover.

He had hung around after Christian had resigned. Mayday had received the request to be on standby in Gorrib with some trepidation, but Gabriel had told him he was a last resort and that the situation with Hemlock probably wouldn't come to a full resurrection. In any case, Mayday decided that he hadn't had the full benefit of his permits yet and that he could have much more fun with them here than in dreary old London, where it was becoming harder and harder to shock the drugged-up Soho crowd with the mere sight of a drag queen floating in mid air. Besides, even *sans* special powers, Mayday's attention-seeking appearance hadn't served its purpose so well in years. An ambiguous wardrobe and a fearless nature promised all sorts of adventures in this remote outpost, and he already had his eye on a couple of farmers.

'City life is so *passé*, Christian. It's all, here we are being gay in a gay ghetto; everyone having dinner parties; Sunday afternoons in the Conran Shop. *Please*. Where's the fun in that? The mystery? The *romance*? Give me a nice big beefy lad living out in the middle of nowhere who's just happy I'm not a sheep.'

Christian was horrified at what he saw as Mayday's flagrant exploitation of the confused love-hungry country Irish bachelor, but he had to admit that his own reasons for not hurrying back to London weren't entirely without motive.

Although he had no reason to stay here now that he had resigned his post, Christian had found himself reluctant to leave this place and its people, whom he had become fond of. Particularly Rose, especially now that she was on her own and seemed to be relying on him for support. He had not heard from the department regarding his resignation and although he hadn't had his papers through, was living life as if he were mortal. With no instructions coming through, he had nothing in London to go back to, but more than that, with no instructions, he wasn't sure what to do next. He was so used to acting on orders, being part of the grander scheme of things, being told to go here and go there that, without the rule book, Christian was feeling lost. It was all very well and good fixing people up and being generally considered a nice guy when that was your job, but now that he was just like the rest of them, Christian was curious to see how he would cut it. Would he still be a decent citizen once he wasn't under orders to be 'good', so to speak? Or, with no higher moral force to guide him, would he go to the bad altogether and become an intolerant bitchy queen?

Fear of this was probably what prompted him to allow Mayday to work his 'magic' on Rose. Although she was reluctant to let this terrifying creature cut her hair and reorganize her wardrobe, Christian knew that Mayday would do a good job. He had worked as a hairdresser, fashion designer, make-up artist, window dresser, and fashion stylist in his hundred or so years. Even if he drove his old associate mad in the process, it would have been criminal for Christian to deny Rose this opportunity.

'You're not going to *be* blonde. I am just *slicing* some blonde through the front. Its two quite different things, dear,' said Mayday, raising his eyes to Christian as if he couldn't even begin to imagine how somebody might not be able to make that distinction.

Rose looked at her face framed with a dozen foil wraps and felt like an extra from *Doctor Who*.

She was beyond nerves at this stage. The two gay men had been in her house since the night before and, 'We're not leaving until you are *transformed*, dear. Sacred Heart of Jesus but those curtains are a *fright!*'

So far Mayday had gutted her wardrobe, identifying 'key pieces' and filling two sacks for the Vincent de Paul. She'd had her legs waxed, her eyelashes tinted, her skin buffed, her cuticles melted, her nails (hands and feet) French polished, her ears pierced, eyebrows plucked, her roots 'volumized' and now it was time to work on the hair.

Up until recently, Rose would have found a way to avoid this intrusive assault on her personal appearance. But, while she was coyly insisting they were 'going to too much trouble' and expressing worry that she 'wouldn't be able to live up to a blonde bombshell hairstyle', secretly she was rather thrilled at all the attention.

It had been one month since she had left Brian, and things had moved on more quickly than she ever could have imagined. She had missed him at first. Actually, she hadn't at all; it was just an emotional tick that she developed to pretend to herself and others that the past twenty-seven years hadn't been a complete waste of time.

'Do you miss him?' Dympna asked her when the two old friends were rekindling their friendship over lunch in Keegans.

'Of course!' Rose insisted.

'Could you just *kill* that Malone woman?'

'Absolutely!'

But even as she said it, Rose realized that in actual fact she felt nothing towards Regina Malone except a vague gratitude. If it hadn't been for Regina, she wouldn't be sitting here wearing a new two-piece that she'd picked up on a day trip to Galway with Christian, lunching with an old friend. If it hadn't been for Regina she wouldn't have had Davy down in her old family home the night before cooking pizzas and decorating her old room to get ready for him to move in with her. If it hadn't been for

Regina she wouldn't have flown over to London with Mary to visit her sister and applied for a job in Kingsbury as senior manager in the new Sainsbury's there. If it hadn't been for Regina, and Christian, her life would not be opening up in front of her as it now was. Christian was always saying to her, 'You should have done this years ago.' Part of her felt that she should never have married Brian at all. But then she wouldn't have her kids. The gap between having wished she'd never met Brian and the thought that she should have left him years ago was a narrow one, and impossible to measure. But it was driving her forward, filling all the pools of possibility that her marriage had drained.

'You know, Dympna, I just don't think I can bear to talk about it.'

That, at least, was true.

As were the tears that streamed down her face when Mayday swept the last section of newly blended hair from the barrel of his large curling brush.

'You look fabulous, darling!' he announced with confidence.

'It's true,' added Christian softly as he stood behind her and held her look in the mottled mirror of her mother's walnut dressing table.

As she looked at herself, Rose realized that not only did she look fabulous but, more importantly, she looked different. And in looking different, she realized that she felt differently now. About everything. In just one month, it seemed that everything had changed. Her kids were talking to her, and she was listening. While they were in

London Mary had opened up about Theo and her reservations about marrying him. Rose had advised her not to enter into a marriage unless she was sure it was what she wanted. She told her that she had plenty of time and that she was a beautiful young thing and not to be worrying. There was nothing revolutionary in what she said, but it seemed to make Mary feel better and for the first time since Mary was a girl, Rose felt as if she had given her daughter something she needed that wasn't food. The two of them had got on like sisters, giggling over their Bacardi and Cokes in the Wig and Ferret in Kingsbury while they got chatted up by a couple of her brother-in-law's workmates.

Davy was moving into the house with her on the pretext that he didn't want to live with his father, but Rose knew that this skinny young man wanted to look after his mother. She was precious to him, but for years she had worked so hard to hold Brian's attention she had hardly noticed that her squabbling son was now the real man of the house. She was seriously considering moving to England, starting a new life there. A month ago she could not disturb her routine enough to meet a friend for lunch because routine was her life. Now her life was different. It belonged to her again and she had the freedom to make of it what she would.

These two strange men, Christian and now this Mayday, people she hardly knew, were a part of making that happen. Nudging her forward, pooh-pooing her fears with the flick of a wrist and engulfing her in their glamour and confidence until staying still seemed a more exhausting option than stepping forward. Where did they get this generosity, this tenderness from? Why were they bothering with her at all? The two pretty men were looking at Rose looking at herself in the mirror, smiling at their handiwork.

'Delighted to have been of service,' said Mayday to her gaze of thanks.

'I feel so useless,' she said. 'You have done all this for me – is there anything I can do for you? I'd cook you a meal but . . .'

Christian butted in before she got the chance to let Mayday know that his senior manager hadn't even been granted a food amnesty permit. Plus, Christian wasn't entirely sure if he'd been made mortal yet and, although he thought he might have felt a hunger pang earlier that week, he wasn't going to chance eating until he was sure.

'You could sing for us.'

Mayday looked at him poisonously but said nothing. Rose looked confused.

'Moses says you have a marvellous voice.' He added, 'He says you can call the very angels out of the sky.'

Mayday spluttered slightly, but Rose was so taken aback by the request that she missed it.

'He said that?'

'He did surely. Didn't he, Mayday?'

'Oh *absolutely*. Never shuts up about your singing.'

'Sing us something now, Rose.'

'Well, I don't know, I . . .'

Then she looked at the pair of them. How could she refuse? Maybe they were just making a fool of her, but sure, what harm? After all they'd done for her she should be happy to go up for Communion naked if it amused them.

'What'll I sing?' she asked.

'Something religious,' said Christian firmly. Mayday gave him a nervous look.

'*Ave Maria*?'

'Oooooh,' Mayday cooed with genuine delight. 'I *love* that one.'

They were the oddest pair, but Rose stood up, took a deep breath, closed her eyes and began to sing.

And as she sang, Rose became lost. Lost as she had been when singing as a child in Mass. Although it was cloudy outside, she felt a warm light pulling her up towards the high notes as if the sun was flooding through the tall stained-glass window of the church, dappling her face with its colours. She kept her eyes closed and she opened her voice out into the words as if she were a young innocent again and singing for the Pope himself.

If she had opened them she would have seen her audience glow. Not just with pleasure, but actually physically glowing white. They knew it was bad form to let their auras glimmer in the presence of a mortal, but her celebration of the Blessed Virgin was, quite simply, too powerful to resist.

When she was finished she turned to find the two men looking slightly shaken after their private rapture.

'That was fantastic, Rose,' Christian said.

'I'll say,' said Mayday with a lascivious grin plastered across his face. 'Anyone got a cigarette?'

Christian gave him a shin kick.

'Rose, you *must* sing at the karaoke finals. Mustn't she, Mayday?'

Mayday hadn't a clue where Christian was going with this, but then he never had much of a clue about anything after a good ecstatic transportation. Best just row along and ask questions later.

'Absolutely must, I insist.'

'But what about London, Christian? What if I get this job? What if . . .'

'Oh London-glumdum,' announced Mayday, getting into his stride. 'Leave on a high. Win the karaoke or whatever. We'll do an upstyle! We'll run up a frock! You'll wear feathers! It'll be fabulous!'

Mayday looked at Christian for approval on his flimsy line of argument and received a cold glare.

But Rose was convinced. Mayday was right. She should start her new life on a high. The whole town would be there and she would go along and show them what it was all about. The new her.

'I'll do it!'

The county karaoke finals would be where Rose Fitzgerald would sing the swansong to her old life.

29

Mary tore the photograph of herself and Theo out of *Romantic Moments* magazine and started to trim around the edges with nail scissors. Sandra snatched them off her as she was passing.

'Gaaaah, Mary, don't use them! They're imported from France. Cost me a bloody fortune.'

'If they can cut the horns off that 'aul Malone bitch then paper won't do them any harm.'

'I suppose.' Her new boss leaned across the front desk of Tasty Talons nail salon and looked at the picture. 'You're better off without that bollix. What the hell are you doing cutting out a picture of him?' She looked down at Mary's hurt face and tried to turn it into a joke, 'With my good nail scissors!'

'It's the first time my picture's appeared anywhere. I *am* in the picture too, you know.'

Poor kid. She was being defensive and small wonder. Theo going off like that with her best friend before she had even had the chance to blow him out. It was humiliating for her. Sandra knew something about humiliation, but she knew more about how to chew it up and spit it back at those dishing it out.

'Well cut his head off then.'

'I can't do that.'

'Course you can, here,' and she grabbed the sheet and scissors, then sliced straight through his neck with a tiny snip. 'Isn't that better?'

Mary felt like crying. That was the only evidence left to her that she had ever been engaged to Theo Malone. He was with Ella now. Ella. Her beautiful, brilliant, deceptive, sex-mad, ex-best friend. Sandra was her new best friend. How sad was that? She couldn't get a man so she had to cling to the hem of another woman who did have men following her around. Was there not a girl less pretty, less hopeless, less frumpy than her in the town she could hang about with? Jesus she couldn't even get that right. Perhaps if she hadn't have gone to London in the first place, certainly if she hadn't agreed to Ella's suggestion that she have a word with Theo on her behalf, get a feel for how he felt about the marriage, this would never have happened.

She got a feel all right. They ended up in bed.

At least Ella had had the decency to tell her. She felt terrible; they'd secretly fancied each other for ages but they hadn't acted on it for fear of hurting her; it was love, Ella said, they weren't able to contain themselves. And this was supposed to make Mary feel what? Better?

She was angry, but again, according to Sandra, she couldn't get that right either and wasn't half angry enough.

Mary had bumped into the Englishwoman the day after it happened and blurted it all out. There was no point in being coy about it, the whole town would know soon enough. All this on top of her mother and father splitting up. She wouldn't be surprised if it made the front page of the parish Catholic newsletter.

'Right,' Sandra said. 'What you need, girl, is to get a whole new life. New hair, new nails, new wardrobe, new job, new man – the works, and I'm going to help you on every front. I'm opening a salon in town in a couple of weeks. Why don't you come and work for me?'

Mary agreed because no one had ever offered her a job before and she didn't think she could face the mortified pity of her workmates at the town council. They were all dull, hopeless cases like herself, except they were *all* married. They had clubbed together for a Waterford crystal vase for her engagement. God knows, but they probably had the wedding gift bought already.

She had handed her notice in, then taken sick leave and started with Sandra almost immediately, putting together paperwork, having price lists designed and printed, taking bookings and organizing the wages. It was nice work, but she'd have enjoyed it a lot more without her boss's interference in her personal life. Like Sandra, the foreign girls that worked there were also stunning looking as well as being lovely, kind people. She knew that her revamped hairstyle and their insistences that she try a new top or come lingerie shopping in Galway were all meant to be making her feel better, but they didn't. They made her feel worse. Mary looked a bit better on the outside. A bit. But on the inside she knew she was still ordinary. A tapered bob and a pair of sling-backs weren't going to make her special, loveable *or* loved. They were just going to make her into an ordinary frump who was trying. When you tried, you failed. If Theo hadn't taught her that, her brief stab at Weight Watchers certainly had.

And then there was Rose. Her reliable stay-at-home mother was overtaking her in the adventure called life. She was glad for Rose, but her happiness was only proving a terrible point to Mary. It wasn't her lot in life, her bad luck, her family, the misfortune of having been born in Gorrib, that was making things bad. It was her. Mary Fitzgerald. Too dull to try. So dull, other people had to try for her. Ella, she had tried in her own way and had finally given up on her in the worst way. That's why she couldn't even get angry with her. Ella had tried, and tried, and tried, and then there was a small crack in her loyalty and slippery Theo had slid in. And why wouldn't he? Ella was pretty and funny and unafraid. Theo was handsome and clever. Weren't they just getting on with it? And now Sandra, the girl who had it all, was trying to help her too. Change her. Give her confidence. Mary just wished she wouldn't bother. The truth was, she didn't want to change. She wanted to things to just stay as they were now for a while and be left alone.

Going to England with her mother had proved a disappointment for her. She had thought that London would be full of interesting characters like Mayday and Christian, and somehow imagined that being there would change things for her. That she would fall in love with the place and perhaps want to stay. But Kingsbury was just relations and shops and rows of houses and cars and buses and millions of strangers and so much life that even though her mother was with her, Mary felt overwhelmed by the size of it and alone in a way she never had done before. So she came back more resigned than before.

She reached mournfully into her desk drawer and pulled out a jam doughnut.

Sandra gave her a look and Mary replied with defiant sarcasm, 'Three for the price of two in Duffy's. Don't suppose I can tempt you?'

'Bit early in the day for me, Mary.' Sandra smiled. 'Ooooh, hello, look who it is.'

Sandra stuck her head out of the door and shouted down the street, 'Hey, Vinny. VIN-CENT! Damn, he's gone. I *do* like that man, haven't seen him for weeks.'

Sandra knew that Mary had gone off with her neighbour that night after Bosanova but she wouldn't be drawn on the subject. Mary liked Sandra, but that kind of confidence was something that could only be shared with someone she had known for a long time. Someone who already knew everything there was to know about her so there was no need to spell things out. Someone like Ella.

Mary shuddered and got on with her doughnut. No point in even thinking about that one. If the Theo thing was bad, the virgin farmer incident was one that she *would* rather forget.

30

Sandra hadn't been down to the bar for weeks now.

'Let her get on with whatever filthiness she's up to next; I'm sick to the eye teeth looking after the lot of you,' said Mags to Christian's enquiry after her English niece. 'Eat up that pudding now, there's a good lad. I'm glad *someone* around here has an appetite for my cooking,' she added, giving Mayday a fond pat on the shoulder as he tucked into his morning fry.

Christian was *dying* to start eating, even if just to please Margaret, over whose affections he and Mayday had become quite competitive.

She had asked Christian one day about his own mother and he had stated rather vaguely that his own mother was rather remote and had so many children she didn't know what to do with them all. Mayday nodded through a mouthful of apple tart that his mother was the same.

'Well she sounds like an awful woman altogether,' Margaret stated as she dusted the statue of the Blessed Virgin that had pride of place on her mantelpiece.

Mayday and Christian realized now why they were advised never to get intimately involved with mortals. They knew it was wrong, but they couldn't seem to resist the old bird's charms. Margaret fussed over them and had made this place feel like the first home either of them had ever had. The BVM was always there for them, they knew that. But she didn't (*couldn't*, they frequently reminded themselves) fill a hot-water bottle or cook a fry or say, 'What time do you call this?' when they arrived in late. Having a real mother was possibly the one thing they envied in mortals.

Moses would have contested that emotion, if he could have drummed up the inclination to talk at all these days. Sex with Sandra had awakened something in him. An old discontent that he had hoped he'd killed off years ago. Desire. Perhaps his mother was right, it was a sin. It sure as hell felt like a punishment.

He didn't love Sandra after a fashion or anything like it. For a few days, maybe a week or so, after it happened, Moses was buzzing. There was no specific intention, he just found he was splashing himself with aftershave, checking the socks for holes, choosing the good briefs over the baggy old Y-fronts he'd had since the seventies. His head was telling him nothing was going on, but his body didn't believe it. Then, as is often the case with these things, something stupid set him off. The mother was downstairs with her geriatric gal pals practising for the karaoke finals. The three of them were acting up in front of an audience of refugee men and then, as if it were in a frame frozen from a film, he saw one of the old lads throw his mother a wink. Out of nowhere a feeling of panic flooded through him. He didn't think about what it meant. Moses didn't go in for analysis, especially when it came to his mother. But he found that when the moment passed and the world started moving again, he did not feel inclined to join in. He withdrew, which was not like him at all. There was something fundamental missing from his life. A romance which, as he'd just realized, even his mother was still capable of enjoying. It had been there once; even after Rose had left him, the feeling he might charm and be charmed had lingered for a while. Now it was gone. The enchantment, the magic of love. The belief that one day it might happen for him. All that was left was his cock and the empty desire to stick it into his cousin. And knowing that, even that desire evaporated too.

He had become morose and intolerant. The perky camp presence of Mayday and Christian irritated him. His mother's constant fussing over them and her girlish excitement about the karaoke finals seemed inappropriate and ghoulish given her age.

He had stopped writing altogether. What was the point? Nobody ever heard anything he wrote, nobody was interested, and in any case, he had nothing to write about any more. What did he know, stuck in this god-forsaken hole, still living with his mother?

Then, the final insult.

'Rose is thinking of moving to England.'

'Get away!'

Meena Murray and Breda Fitzgerald were waiting in

the front bar for his mother decked out, Moses was horrified to note, in tracksuit bottoms and trainers, with their best cardigans on top.

'She was round yesterday, brought me up a lasagne. I don't care if she left that fool of a son of mine, she's still my daughter as far as I'm concerned.'

Moses felt a tearing in his head, but he couldn't walk away.

'And sure, what'll she do over there?'

'She has a sister in Kingsbury, and she's only gone and got herself a job.'

'Get away!'

'I'm telling you.'

'Where?'

'In a supermarket.'

'Get away!'

'Running the show.'

'Get away!'

'Manageress.'

'You're not serious?'

'I am so. Deadly.'

'What will you do without her?'

Moses stopped listening then. *What will you do without her?* And there it was. The end. Rose had not been with him for years. But she had always been around. That was the thing about Gorrib. Things never came to a proper close because on some level the same things, the same people, stayed within reach. There was always easy access to the past. The promise that one day things could go back to the way they were. The post office might get a refit, but it was there in the same place it had always been. When people died they left behind them neighbours with anecdotes who could be relied upon to fill in the gaps. People emigrated to England, lots of them, all the time. But they always came back some time or another, and if they forgot Gorrib entirely, Gorrib never forgot them. Twenty years later returning emigrants were always astonished at bumping into old schoolfriends who could remind them of details in their life they had long since forgotten themselves as their memories had been wiped by the vastness and the stresses of city life.

Moses knew that if Rose went to England she would never, not in any real sense, come back. Although he was not prepared to admit it, he knew that she would take a part of him with her. A part of him that could never be replaced.

But there was nothing he could do about that now. All he could do was leave the question hanging in the air above his father's bar, with the ghost of a girl in a white dress standing in the open doorway.

What'll you do without her.

31

Shortly after his aborted night of passion in Bosanova, Dermot went back to Dublin to sort out his affairs. It was an interesting trip. Satisfying in the business sense, but depressing in the sense that he was revisiting a life that didn't feel like his own any more.

The hotel was no longer his. Swallowed away from him with a single signature. He drove past it on the quays on his way into town and could hardly believe, seeing its stature and style, that just a few weeks ago it had been under his control. He stayed in one of his flats in Rathmines, which had recently become vacant. It felt odd to be in Dublin and was somehow more comfortable now he was staying in a sparsely furnished bedsit. He had thought about booking into a hotel and calling up one of the girls to come and keep him company. But it was more what he felt he should be doing than what he wanted to do. In the end he did neither and just spent his time there diligently going through his accounts and passing responsibilities for day-to-day property management and sales to his rental agency and solicitor. He had gone out for dinner one night with his accountant, John Ward. He liked John. He was a serious, dry sort of a fellow, but Dermot trusted him. The early part of the evening had been fine as the two men pragmatically discussed the best way for Dermot to handle his affairs from the country during what Dermot was now calling his year's sabbatical. Then a gang of their old business associates arrived. 'Friends' that John had told to pop in; give poor Dermot some support. They were all full of business talk: the next 'big deal', where to go next. Leeson deserved a second chance. 'You'll bounce back, son,' one of them said. And it was then, in that moment, that Dermot realized that 'losing' the hotel meant, to them and previously to him, failure. He had lost the hotel, and in doing so he had lost the game. Because, Dermot realized, that is all this was. A boy's game. Acquiring things that you were too stressed out or tired to enjoy. For what? A slap on the back from one of your associates. He still had more money than he needed, certainly for the frugal life he was leading in Gorrib. The only thing he had 'lost' was the admiration and respect of a bunch of men who considered him part of their peer group. A group that success and status initiated you into, and failure to conform to their ludicrous and shallow rules propelled you out of. Looking around the table, Dermot realized that these people were not his friends. Vinny was his friend. He helped him, kept him company and expected nothing in return. Vinny neither knew nor cared who he was or where he came from. He took Dermot at face value. Vinny was decent. This crowd wore their decency like a badge. Not one of them had called to see how he was after the hotel went under, yet here they all were bragging in front of each other about how they could help him get 'back on his feet'. Offering membership to their golf club; corporate box tickets for the game on Sunday; to cut him in on some new deal, some bigger, more important deal than his hotel because it was theirs. But Leeson wasn't playing their game any more. He wasn't up for a rematch. Not because he couldn't any more, but because he didn't want to.

Back at the house in Gorrib a few days later, Dermot wondered about the wisdom of turning down their help. It wasn't that he didn't want to be here. He still had the house to finish and the slow pace of life here did seem to suit him. But having made that initial leap back and getting stuck into sorting out his businesses, Dermot realized that there was a part of him that didn't want to let it all go. He was too good at it and while he could do without the bullshit of business lunches and gold handicaps, he enjoyed the money part of it. Not spending it so much as watching it grow. He thought, wistfully looking out on his messy back field, that perhaps he would get the same buzz from cabbages. But he knew in his heart and soul that he wouldn't.

He had no milk in the house, which gave him the perfect excuse to wander over to Vinny's. It was nearing six, so there'd doubtless be some tea in it for him if he hurried along.

Vinny was out back in the lab, so Dermot let himself into the kitchen and stuck the kettle on. A nice ham sandwich now, he thought, would be just the man to settle him back. Vinny always had a fresh sliced and a pack of ham in, and as Dermot was rummaging around on the dresser he spotted a thick wodge of official white envelopes wedged behind the bread bin. He slid one out for a peek. They were bank statements. Unopened. Weird. Why would somebody not open a bank statement? Maybe he was strapped for cash? If he was, Dermot would like to help. So it was entirely with good intention (and not at all out of blatant curiosity towards another person's financial affairs) that, checking through the window that Vinny wasn't coming, he carefully eased the envelope open with the steam from the kettle.

Merciful hour of Jesus, the guy was loaded!

Two hundred and fifty-seven thousand, *thousand*!, euros just sitting there in his current account.

He closed the envelope and placed it back with the others. He checked and found that all the envelopes were identical so the chances were there was nothing in the way of other investments. Just this lump sitting in a current account. God, thought Dermot, what you could do with a lump sum like that as capital. You could own Gorrib. Bring that into the bank and see how much they'd lend you. Now, there was a sum lying dormant that Dermot could make grow. And grow and grow. Vinney spent nothing. Not that he was mean but there was nothing to spend on down here. All the same, thought Dermot, it's a crime, to have that kind of money just sitting there earning nothing. A *CRIME*!

There was no way he could just blurt it out. So he made the sandwiches and the tea and waited for Vinny to come back in.

'You're back from Dublin so.'

'Two sugars is it?'

'Three.' Then, 'Thanks,' as Dermot put the sandwich down in front of him.

Vinny had been in quiet, depressed form before he left, but Dermot had assumed he would have cheered up or got over whatever it was that was bugging him by now. He obviously hadn't. Best not bring the money thing up just yet.

But he couldn't help himself.

'Business good?'

'Ahra, it's all right.'

'Busy?'

'New order there in last week from a crowd in Italy.'

'Yeah?'

'Cockroaches. I've a thousand of the bastards out there now ready to go.'

'And how much will you get for them?'

'I don't know. Five euros a roach maybe?'

'Jesus, that's a lot of money there, Vinny.'

'I suppose.'

'Tell me,' Dermot decided to just go for it, 'have you ever thought about investing your money in . . .'

Vinny got up and stuck his plate in the sink and started clattering about the kitchen.

'. . . property or business. I mean, you must be doing awfully well with the lab and all, and—'

'Oh for God's sake, Dermot, can you not see that I've too much other stuff on my mind right now?'

Whoaaah! This was not like Vincent at all. Snappy. Something was going down. No point in dancing around it.

'Like what?' Dermot asked straight out.

'I don't want to talk about it,' Vinny's voice was smaller now. Like he'd regretted saying anything at all.

'Well then let's talk about money.'

'I don't want to talk about that either.'

Vinny stood with his hands resting on the butler sink. He was breathing heavily and, even from the back, Dermot could see that he was raging. Vinny was huge and a weaker man would have walked away and opened up the conversation again when he calmed down. But Dermot was more than a fair-weather friend, and he could see that this man needed to get something off his chest.

'Well then, let's talk about the other thing.'

'I'm tired. Come back tomorrow, Dermot. I'm not in the humour.'

'Well, funny that, because I am.'

Vinny turned and glowered at him and, for a moment, Dermot thought he might hit him. He knew that look. Men like Vinny didn't get depressed. They got angry. He wasn't angry with him. He was angry with himself.

'Dermot, there's nothing you can do. I'll be grand, just leave it for tonight and I'll be over in the morning to . . .'

'How do you know I can't help unless you tell me what it is?'

Vinny stared at him and Dermot saw him weaken.

'I'm not going anywhere, so you're as well off telling me as not.'

The huge man came and slumped at the table. He gripped the edge of the table and closed his eyes. He was mortified.

'I was rejected by a woman.'

Ah fuck. Was that all?

'Join the club. I haven't had a woman in months. Can't get it up. Nothing to be ashamed of. Women are funny creatures. You see the thing about women is—'

'I've never had a woman.'

His voice was so small now it was barely audible. But Dermot heard him all right, and he wasn't going to ask him to repeat it.

'I see.' He was beginning to regret starting this conversation. This was turning out heavier than he thought.

Vinny on the other hand, now that he had started, was unable to stop.

'I bought her home from the disco and we talked, then she got into the bed and I said I'd never done "it" before and she got really annoyed and she left.'

'I see.' Dermot had seen a film once with Barbra Streisand as Nick Nolte's therapist. All he had to do was be Barbra to Vinny's Nick, so he just nodded and said, 'I see,' in the softest most sympathetic voice he could manage.

'Then I saw her coming out of the lab, and when I

went down later there was a rake of roaches out so she must have seen them and got frightened because she run off.'

'I see.'

'And I tried to run after her but I couldn't because she got picked up on the road by somebody and I couldn't catch up.'

'I see.'

'And then I didn't see her for ages because she had gone to England and then she came back and I seen her yesterday in the town in the new place where the women get their nails done or something but she didn't see me because then I was afraid she might see me and so I ran off and . . .'

A spark went off in Dermot's brain. He'd picked up the *Mayo News* on the way down and seen that the English lap dancer was opening a nail salon.

'And this girl was . . .?'

'The one in the disco. That night we went out to Bosanova. The gorgeous one I was talking to all night.'

There was only one gorgeous woman there that night. Dermot had wanted her and he would have been well able for her. And she knew it. So she had picked on poor Vinny. He'd seen the way she was flirting with him. Taken this simple country lad home then laughed at his inexperience. The poisonous bitch!

'Dermot,' poor Vinny's eyes were filling up, 'I love her, Dermot. I can't get her out of my mind.'

'She laughed at you,' Dermot was feeling deadly. Vinny didn't deserve this. No man did.

'I don't care. She didn't mean it. I know she didn't mean it. I want to try again, but I'm too afraid. Will you help me, Dermot? You know about women. Will you help me get her back?'

The poor bastard was crawling. That's what woman like that did to a man. They made you crawl. With their Parisian shoes and their city appetites. A man like him would be able to handle a woman like that but, oh no, she had to pick on a sweet, gentle innocent like Vinny. Typical vicious bitch. Probably knew about all his money. This was heartbreaking, it really was. If it had been less so, Dermot would probably have had the foresight not to say what he said next.

'She doesn't deserve you, Vinny. I've had her already and I can tell you she's nothing but a dirty slut.'

Dermot had played rugby at school, but he'd never had a land like it. His head hit the flagstones sideways and for a second he thought Vinny, who was standing over him, might be putting his hand out to help him up. But the huge fist was still clenched as his host said, with no room for negotiation whatsoever, 'Get out of my house.'

Dermot didn't stop to argue his case.

Vinny had fallen, hook, line and sinker, but he was still Dermot's friend and he wasn't going to let a woman like that come between them.

He staggered back to his house, checked his nose was still intact, changed into his Gucci suit and loafers and headed into Gorrib.

He was going to tackle this bitch once and for all.

32

It was about eleven a.m. when the emergency call came through.

'Mayday! Mayday! Do you read? Copy, Mayday. The time has come, repeat, the time has come. Brendan the Voyager has issued instructions that a specialized military unit arrive in Gorrib at twelve hundred hours, but they are on standby only. Repeat, military unit on standby only. To be utilized only as extreme emergency measure. Do you copy? Mayday?'

Mayday was standing in McGreavy's kitchen with a cream doughnut in one hand and a Diet Coke in the other. He froze, and his hand loosened on the Diet Coke, sending a fizzy dribble of brown liquid onto Margaret's good carpet.

'My good carpet!' she howled, and as Christian leapt across to the rescue he heard Mayday croak in a tiny voice, 'Copy,' and he knew that the call had come through a psychic channel. That was not a good sign. No time for memorandums or plans. This was Arnold Schwarzenegger territory. And Mayday was no action man. Still, thought Christian, not my problem.

'I can't do it, Christian.'

Fuck. He knew this was going to happen. The cowardly shit was all feathers and front. When it came down to it, he lacked guts. Well, so do I, thought Christian, so do I.

'You've made your bed and you're going to—'

'No really. I'm petrified. Look at me . . .'

He held out a perfectly manicured hand (French Golden Glimmer nails courtesy of Tasty Talons, Mayo's first nail salon) and it was shaking. Christian looked him straight in the eye and Mayday began to weep.

'Please, Christian, I can't handle this. You know me, you know what I'm like. I'm all talk. I'm not built for this. I'm not able for it. You've got to help me, please, Christian, I'm *begging* you.'

Humility and Mayday were such an extremely uncomfortable match that it propelled him so far down the patheticness scale that Christian had no option but to relent.

'What are you two whispering about over there like a couple of schoolgirls?' called Margaret. But they were already gone.

They weren't halfway down Church Street when Mayday recovered and was back to his irritating self.

'Will we manifest ourselves down there?'

'No.'

'It'll be quicker.'

'No.'

'It *is* an emergency.'

'All the more reason not to draw attention to ourselves.'

'We can manifest from that alley down the end. I've done it before, no one will—'

'I don't have a permit.'

'How do you mean?'

'I don't have a manifestation permit.'

'What none?'

'Used it up.'

'What like, no permit at—'

'No.'

'What about flying then? You must have a flight—'

'No.'

'No flight?'

'No.'

'No manifestation?'

'No.'

'How about transubstantiation? We could turn ourselves into cows or rabbits or something if things get a bit . . .'

Christian stopped and glowered at him in a way that was, frankly, confrontational.

'I have no permits, Mayday.'

Mayday went silent for a minute, and for one glorious moment Christian thought he saw something that remotely resembled gravitas. He was wrong.

'What – none?'

'That's right. I have no permits.'

Mayday blinked.

'This is not a game, Mayday. All we need is the word of the Lord.'

It felt good to sound devout, even if Christian didn't mean it. This was going to be horrendous, no doubt about it, but only a martyr would go into a situation like this without a veritable army of permits under his belt.

'Yeah *right*.'

Mayday was pissed off and probably genuinely terrified, which was, Christian decided, a very good thing given his manipulative performance in the kitchen.

'Jesus managed,' Christian said with a tone of such pious fortitude he knew it would send Mayday round the bend.

'Oh please! Miracles every five minutes? He got away with—'

'Mayday!'

'Yeah, yeah right, somebody up there's listening.' Then in his prettiest girlie voice he added, 'Christian, do you really *need* me there today? I mean, you seem to have this whole thing—'

'Don't even think about it.'

They walked the rest of the fifteen minutes' journey in silence, Mayday wondering how long before he could reasonably call on the Field Unit that he knew was in place, and Christian privately cursing God and all belonging to Him in the hope that now he was mortal they were no longer able to listen in.

Both angels were so absorbed in their thoughts that they didn't notice that the black storm clouds ahead had a tinge of Lucifer about them.

When they reached Hemlock's place the sky was almost black. The door to the caravan was ajar and gently swinging on its hinges with a creepy 'Eeek-eeek. Eeek-eeek'. It was pure Hammer Horror. Morticia Adams make-up and a casual interest in S&M was one thing but *this*, Mayday realized, was quite another.

'I don't like this one bit.'

'And Christian makes two. Come on, dear, let's get this thing over and done with.'

But Mayday wasn't moving.

'Supposing *he's* in there.'

'Who?'

'Satan,' he whispered, in case the dark angel might hear his name being uttered and call, 'Coo-ee, boys, I'm over here!'

'So what if he is?'

And it was only as he said the words that Christian realized that he wasn't afraid. The only reason this job had ever daunted him was the fear he'd bugger it up and fail to get his promotion. That wasn't going to happen now, anyway. That aside, he had nothing to be afraid of. He was a good angel; tried to serve Him well. So he'd bent a few rules and used permits to perform party tricks a few times. He had nothing to fear from the Dark Angel, the ugly old goat. If he appeared in the full regalia, Christian had seen enough pictures not to get a shock. 'See you're feeling a bit horny there, Lucy?' he'd say. It wouldn't be pretty, but a queen on top form had enough lash in their tongue to whip the most macho of all devils into a corner. He felt sure of that.

Being nearly mortal himself now, he had some sympathy for Hemlock. Some might say that if the Devil was sniffing about, the old man must have given him some reason. No smoke without fire and all that. But what had poor Ignatius done except fall in love and not be able to handle the rejection? He was weak. Weakness wasn't a crime, it was a lesson and some of us, Christian thought, looking at the point of fact in the pink plaits quaking in front of him, learn quicker and better than others.

'Go on then, you big fairy,' he said, nodding back towards the road. 'You head back.'

'There's a Field Unit back in the bar on standby. I'll send them down for half twelve,' said Mayday, already on the move.

'If I need them I'll call,' Christian said, already realizing that he'd no psychic powers and no permit to use them even if he had.

33

Sandra never did ask the girls about the lap-dancing club.
In fact, one month on she could hardly believe she had
done it herself for all those years. She had enjoyed it,
sure she had. If you did a job like that without enjoying
it, you were in big trouble. But this – starting up her
own business – this was so much better.

First up, Sandra was a dominatrix. She loved to be in
control. It wasn't easy when you were working for the
collection of exploitative sleazebags she had encountered
over the years, but she had managed it. Never had any
problems with the punters either, never met a man yet
that couldn't be whipped into shape if she set her mind
to it. A bunch of hardworking grateful women were a
cinch after that. She had half the money for the six-
month lease saved already (her parents' extension would
have to wait) and a low-cut top, a broad smile and a set
of projected earnings for the next few months were all
she needed to borrow from the bank. She had loved
sitting down with Mary and going through the figures on
the computer. Sandra had always had a good head for

money but she had never used a computer before. She was astonished at how quickly Mary could negotiate the complicated-looking screen and was doubly delighted when, under her PA's instruction, she hooked up to the Internet and had a great rummage around looking for nail products to import.

Importing products. Having a PA. Premises. What a buzz! The local paper had even taken her picture and done a piece headed 'Gorrib Girl Makes Good'. So there it was, officially, in black and white, she was a local. Gorrib was her home. Finally, she was putting down roots.

How scary was that!

She hadn't thought about the move in terms of staying around. She had just seen an opportunity and gone for it. But now, sitting in her chilly rented bungalow looking at her own smiling face in the *Mayo News*, drinking yesterday's coffee, heated in the microwave because she had forgotten to buy herself milk or coffee, reality began to dawn.

Six months, that was how long the lease ran for. Then there was the staff, she couldn't just walk out on the girls or Mary when the lease was up. This was a major commitment. A lifetime commitment. Shit. She hadn't thought of that. Was this what she wanted? Was this the place that she wanted to stay in for – hullo? – the rest of her life? It seemed like an awfully long time. No more jetting off when she felt like it, although, she justified to herself, she'd be able to well afford to if the salon did well. She might have to buy a house; she couldn't live in this place for ever. How would she cope with no shoe shops, no sushi? Would she ever get a Brazilian wax again?

Sandra shivered, then wandered into the bedroom to get a cardigan. She had left her favourite one in the salon, so she went to her large suitcase to get another and – bam! it hit her. She was still living out of a suitcase. She had been testing herself. Trying to make friends, getting back in touch with family, taking a break from the relentless travelling, the running, the being on her own. She saw she could do it. Then she'd seen another opportunity, for a career change, and had tested that out too. It worked. But she hadn't unpacked her suitcase; hadn't emptied out her belongings properly, then put the lid on her old life and tucked it under the bed. No. It was still there open. The yawning leather lid spewing out a chaos of clothes saying, 'Come on there, Cosmo chick, throw everything back in and we'll head off again. Who knows what's around the corner?'

But Sandra had been around enough corners. There were shoe shops and sushi, good Brazilian waxes and bad Brazilian waxes; there were men and there was money and the cold comfort of always knowing that you were in charge. No parents to criticize you, no friends to judge you, no boyfriend to control you. It had been reason enough to keep her moving through her twenties, but the don't-fuck-with-my-freedom mentality had worn thin. Since she had come here she had created, if not a home, at least an openness to the idea of it. She looked around at the bungalow and realized that she hadn't made much of a job of it. Sandra had spent most of her adult life being on her own, but she couldn't say that she had lived on her own as such. No fixed abode.

Starting now, she decided things were going to change.

In five minutes flat she emptied the suitcase, hung up all of its contents and threw the empty vessel under the bed. It was a sunny morning, so she put on a jumper and her new wellington boots and headed down towards the garage.

When she was about ten minutes down the road, the sky clouded over and it started to rain.

34

The salon was closed, but Mary was in doing some paperwork. She had nothing else to do. Rose was out on a shopping trip to Galway with Christian getting her outfit for the karaoke finals and Sandra was at home. Her father had virtually stopped speaking to her since she started working for Sandra, with whom it seemed he had been planning some business venture, so the atmosphere in the house was untenable. There had been some talk of him selling the house and moving down to Limerick where his brother had a car dealership but in the meantime she and Davy were spending as much time as possible with their mother in Church Street. Davy had plans to move in there full time, but Mary wasn't so sure. Even with her mother moving to London on the cards, she knew it was time she started to stand on her own two feet. The problem was, she had to find them first.

There was a man banging on the window.

If he had tried the door he would have found it open, but Mary went out to him and he stormed in past her.

He was a good-looking city type in an expensive suit. A supplier no doubt, although he had no case with him.

'Can I hel—'

'Where is she?'

'I'm sorry, sir?'

'Where is she? Shirley? Sandra? Whatever her fucking name is. Where is she?'

He was annoyed about something. Mary had come across enough dissatisfied customers on the front desk of the council offices before now, but never someone so handsome, so well dressed, so . . . he was marching down to the back of the salon.

'Get the fuck out here, you English bitch, I want a word with you.'

His words echoed through the empty salon as he kicked open the doors to the small toilet and the product storeroom.

Mary should have been scared, except that she had lived with Brian Fitzgerald all her life.

She stood by the door and fixed him with a formal stare.

'Miss Gallagher is not here at present. May I help yo—'

She was cut short as the man collapsed into a nearby chair. His breathing was fast and he looked as if he was going to explode. Davy had suffered from asthma as a child, but this guy didn't seem to be grappling for an inhaler, so she emptied out a paper bag of nail tips from her desk and ran over to him with it. She held it up to his face and said, 'Breathe in, breathe out.'

The combination of his head resting on her comely breasts and the sensible, soothing tone of her voice calmed him down.

When he was breathing properly again, she handed him a glass of water.

'You'd want to watch out for that asthma. My brother has it. Man your age should know to have an inhaler with you all the time.'

'It's not asthma,' he said. 'It's a panic attack.'

'Sure, what's a handsome fella like you got to panic about?'

Just like that, Mary was flirting. She recognized him now. He was the dishy Dublin guy Vinny had with him at Bosanova that night. She had thought he was more Ella's type than hers, but how wrong she had been about that. Now she had him all to herself. But he didn't recognize Mary. He was looking for Sandra. Of course.

'When I get angry like that, I can't control myself.'

I bet you can't, Mary thought, but stopped short of saying it, instead asking, 'And what are you angry about? Sandra by the sounds of it.'

Some grand passion no doubt. Something she would never know anything about. Still it was gossip, and Mary was a good small-town girl with gossip in her blood.

'Yeah, well.'

But he wasn't getting off that easy.

'Turned you down did she? Stood you up?'

'Ha!'

Oooh, nearly there. Just one more inflammatory question and she'd have it out of him.

'Well, Sandra can pick and choose, can't she? If I had a pound for every time a man came in here chasing after Sandra, why I'd have a . . .'

'She's a fucking bitch. Do you know what she did?'

'Ah, she's a lovely woman, I can't imagine Sandra now doing . . .'

'She took a friend of mine, a lovely, simple country lad and she tried to seduce him.'

'You're jealous by the sounds of it. Who was he, this friend?'

No point in only getting half the story.

'Never you mind. Let's just say he's a good friend of mine and he's not very experienced with women.'

Vinny! Sandra and Vinny. No. Can't be right.

'And when was this then?'

Mary was enjoying this. She had been so wrapped up in her own misery for the longest time that she had forgotten the simple pleasures of getting stuck into other people's business. She'd been so afraid of being the victim of people's gossip, but now she'd managed to turn the tables right around. This was great.

'A few weeks ago, at a disco. Anyway, he has only gone and fallen in love with her and I know she's only stringing him along. He's not her type.'

'And you are, I suppose?'

'No, I'm not saying that, it's just that . . .'

'You want her for yourself?'

'No it's not that, it's more like . . . Do I know you?'

He was changing the subject, but a thrill shot through Mary.

'You might do.'

He narrowed his eyes.

'Weren't you in Bosanova a few weeks ago with Sandra?'

'I might have been.'

She was getting coy and giggly now.

'And weren't you with another girl too, talking to Vincent, the farmer?'

'Maybe.'

A squat dumpling of a woman with a face like a bap. He seemed to remember Vinny making an unnecessary fuss of handing her a drink.

'Did you go home with him that night?'

This conversation was taking a direction that Mary didn't like. She went all tight-lipped, then the handsome man glowered at her nastily and repeated, 'Did you go home with him that night?'

'I might have done.'

He stood up and towered over her.

'WELL DID YOU OR DIDN'T YOU?'

'Yes.' she muttered.

'And did you or did you not sleep with him?'

'Well I . . .'

'DID YOU OR DID YOU NOT SLEEP WITH HIM. YES OR NO?'

Your man was looking frantic, like he might start with the mad breathing again, and the paper bag mightn't work this time.

'Yes, no, well, oh!' Mary wailed.

Then it was over. The man seemed relieved. He

wasn't going to ask for details. She wouldn't have to tell him she was a virgin although Mary didn't know that, experienced ladies' man that Dermot was, he only had to look at her to know.

'Right,' he said, and walked out of the door. Leaving Mary to figure out the fact that, as Vinny had slept (sort of, nearly, whatever), with her and not Sandra that night, as Dermot had initially suspected, then that meant Vinny was, in all probability, in love with her.

35

Hemlock was beginning to think that perhaps he should have visited a doctor. Had a go, at least, at putting off this nasty endgame that was now well underway. He hadn't been able to keep anything down for days, not even whisky – a bottle of which he had kept back for when his last moments came. It didn't matter now. Although it was only late afternoon, the inside of the caravan was dark. The weather was raging outside, he could hear rain lashing down on the roof, but the air inside was as still as death. Despite that, the candle kept puffing out and he could sense an invisible presence breathing alongside his own phlegmy rattle.

He felt nauseous and the pain from his rotting liver thrummed relentlessly inside his abdomen. Cursed mortal body. He'd be glad to get rid of it. If only it were that simple.

For Hemlock had already decided that he was, if he could, going over to the Other Side. He was halfway there already, and besides it was the sensible option. He'd partaken of precious little that could be called fun during his time here on Earth, and who in their right minds would turn down an eternal orgy. He deserved a break.

Lucifer, in his petty, egotistical way had taken over the weather. Big deal. Even Hemlock knew that it was going to take more than a few dramatic clouds and a spot of rain to win this battle. God wasn't going to give up that easy.

The battle was won by whoever could inhabit Hemlock for the longest time in this last hour, and the clock was already ticking. The aged figure lay in a ragged bundle on his fetid couch and willed himself into thinking of all the glories Hell had to offer him. Endless consumption of any manner of mind-altering substances; virgins of every sex, colour, creed, denomination and degrees of willingness to empty himself into; and the food menu was pretty good too. Never the same two days in a row. Foul-mouthed and wicked chefs got special dispensation if they agreed to cook for the Dark Prince and his Executive Officers.

It was looking pretty good for a clear passage into the bowels of Hell except that Hemlock hadn't reckoned on the Other Fellow excavating his buried conscience. If he had thought that he had one, he might have been better able to deal with it. Hold the bad thoughts steady without regrets and realizations flooding over him. There he'd be, flagellating some trussed-up sinner and making a right good job of it too, when up behind him would pop old Maisie Cassidy from Ridge Row, with a pathetic spin in her voice saying, 'You urinated on my beloved dahlia's back in '81, and they've never been the same again.'

'Eat shit you wizened old bitch!' he'd retort bravely, but Hemlock would feel just the tiniest tinge of guilt. In the battle between conscience and will, that was enough. When anyone, even a bad-bastard fallen angel like Hemlock, is near death, God has the canniest way of amplifying the smallest regret into a full-scale beg-for-forgiveness guilt attack. Hemlock was having to concentrate very hard to keep his God-given conscience at bay.

It was hard work, and it was made all the harder now by the sudden entrance of that smarmy fairy he'd seen slingeing around the town flinging the door open and announcing, 'I am an Emissary of Our Lord.' He was holding aloft two twigs in the sign of the cross as he continued, with very little conviction, 'I cast you out noxious vermin in the name of God the Father Almighty, Jesus Christ His only begotten son and by the Holy Spirit. Um . . . come out, come out there, ye unclean demon 'til I, um . . . bind you with the unbreakable chains of . . . um . . . adamantine and cast ye into the abyss of Hell.'

Hemlock felt like laughing but he was in too much pain. He quite rightly guessed that Christian had never done this before and hadn't the first hope in Hell of knowing what adamantine meant. Lucifer must be petrified. Really. With a bit of luck the eejit might start flinging Holy Water around the place, then we'll see if his Latin is up to scratch!

'You'll have to do better than that, ducky,' he growled from his dark corner. 'Now if you'll excuse me, I'm initiating a Black Resurrection over here for my new master, so you carry on there like a good lad and we'll mind each other's business.'

Was this the best God could do? Hemlock was feeling more confident now. If the nancy started bothering him, so much the better. The drunk's propensity for wickedness was always stronger when he had somebody to rail against. Slagging off an 'Emissary of our Lord' (although by the looks of him he was no archangel – low-ranking cupid was a better guess. Was that all God thought of him?) was perhaps just the distraction he needed to stop his conscience seeping through into his mind.

In fairness, Christian knew he was winging this whole exorcism thing. He wasn't even qualified to administer extreme unction. Crows were gathering outside. Hundreds of them on the telephone wires and fences all around the small roadside site. Their excited cawing was deafening as they waited and wondered what it was that had drawn them suddenly and inexplicably to this place, but inside the caravan Christian could hear nothing. Nothing bar the rasping breath of the dying man in the corner and his intermittent cackling as he communicated with his dark lord.

The cupid stood in the dank interior and looked around. As his eyes adjusted to the gloom he saw the scattered debris of this sad life. Rusting tins with spoons discarded in the half-eaten contents, empty cans of beer everywhere. Amid the chaos were signs that someone might have been trying to make a home. A filthy square of carpet thrown in the corner as if it had once been used to wipe feet had been rescued in from the rain. Six dusty jam jars lined up behind the sink, the beginnings of some discarded collection. A piece of twine tied in a bow in the middle of a pitiable remnant used as a curtain. Small scraps of evidence that perhaps there was a soul here worth saving. Christian decided he must at least try.

'You must be in a lot of pain.'

'Oh piss off.'

'Can I get you anything?'

'You a doctor?'

'No.'

'Got any whisky?'

'No.'

'Well then, like I said. Piss off.'

Christian saw there was a bottle of Jameson just out of Hemlock's reach.

'Would you like me to pour you a drink?'

The patient shot Christian a look of pure spite. 'Sorry, Pollyana, I seem to be all out of ice and lemon,' but as he leaned across for the bottle a pain shot through him and he drew back into his bundle.

Christian took it and handed it to him. Hemlock drank deeply from the neck, then almost immediately spewed up a cupful of thick, yellow mucus.

The cupid drew a clean white handkerchief from his trouser pocket and started to mop (he could say he always kept one in reserve for circumstances such as these, but frankly the worst it had ever seen before was the occasional damp bus shelter seat). Hemlock growled and snatched his head away.

'You're a regular Mother Theresa, aren't you.'

309

'Ignatius, this must be hard for you . . .'

'Actually, I'm enjoying myself. Haven't been touched up by a cutie like you for years. Give us a kiss then.'

And he puckered up his putrid mouth.

'I can help you. God sent me to . . .'

Hemlock's face drew back into an extreme grimace.

'Actually, do you know what, handsome? You can spare me. I would like it now if you would kindly fuck back off to where you came from. Please.'

'I'm not leaving here until . . .'

'Oh fuck you and you mother and . . .,' then his face went all straight again and for a moment he looked almost human.

'I want you to go. Will you do that one thing for me? Will you kindly fuck off now? I'm on my way to Hell, and if you're caught hanging around here you'll only get the blame.'

'Fuck,' thought Christian for a moment. 'He's right.'

'And you know what happens when he gets mad?' Hemlock shrugged his shoulders and gave an apologetic grin. Pus poured through his four remaining teeth. Christian was balking. This whole thing sure was revolting. Unhygienic even. But it was just a weak moment. At least he had Hemlock's attention now, and he was just thinking where best to go next with it when . . .

'Excuse me. Hello? My car ran out of petrol just outside and it's pissing down so I, um . . .'

Dermot thought perhaps he should have waited in his car. No perhaps about it. He *definitely* should have waited in his car. But he was here now, and these two men were looking at him as if he had just landed out of a spaceship. Out of ludicrous awkward politeness he said, 'Lot of crows out there. Lots. Got a bit of a crow problem going on there.'

The two men just stared at him open-mouthed. A very strange pair. A good-looking guy he felt sure he recognized and a bundled-up wretch who he guessed the smell of vomit was emanating from.

'Well, I won't trouble you. I can see you're busy so I'll just . . .'

As he started backing out of the door, the younger man rose and held his hand up as if telling him to stop.

'No really, I'd best be . . .', but Dermot found that his feet were rooted to the spot.

It was dark and he could barely make out the shape in the corner, but he could feel himself become fixed in the man's eyes. They were suddenly wide with shock and held in their strange shimmering blueness a terrible pleading.

'Only begotten of the Father.'

The younger man said it in almost a whisper but the impact on the old one was obvious. He blinked and his features crumpled into a fuzzy mess.

'I've lost,' he said. 'All that I have lost.'

Dermot's mind went blank with confusion. Shock. He knew that there was something shocking going on, but his mind could not begin to compute what it was. His legs started to go from under him, and the young man broke his fall and led him over to the pile of rags.

Dermot sat down and found himself transfixed by the

ancient, terrible face. He did not want to look, but he seemed to have no will to look away. So he looked, and what emerged slowly in front of him was his own face in thirty, forty years' time. It was not obvious. The similarities were hidden behind the dirt and the ravages of time and terror. It was not in the blueness of both their eyes, or the soft scowl on their brows or the lines of their noses or the way the flesh fell across their mouths. It was in the streams of their blood now meeting. The river's end. The beginning of a man who finally knows where he has come from and the end of a man who could never accept who he was.

Hemlock reached out a gnarled hand and Dermot took it.

Then he was gone.

36

'There is no such thing as bad weather, only *unsuitable* clothing.'

As Sandra pulled the hood toggles on her rainproof jacket and trudged back out of the shop garage into the rain she smiled to herself at Aunt Margaret's saying. The old woman would curl her nose and drag the word 'unsuitable' out as if it deserved special pronunciation when applied to her English niece.

Sandra's smile fell as she remembered the minor estrangement. Even by her own definition she had proved to be 'unsuitable'.

The easy-going lap dancer had never given much thought to whom she did or didn't have sex with. Not indeed that she was at it every night of the week, or anything like it. But when an opportunity presented itself, and she was in the mood, Sandra was a voracious lover. To her, sex had always been a purely physical thing. An extension of the seductive powers of her job. She revelled in the casual nature of her encounters and left in her one-night-only wake a trail of men all over the world whom she knew remained interested in her. She would seduce, satisfy and be gone. No hanging around for the messy emotional complications to set in. She was free-spirited and independent, and in her short, sharp, shock treatment of men, she fancied she maintained a certain mystery. Enough at least to keep her ego intact and convince herself she was more than a common slut. Sometimes she thought she might like to be loved. When she was tired and came in from a gig to an empty hotel room she thought it would be nice to have somebody to talk to. But the price of having a man telling her what she could and couldn't do, trying to control her, seemed a high one to pay for the little affection she required. Her life was exciting and adventurous, and her sex life was just something that she slotted into that frame.

But she had taken her eye off the ball with Moses. There was already a friendship and a love of sorts between them. She hadn't thought it through, she should have held herself back. The consequences of her actions hurt, and that surprised her. Hurt was something that she had successfully avoided for most of her adult life. And she realized that she was avoiding it now by not having been down to McGreavy's in weeks.

She had made a few friends. Mary, Vinny (when she could get hold of him) and the girls in the salon. But Moses and Margaret were special. They held a certain status in the town because of their longevity in business and their involvement with the community. Sandra had enjoyed the novelty of being part of an extended family, and knew that she had thrown it away with her careless attitude to relationships and sex. Perhaps, she realized, as she pushed against the driving wind, she wasn't quite as smart as she thought she was.

On the other hand, she knew she wasn't a bad person. Feckless, perhaps, when it came to men. But she had justified a lifestyle that had been unconventional and generally disapproved of for so long that positive thoughts about herself and her lifestyle had become an automatic part of her emotional make-up. She was, despite her seduction of Moses, a nice person. A kind person. Hadn't she given work to the refugee girls? Didn't Mary like her? And Vinny? She wasn't going to run away. No, she wasn't. She wasn't going to be chased out of town by a minor indiscretion. She going stay right here in Gorrib and build a life. She was going to . . .

Then she almost fell over him. He was sitting on a flat stone at the edge of the road, being mercilessly rained upon. His suit was soaked through and he wasn't even trying to protect himself from the driving rain. She recognized him, vaguely. He was that friend Vinny had with him a few weeks beforehand at the disco. No, wait, she thought she knew him from before that.

But she didn't have time to wait. The poor guy was shaking. Rain poured down his face, but she could see it was streaked with tears. He had been crying.

The rain stopped. Suddenly, just like that, but the man continued to shake.

'Are you all right?'

But he didn't seem to hear her.

Sandra took off her windcheater and put it around his

neck. It was too late as he was already soaked, but she was near enough her front gate to carry him if she had to.

'Come on,' she said firmly, and hauled him up onto his feet. Dermot staggered alongside her until they reached her house. She sat him on the sofa and removed his wet clothes, then grabbed a towelling gown from her newly inhabited wardrobe and put it on him. She eased his arms into it as if he were a placid child. There was nothing physically wrong with him. She could see that. But the poor guy was in shock of some kind. Sandra dragged over the two-bar electric heater and put the kettle on.

A few minutes later she handed him a cup of hot, sweet tea. Her mother's antidote to every ill.

'Here,' she said. 'Drink this.'

'Thanks.' Once he spoke, she knew who he was. The guy from the lap-dancing club. Mr Heart Attack – not. He was a long way from home. Sandra's curiosity was further piqued but there was no point in her sitting staring at him. He'd tell her what was up if and when he felt like it. So Sandra moved around the kitchen, washing up and thinking quietly to herself that she must do something about this hideous rented crockery and wondering if Mary could manage an afternoon in the salon alone so she could nip up to Galway and get some new curtains. Anyone looking in might have mistaken it for a regular west of Ireland domestic scene. A silent man lost in his own thoughts while the woman fussed around the kitchen. An hour passed like that, in which time Sandra surprised herself by turning the curtains around so that the swirly pattern was pointed out, covering the Formica table with a cream cotton shawl and filling a vase with wild flowers from her front garden and plonking it in the middle. Was it that easy to make a home?

The man was still sitting by the fire, but he had come to and was watching her. She blushed slightly as she realized she hadn't even taken her wellingtons off and had, briefly, forgotten he was there.

'Would you like something to eat?' she asked. 'I haven't anything in but . . .'

He was fine now, although he still looked terribly sad.

'Where are you staying? I can drop you back.'

His eyes started to fill up. Dermot didn't want to go back to that house. Not now, in any case. Maybe not ever. He couldn't go to Vincent's so he had nowhere to go. He felt as weak as a kitten, and he hated it. How long had he put off these tears? *All that I have lost*, the old man had said. *All that I have lost*. In the past few months, with the impotence and losing his sex drive, his business and, at times, his sanity, Dermot had felt he was losing it. He knew now that whoever he had loved, or should have loved, or had the right to love, had been lost to him a long time ago.

But Sandra didn't know any of that. All she knew was that there was a man crying on her sofa. Without thought or contrivance she sat beside him and she folded the sobbing man's arms around her body and welcomed his tears with the careful comfort only a woman can give.

Later, by the shallow sun of the early evening, they made love. There was no porn or pride left in either of them. Just the artless coupling of two souls finding a home in each other's arms.

PART FIVE

good vocations

FIELD REPORT SEVEN

So Gabriel calls. No memos mind you – *calls*. And he says, 'God wants to see you.'

'Oh does He now,' I say, all cool like.

'Yes,' he says. 'And He wants to know if you'd like Him called into your presence as anyone in particular.'

I couldn't believe it. God! Requesting an audience with *moi*! But I didn't let on. Keep it cool, says I. You've resigned your post. The guy's mucked you about big time over this whole Hemlock business. Hold firm. Don't get caught up in the whole celebrity thing.

You could tell Gabriel was *very* pissed off. Having to call me up like that and speak to me in person. He's a big one for protocol is our Gaby. Loves his memorandums and keeping us mere field workers at a distance. I can just see Himself bawling him out and going, 'NOW! I want to speak to him NOW!' in that big booming voice of His. Must have made him feel a right lowly twat.

'Let me see now, who do I fancy meeting?'

'This is *GOD* we are talking about, Christian.' He

wasn't impressed with my lack of fawning. Loves a good old fawn does Gabriel.

'The boss, eh?'

'*Our* boss.'

'Not mine, sweetie. Not any more.' I knew that would send him close to the edge. If the Big Man was looking for me it was because He was afraid I'd be tainted by the hand of Satan. Gabriel is my line manager, so if I moved across to the Other Side, he'd be the one taking the penance.

'Don't push it, Christian. Just give me a name. You know He's going to come anyway and if you don't give me a name – a sensible one, mind, I'm not going back there with a daft request – He'll give you the full monty, and I don't think even a cocky bastard like you would be able to manage that.'

I could have gone on. Why doesn't he bring me up there, etc. Dragged it out a bit, but I decided to give him a break.

'I want Him to appear as Margaret McGreavy.'

There was a silence as Gabriel girded himself.

'You know He doesn't do "live" Catholics.'

'His problem.'

More silence. I was enjoying myself, I really was. Except that, underneath the tease, I did want God to inhabit Margaret's soul. She was such a good woman, a holy old thing, in a funny way. I thought it would be a buzz for her. A minor miracle. She wouldn't tell anyone. I knew that. And I knew G knew it too. He'd go for it. I was sure because my motives were pure. I mean, I was willing to sacrifice an afternoon gassing with Ghandi or Jackie Kennedy for the enhanced spiritual vibe of a friend. But then that's just the kind of guy I am. Nice.

But Gabriel didn't think so. Well he huffed and puffed, but I wouldn't back down so he had no choice but to go back with my request.

I was a bit worried afterwards. Well, you would be, wouldn't you? I mean this is *God* here. A guy that's used to calling the shots. Does not like being told what to do, by all accounts.

I was beginning to think maybe I'd blown it when I'm sitting in the kitchen with Margaret later that night. It's still the day of the resurrection and she's exhausted trying to figure out where the six dishy guys that are the field unit have come out of. I'm keeping schtum. She's worn herself out speculating and drops off to sleep, like she often does in the middle of the afternoon. Meantime, *I'm* wondering whether to chance taking a slug of tea. Just to see what might happen. Then suddenly the old bird is sitting bolt upright in the chair and staring at me with this fierce glower.

'I wouldn't do that if I were you.'

There's a loud echo in her voice and it's about four octaves lower than usual.

She looks up towards the ceiling and says, 'Will somebody turn the bloody volume down here, I am *NOT* performing *OPERA*!' Then smiles at me apologetically and says, 'Can't get the staff,' as the voice goes back to pure Margaret.

'Hope I didn't give you a fright there, lad?'

I smiled weakly. What could I say? This was God. Inhabiting the body of an old woman. Of course He gave me a bloody fright. I coughed to stop my voice from squeaking. Nothing G hates more than a timid poof. So I'm told.

'No, sir.'

'Sir? Sir? What's all this 'Sir' nonsense? God will do. You can call me Harold if you like. Our Father who art in Heaven, Harold be thy name.'

Then He let out this huge laugh, 'HUR, HUR, HUR,' and the heavy echo started again.

'DIDN'T I TELL YOU TO TONE IT DOWN?'

I was petrified in my seat. Perhaps I should have requested Santa Claus after all. Mags in her favourite yellow cardigan with the Almighty's gob on her was creeping the shit out of me. *The Exorcist*, only sillier.

'Yes, God.'

'Yes I frightened you or are you just being servile?'

'No, you didn't frighten me and, er . . .'

'It's all right, lad. I don't mind servility as a rule. It's one of the few perks of my job. Hur, hur, hur.'

He was a cheerful chappy, which, given the stern face He was inhabiting, wasn't making me feel any the more comfortable.

'Now. I understand you've resigned your post.'

I could have grovelled and said there'd been some mistake, etc., but He had gone to all this trouble and I knew He'd be bucking if it was all for nothing, so I was as honest as I could be.

'Well I . . . um . . .'

'Don't beat about the bush, man. You've resigned and I know why.'

'Well I . . .'

If He knew why, then *why* did He bother asking?

'I know everything, Christian. *Ev-ery-thing*. Do you understand?'

'Yes, well, of course.'

'I can read minds, you know. And hearts, and souls when it comes to it.'

'Of course, sir, *God*, I . . .'

'There is not a thing in this universe that passes by these,' and He stabbed at Margaret's spectacles, 'peepers. All seeing, all knowing, that's me.'

Clearly there was no practice what you preach when it came to humility.

'So out with it, man. OUT WITH IT!'

He'd forced me into a corner. I hadn't wanted to criticize the department, but perhaps this was an opportunity for me to air some of my views.

'Well, I don't want to appear crit—'

'He's been at you, hasn't he?'

I was confused.

'Who?'

'Satan. Lucifer. The Prince of Darkness. He's been at you.'

'I don't know what you . . .'

'Don't lie to me, man! He's made you an offer you can't refuse. He's got in amongst you.'

'No, you've got it all . . .'

'Tugged at your twig, nudged at your naughty bits,

twisted your halo. Don't come the innocent with me. I know all about you, Christian. Don't think I don't know because I know everything. This is your God you are talking to here. You mightn't have made your mind up yet, but I know you've been tempted . . .'

'Oh, SHUT UP!' I still can't believe I said it. 'I have not been "got at" by Lucifer, in fact quite the reverse.'

What I still can't believe is that He *did*, shut up. I suppose no one ever talks to Him like that.

'If you *must* know I had an epiphany.' He looked confused now, and I had Him. Even God is mystified by how epiphanies happen. If He could figure out how they work, He'd zap every human on Earth with one and there'd be no more wars or nastiness anywhere. Boring, but it would make His job a lot easier.

'But Hemlock said . . .'

Oh now this was *too* much. Believing a known sinner above one of His own. Charming.

'What? *What* did he say?'

'Well he said that he was just about to launch into a Novena when you walked in with a horned goat's head and started . . .'

'That is *so* not true! Were you not watching?'

Margaret's head bowed slightly and He looked across at me over her glasses.

'I was busy.'

I couldn't even speak, I was that flabbergasted. Class One emergency, my job on the line, my spirit, my very faith in danger and He couldn't even be bothered to check in!

'What?' He said, defensive now. 'I'm a busy guy!'

'You're supposed to be All Seeing, All Knowing!'

'Yeah well, sometimes we all need a day off, you know.'

He looked sly then, as if He didn't believe me.

'So Hemlock was lying?'

'Dur, *yes!*' Then it occurred to me.

'I suppose you let him in then – to paradise?'

'Reduced sentence in Purgatory. Down from a hundred to fifty. I thought on account of coming clean about the son and . . .'

'. . . blowing Satan's messenger in the goat's head off?'

He looked briefly mortified, then drew Himself up in the chair again.

'So if you haven't gone over to the Other Side, why did you resign?'

So I told Him. Everything. The officious memos, permits not coming through, how I was fed up with the bureaucracy. That I felt the whole job was becoming more about the running of the department and less and less about saving people's souls. I even said that sometimes I felt estranged from His presence and wondered who I was working for. That all I needed was to know that He was there. A pat on the back from time to time. I acknowledged Him for taking the trouble to see me, and He nodded sagely in reply. I went on and on, and guess what? He listened. *He* listened to *me*!

When I had finished He said, 'Christian, you have made some very good points there. You know, and I have never said this to anyone before, but I often wonder myself if even the best of us aren't sometimes missing the point?'

Wow. God confiding in me.

'How do you mean?' says I.

'Well, look at religion for instance. I mean, it's all very well praising me and burning incense and kneeling in my direction every morning and all that, and I'm not saying it's not gratifying to have a spot of ceremony performed in my honour from time to time, but, you know? It starts a lot of fights too. Arguments. Wars.' And He sucked His teeth as if He didn't quite know what to do with the word alone, never mind the wars themselves.

'And what is the point?' I asked. Here it comes, thought I, the Meaning of Life from The Man Himself.

'The point?' He said, as if He couldn't believe I didn't know. 'Well, just to be nice. Bit of love and respect like. Just be nice, you know?'

I did, and the two of us sat and reflected on this for a few seconds, and it all felt so nice and normal that I said, 'Fancy a cup of tea?' and God said, 'Oooh, you know what? That *would* be nice.' I didn't know if it was Him or Margaret talking, but I knew that as a devout Catholic, and a live one at that, she was sure to be getting in amongst Him on some level.

I drank the tea, any digestive hiccups doubtless sorted by His presence, and it was very nice (my first cup in forty-odd years, it wanted to have been). We talked about where to go from here.

'The department needs angels like you, Christian.

Cupids who aren't afraid to speak their minds, shake things up a bit.'

He explained that the reason I had trouble getting permits through was at least partly due to the fact that I was so effective and highly regarded that they were deemed unnecessary a lot of the time.

'Poor Mayday needs all the help he can get,' He said. 'You're in a different league altogether.'

Then realizing it might sound like He was fobbing me off, added, 'But I take your point about the expenses. I'll have words with James the Less and we'll see if we can't organize you a decent salary.'

I was afraid to ask about the promotion but He stepped in, 'Paris is a very expensive city.'

I was thrilled but didn't let on. I had more to ask for yet.

'Seeing as you're here,' I said. 'There is one request you might be able to grant me. I know the whole Moses/ Rose rematch has been cancelled now that Hemlock is dead, but I'd like to try one more thing.'

He hummed and hawed and said He'd see what He could do for me, but I knew it wouldn't be a problem. Again, pure motives. Gets Him every time.

We finished the tea and He said, 'I'm off now. It was nice talking to you, Christian. Really nice. And I like your choice of person, she feels very – serene.'

High praise indeed.

'Although I'm not sure about the cardigan. Yellow isn't really my colour, huh, huh, huh.' and Margaret's head dropped back into sleep as God giggled quietly at His own joke.

37

Vinny felt bad about hitting Dermot. He had never hit anyone before. But even the following day, thinking about it (as if he had been able to think of anything else) he did not see that there was anything else he could have done. He was protecting Mary's honour. Besides, the punch was something that he could use to push the hurtful fact of her having slept with Dermot to the back of his mind.

He went methodically about his business the next day, checking the temperature of the roach eggs, meticulously counting and ferrying them from one plastic box to another. But he found it hard to concentrate. With the discovery of every fully hatched roach, the image of that sweet plump girl being mercilessly hammered by that city slicker who called himself a friend kept creeping back into his mind.

At lunchtime, he went back into the house for his tea. The postman had been and on the mat was another one of those cursed envelopes. As he was shoving it in behind the bread bin, a wave of depression washed over him. All these letters. How much money did he have now? He didn't know and he didn't care. He was stuck here alone, without even a friend to drop by in the evenings to keep him company. Without even Dermot to take him into town and help him find a woman. Another woman. But even as he thought it, Vinny knew it was hopeless. When a solid, sensible girl like Mary was annoyed at his lack of experience, who else would have him? If indeed, he would be satisfied with anyone else. Now he had tasted the delights of Mary Fitzgerald; seen her sitting up in his bed in one of his shirts nursing a cup of cocoa; known the steady breath of her sleeping in the bed beside him, he knew he could never go back.

Never.

As the envelope slotted behind the bread bin, a framed picture fell off the dresser shelf above him and he caught it before it crashed to the floor. It was a photograph of his mother, taken not long before she died. He put it back on the shelf, but it fell again. Then again. The shelf is unstable, he thought. I'll tighten it up. Vinny didn't like things to be out of place. He laid the picture flat on the top of the bread bin and as he was rummaging about in the dresser drawer for a screwdriver, it fell again. He picked it up from the floor and he looked at the image of Kathleen Rouse in the new hat she had bought for his brother's wedding in Australia. She had never made it. Diagnosed with cancer five weeks before the big day, she had lasted only a month.

'Do you want me to take the hat back to the shop in

Galway for you, Mam?' Vinny had asked. He was only trying to help.

'I do NOT,' she had growled. 'And I'll not be buried in it either. You don't let your father bury me in a hat, you hear?'

Vinny had hated it when she talked about her own death like that. He had so wanted her to get better, chose to believe that she would be there for ever. But Kathleen knew, and she was a forthright woman. 'Be prepared,' she always said. 'I'm just preparing you for when I'm gone.' She said all sorts of things in those last weeks. 'See that hat,' she said. 'When you get married now, Vincent, I want that contraption to feature at the reception. I won't be there myself, you've dawdled so long in finding a wife. I don't care if the priest wears it or if you wear it yourself and the whole town laughs at you. I'll not have that hat wasted.' She was joking, but only half so. People thought his mam was making an eejit of him, going on like that as she did, but Vinny knew she always had his best interests at heart. She wanted him married. Wanted him to continue being loved after she was gone.

'As long as she's strong and sensible, that'll do. You're a clumsy 'aul eejit so don't be hanging around for years and setting your sights too high.'

His mam would have liked Mary, that was for sure. She was local and chatty and there was nothing fancy or silly about her. She was sensible and strong. His mother's words. Not his.

But then maybe the same description could apply to him. He was strong, certainly physically.

But would a sensible man not be able to open his own bank statements? Would a sensible man not have handled Mary better that night? Scooped her up into his powerful arms and let nature take its course, instead of blurting out what he had.

Vincent grabbed the latest envelope back from its hidey hole and tore it open. He was shaky looking at the total figure. Noughts. Lots of them. Enough, at least to dicky himself up like that snake Leeson. Enough even, perhaps, to swank down into the town in a fancy car and impress a woman into turning a blind eye to his lack of experience.

It was worth a try.

The karaoke finals were on that night in McGreavy's and Mary was sure to be at it. Everyone in the town would be there. He'd take a chance.

Vinny checked the time. Two o'clock. He had four hours until Gorrib closed up for the day. The bank first for a major cash withdrawal. Then half an hour in Doherty's menswear and the most expensive suit, shirt and tie they could offer. Then the Mazda show-room. The Mazda dealer, Paddy, was a bachelor and often ate his tea alongside him in Keavany's. He'd sort him out with something flash. Something a woman would like, mind. Then it would be up to Katie's Gifts and Gee Gaws for a big rake of flowers and chocolates even. He might even go mad and get her a Waterford crystal vase. Women loved vases. His mother certainly had.

With all the armoury he had in his possession, Vincent Rouse was going to land himself a wife this night. And not just any 'aul wife either, if he had his way. The best wife in the whole wide world. If it killed him.

38

His mother was going mad. Wishing to respect his mother's privacy, Moses had only caught some of the bizarre conversation that had taken place between her and Christian, who was as odd as they come anyway, but there had been a lot of talk about God and the Other Side. He was worried that his mother might become gripped by the mania that sometimes caused old women in this area to throw themselves into the river as penance for rearing a wayward child, or their son marrying a Protestant, or some other unspeakable sin they imagined they were responsible for.

As a result, over the following few days, Moses resigned himself to playing the dutiful and caring son. His mother and her chums were favourites in Connor's betting shop to win the karaoke. Word had spread that they were going to be doing a geriatric version of Destiny's Child, which did nothing to allay her son's fears that she was losing her marbles. In addition, Margaret had taken delivery that week of a Lavazza Espresso machine, which she had ordered from Dublin without consulting him. It was, she said, to be able to provide a better service for her daytime customers, particularly the shady moustachioed winker whom she seemed to be paying some special attention to.

It was only a couple of hours to the start of the county finals and Moses was busy preparing the bar. It had not exactly come as a surprise to him when Christian and Mayday offered to 'style' the bar for this big event, but even still, he was impressed with the job they had made of it. The back of the stage was hung with silver curtains for the singers to perform in front of with all the 'messy' equipment hidden behind. Moses had employed Liam Brennan to do all the technical work that evening, as he himself was an associate consultant on the adjudicating panel. His power to sway them one way or another was something that had enraged his mother in past years when she hadn't won.

' "The Boys from Donegal" just doesn't cut it, Mam, in this day and age,' he had said last year. 'You want to try something more modern, upbeat. A foot-tapper.'

He was beginning to regret this advice with the alarming thought that his mother and her cronies might emerge in sequinned boob tubes and hot pants to belt out the Destiny's Child hit, 'Bootylicious'. It didn't bear thinking about, but the old woman would not be drawn on the matter of their performance or wardrobe that night.

The bar and beams were strung with fairy lights. It was a veritable fairy grotto, which Moses was at a loss to work out how they had achieved. The lights were diaphanous and delicate, with no strings or flexes or plugs to be seen anywhere. The whole 'fairy' effect was further enhanced by the presence of the six stunningly handsome and eerily identical men who had mysteriously arrived in the town the week beforehand. Were they tourists? Not fishermen certainly. Mayday latched onto them initially and said they were his sextuplet cousins from New York, but when put on the spot he was at a loss to further explain their presence and didn't seem to know where they were staying even.

The six of them sat now, as they always did, in a corner booth, without a drink between them. When they saw Moses, there was a whispered consultation as one of them fiddled about with some money as if he had never seen the stuff before. Once they seemed to agree on how to go about ordering drink in a pub, one of them came up to the bar and grandly ordered six Club Oranges and a packet of Tayto in a strange accent, the likes of which Moses had never heard before. Singsong and unnaturally high-pitched. He brought the drinks back to his friends, one by one – handing them out like they were gold dust, then he counted his change, nodded at Moses, and the six of them sat there mute like a collection of statues, not touching the drinks or crisps.

Weird.

Moses normally enjoyed the county finals. He had hosted the competition for five years now, and sat on the Irish Karaoke Committee, driving up to Dublin twice a year, once for their annual conference and again for the national finals. He had made friends with some great guys from all around the country; a few of them would be up tonight.

'Jeez but you have a great setup, Moses,' Frankie Fiddler said every year. Frankie had sung with the showbands, then packed it in to travel all around the country doing karaoke gigs. 'More money, Moses, when you're a lone operator. He was forty-nine, and two years ago Moses had switched on the *Late Late Show* and seen Frankie perform his self-penned Eurovision song for Ireland. It wasn't a bad track, though not a patch, Moses knew, on his own stuff. Ireland had taken fifth place that year and while 'The Mean Fiddler' had yet to top the pop charts, he made a living, more or less, out of performing his own material.

Freddie would be here tonight, if he wasn't gigging in England. But this year the mere expectation of his presence filled Moses with a sense of dread. Here he was still in the pub, doing his karaoke nights, hosting an amateur competition, living with his mother. The locals and his friends would say that he was a great man, entertaining the community. 'Here he comes again – The Man With The Mullet,' 'Good man, Moses – haven't gone for the short back and sides yet we see!' Hadn't he the great life altogether with his mother still alive to cook for him, and the grand lovely wee pub to potter about? Wasn't he the lucky bastard though that he didn't have to get out there and lead a life like the rest of them, with a wife to nag him and kids to worry about? Wouldn't they all swap places with him in the morning, the grand wee maneen with his outdated haircut, rotting away with only his mammy in an inherited pub?

Moses had never felt patronized because he had always believed in the good in people. Now, he wasn't so sure. About the good in others, or himself. He wished Sandra would come tonight so he could throw her over a chair again and do what he had done before in front of everyone here. Then they'd know there was more to him than met the eye. He also wished he could go back upstairs and hide his head under the covers and not come down for the whole night, not have to pretend to be the happy host. The two opposite desires collided in him, causing confusion and unhappiness that only distraction could abate.

Moses went and checked the equipment was set up, then went upstairs to get ready.

He stood in front of the bathroom mirror and, barely thinking, grabbed the back of his mullet and hacked it off.

That was one thing they couldn't tease him about any more.

39

Rose was ready. Christian said it. Mayday said it. But most importantly of all, Rose *knew* it. She felt, from the top of her newly highlighted hair to the soles of her sequinned sandals, ready for anything and everything.

Standing in front of the wardrobe mirror in the main bedroom of her parents' house, she couldn't get over herself. She looked like something out of a magazine. One of those polished confident women, upbeat and go ahead, 'Forging through their Fun Forties'.

A small part of Rose still worried about the staying power of this transformation. Could a bit of lipstick and a few new clothes really have healed all the hurt she had experienced in the past few months? Should she not be feeling devastated by the fact that she had lost her husband? By the fact that this new image was telling her that her life up until now had been a failure, a sham? But any doubts were firmly discouraged from taking hold by her two new friends, 'Don't question it, darling. You look fabulous, therefore you *are* fabulous. You just go down there to that pub tonight and you knock them out.' If she expressed any doubt about what she was doing and where she was going, it was only because she had for so long been in the habit of humility. Kept herself at the bottom of the pile because of the ton of shit she'd have to swim through to get to the top. But thanks to Regina Malone and those smutty pictures the shit had been swept away in one grand swoop. Mayday had tried to take possession of them to have them printed onto T-shirts, 'Cap sleeve, fitted numbers? I think they'd look great,' but Rose had declined. She wished Regina and Brian luck in their lives – that was the greatest satisfaction of all.

Rose was all ready for her trip. The bags were packed and bills paid up to date. Davy was already in situ, promising to mind the house while she was gone. His skinny face had gone all stoic when she told him she had got the job and had decided to move.

"It's a good thing, Mam. You go for it.'

'I'll be back in a few months to check up on you.'

'I'll be fine. Don't worry.'

'There's flights from Knock every day. I'll be over and back all the time.'

'It's all right, Mam.'

'You just call me, and I'll send you over tickets.'

'I'll be fine.'

'If you need money or anything at all, just pick up the phone and . . .'

'MAM!'

But she wasn't really worried about Davy managing without his mum, or even Mary, although it didn't feel completely right leaving her so soon after the broken engagement. At least she had the new job to keep her busy, and that nice new friend Sandra seemed like a sensible woman. If it got too grim up with Brian, she could move down here with Davy. Mary she *had* to leave behind because her daughter had been particularly insistent she go.

'At last you're getting on with it. If you wimp out and stay here, I'll kill you Mam! You'll have a great time. You deserve it.'

So the tickets for London were booked for that coming Wednesday. London, Heathrow. Her brother-in-law, Dez, had introduced her to this lovely man, from Birmingham originally, called Kevin. She had met him out one night with Dez and her sister and he seemed to take a shine to her. He was divorced; two grown-up children. Dez had rung yesterday and said that as he was working, Kevin had offered to pick her up at the airport and take her over to theirs. Rose felt a slight shimmer of excited nerves. She wasn't ready for another relationship, but she couldn't say anything to him because he was still a virtual stranger and anything said now would make him assume that she thought that he wanted to have a relationship with her which, the way he had offered to pick her up from the airport like that, she thought he probably did. She didn't want to have a relationship with a divorced man. In fact, Rose didn't really want to have a relationship with any man. Not really, not except . . .

It was silly, but since she had made the decision to move away, Rose had started to think about Moses again.

'Closure,' Christian had said, shrugging his shoulders

and raising his eyebrows and palms simultaneously. 'You've no closure.'

'How do you mean?' she asked, unfamiliar with this American psychobabble concept.

'Of course, I don't *know*, but it *sounds*, from what you've *told* me, that your relationship with Moses never reached its full potential. Never ran its course, came to a natural end. What can you do? You'll just have to go to London and leave behind you an unresolved situation. It's sad but . . .'

Then he shrugged again and carried on ironing her chiffon skirt.

Perhaps he was right. He was right about most things it seemed.

In any case, Moses would be there tonight and she could say goodbye to him then. They hadn't spoken, aside from the common courtesy of a street 'hullo', since that day when he had ignored her by the river. Christian and Mayday had put her in for the competition and she wondered how he had felt about her doing it. She asked Christian.

'He's fine about it, isn't he, Mayday?'

'Fine, yeah. Said nothing to me. Do you know him well then?'

'Moses and Rose used to go out,' Christian explained.

'No!'

'When they were much younger.'

'You're kidding! A moppy-haired little runt like him and a goddess like you? I don't believe it.'

The colour had risen to Rose's cheeks and she had

wanted to defend Moses. Then she remembered that it wasn't her place any more. For a moment if felt like she still loved him.

'Well, you're well off out of it, love. Isn't she, Chris? He's been a right mopey bastard lately.'

'Moping about all over the place,' agreed Christian.

'All miserable and mopey. Head on him like a trapped badger; if I didn't know better I'd say he was . . .'

'In love? Sure, who'd have him?'

Rose left the room and had a little cry. She wasn't sure why. Except she hated hearing people, especially supposed friends, betraying Moses like that.

He'd be there tonight and she'd say goodbye to him then. Whatever coolness existed between them she would melt it away and achieve her 'closure'. Part of her knew she would be unable to leave for her new life without it.

40

There is nothing quite like knowing that somebody is in love with you to move them up a few notches in your estimation. And while Mary had never imagined herself falling for a ham-handed farmer, who favoured brushed cotton check shirts and kept creepy-crawlies in plastic containers in a shed, the news of his pining heart had not past her by.

Put it like this, Mary was interested. Very.

Over the past few days she had racked her brains trying to remember details from that night. All she could really remember was that she was quite drunk, but that he was drunker. He offered her pyjamas and cocoa and had a big silly grin on his face when she got into his bed. He hadn't touched her the whole night through, and the part that she could remember with the most clarity was sneaking into that outhouse, which she thought was a lavatory, and picking up that plastic container full of insects and them falling all over her. She didn't know what she thought she might find in it, or why she had been drawn to investigate like she had, but the contents had confirmed to her that the guy was a grade one nutter. Possibly even dangerous, although he had seemed markedly the opposite. Maybe that had been a bad sign.

But now she had discovered he was in love with her. Even if her suitor was a dangerous, insect-loving innocent, he was still a suitor. And Mary had never had a suitor before. Only Theo, and he didn't count. Just like that. After years of pining and mooning, Theo had been usurped by an odd farmer who, in Mary's mind at least, was not the most suitable of suitors but was a suitor nonetheless. If nothing at all happened, the demoting of Theo in her affections was something she could thank her secret admirer for.

In the days after she had been landed with this remarkable news, Mary had thought about Vinny a lot. He'll be at home now having his tea, she'd think, being in love with me. He'll be out the back fiddling with his insects, being in love with me. He'll be standing there in his kitchen, looking out of the window at the rain, being in love with me. She liked thinking like that. It mightn't be going anywhere, but it sure painted a prettier picture than Theo Malone riding another woman. He'll be getting in to the bed now with the mug of cocoa, being in love with me. And then, bits and pieces started to come back to her. The lovely warm smell of his shirt when she put it on to cover herself up in the bed. Wearing a man's shirt. It was sexy. It had *felt* sexy. His forearms when he handed her the mug of milky cocoa, all hard and hairy. The cocoa. That was sweet now that she thought about it. He'd offered to make her a ham sandwich earlier too.

That was sweet of him. She liked ham sandwiches. Just as she'd been dropping off to sleep, he had let out a little cough then said, 'Sorry,' like he really didn't want to disturb her. Ahhh. That was really sweet. On and on and on Mary went, and the more she indulged herself in thinking about this man the better she felt. The exact opposite of how it had been with Theo. That meant something, surely?

She figured her best chance of seeing him again was to turn up at the karaoke. She was going there anyway, her mother was performing. Theo and Ella knew that so they wouldn't have the nerve to turn up. Sandra couldn't come because she said she had 'other things to attend to'.

'New man?' Mary asked.

Mary's mood had lifted, and Sandra noticed it. Instead of answering she said, 'What about yourself?'

Mary smiled, 'Maybe.'

The whole town was going, but just to be sure she let Sandra know she'd be there.

Vincent was Sandra's neighbour and she had a sly feeling Sandra had hooked up with Dermot; maybe between them they might pass it on.

It was eight thirty now and the place was filling up, but there was no sign of him. Mary was wearing a dress Sandra had lent her. It was tight Lycra so Sandra had told her to wear a thong, which felt like it was cutting her in half. She was perched up on a barstool and had to keep tugging the skirt down so Cozy Maloney would stop gawping at her white thighs.

'Yorra fine birra shtuff there, Mary Fitzgerald, are ye married yet?'

He was seventy if a day. She smiled politely, but inside she felt a hurt indignation that a wiry old goat like that would think her rightful fodder. By eight forty-five, she was beginning to feel fat and silly again. And when she tried to think of Vincent riding into town being in love with her on his tractor (or whatever farm-like vehicle he drove) thoughts of other, less gratifying, parts of that evening started to creep in. The parts involving her. The way she lost it when he said he was a virgin. That was mean. The petty way she grabbed the cocoa off him, as if it were muck. She'd been reared better than that. Sneaking out in the morning without saying goodbye or making the slightest show that she was interested in him at all. And she hadn't been. But she was now. How shitty was that?

She must have hurt him. She knew what it was like to be hurt and now she had done it to somebody else. Except Vincent surely wasn't as big a fool as she was, and he'd surely not be back for more of the same.

Mary eased herself off the barstool under Cozy's watchful eye, and went to the ladies' room to adjust the torture of her knickers. There she was again in the mirror on her way out. Bit of natural lipgloss fighting a losing battle against a plain chubby face. You'll have to do a lot better than that if you want a man, her reflection said to her. Mousy Marys can't afford to go fobbing off farmers at every turn. Who in God's name do you think you are?

Eight fifty-five and the singing was about to start. Mary was being let down by another man. Except this time it was her fault.

She'd go over to the bar now and get her bag. She couldn't face this tonight. Rose might be disappointed but that was too bad.

⬭

Vinny hadn't wanted to arrive too early. Not after what had happened the last time. He was determined to come across as 'cool', so he had left it to the last minute before driving around the block a few times in the car in case she might see him on her way in, then parking the spanking-new Mazda right outside the door. He sat for a few minutes wondering whether to take the vase and the chocolates into the bar with him and give them to her straight away, or say, 'I've a surprise in the car for you,' then bring her out, then she'd see the car and get the gifts in the one go and be doubly impressed. 'I've a surprise in the car' might sound a bit strange though. Like he might be wanting to get up on her or something. He needed to be more specific. 'I've a lovely vase and some chocolates in the car for you – in the *new* car for you.' No. The new *Mazda*. Yes. 'I've some chocolates and a lovely vase for you out in the new Mazda.' Supposing she didn't know that Mazda was a brand of car? 'I've some chocolates and a lovely vase for you out in the new Mazda, which is a car.' No, too awkward sounding. 'I've some chocolates and a lovely vase for you out in my new car. It's a Mazda.' Perfect. Natural, but full of information. Now he just had to get the delivery right. He pulled down the mirror flap.

'Hullo, Mary. I've some chocolates and a lovely vase for you out in my new car. It's a Mazda.'

He practised it smiling, frowning, eyebrows raised, eyebrows down, with and without hand gestures. He changed intonation from excited surprise, 'Mary! I've some chocolates! And a lovely vase!' to flippantly hurried, '. . . foryououtinthecaritsaMazda.'

After a dozen or so practise runs Vincent felt, if not exactly confident, then sufficiently satisfied that he had struck the right note between friendly and masterful.

All he had to do now was remember his lines, and try to keep cool in the face of her astonishing beauty. He checked the clock. Christ it was five to nine! He was almost in the back bar before he remembered to saunter.

There he was. And how!

A huge big fine thing, six foot and then some, with a back as broad as an oak. He was wearing a suit that was slightly too short on the trouser, but you know what? It didn't matter. He had come. There he was. Standing at the bar, right in front of Mary Fitzgerald, being in love with her. Cozy Malone was already sneaking in there looking for a drink when Vinny turned to face her.

'Hullo, Mary,' he said. 'I've a . . . I've a . . . I've a . . .?'

'You've a what?' she said, smiling that big broad smile of hers. 'A stutter, is it?'

Then it just came out. Years later she would tell him

it was what had won her over. They would be sitting up in the top bedroom and she would flick off the TV, which she had him fit on a bracket above the bed, and say, 'Do you remember what you said to me that night? In front of the whole of Gorrib?' And he would always remember exactly, every word, but he would tease her by saying it was the chocolates and the car and ask her where she had hidden the vase. And she would say it was an awful vase and what had he been thinking wasting good money on rubbish. But he would know that she kept it in the house her mother grew up in on Church Street, and filled it with fresh flowers from their garden every week.

'You look great, your dress is nice, I love you, Mary Fitzgerald.'

Then quite without thinking, certainly because he had said it first, perhaps just to be polite, and possibly because the bar had gone quiet and every set of eyes of every sinner in the place were suddenly fixed on them, she said, 'I love you too.'

41

When Christian had said he was going to organize a backing group for her number, Rose had thought he was joking.

It seemed, now, that he wasn't.

McGreavy's was hopping. The singing was supposed to start at nine, but it was nearer half past when Rose arrived. Every inch of the bar was taken, people squeezing sideways in between the old regulars who held their positions as usual, stoically occupying their stools as if it was a normal Wednesday night. There were people in from Ballina, from Westport, from Sligo. At least two had come as Elvis, one man was blacked up in a red leather biker jacket, whom she assumed was a Michael Jackson, and there were assorted girls in glittery sexy get-up, the result of the drive to get more young people involved in what was rapidly turning out to be the community event of the year. Family groups huddled around the tables on low stools, mothers and aunts with their adult sons ferrying whisky and fags over to them so they wouldn't lose their places. The people in the front bar were the latecomers who wouldn't see the action on the small stage in the back bar, but by popular demand the Irish Karaoke Committee had sent up a man to install a video link between the two tiny rooms, so there was a huge screen erected above the doorway that led out to the back bar. The McGreavy night was legendary among committee members in both the quality of the performances and the mighty craic therein. It was something worth catching on film.

Rose looked at the screen and saw the handsome young DJ Liam Brennan going through the hosting spiel.

'We'll be starting the singing now, ladies and gentlemen. Could I remind you all to keep back from the stage. I know it's a busy night, but can we please make sure we clear a path through the crowd to let the performers up to the stage. We've a lot of acts to get through and the judges have a tough job ahead of them. Speaking of which, can we have some drinks up here for the committee please. Brendan, what're you having?'

Ordering drinks over the mike for the judges was all part of the fun. A tradition that Moses had started five years ago. Rose wondered why he wasn't hosting the event himself tonight. Was there something wrong?

On the screen in front of her, Regina Malone's substantial cleavage was caught in close-up as she pushed past Liam to get to her seat right in front of the stage. She had her eye on one of the judges from last year and had commandeered the best seat in the house early.

'Get outta the way, y'aul trollop!'

'Come back! Come back! 'til we get a right look at your diddies, Duchess!'

'Where's that dirty dog Fitzgerald when you need him!'

Then the heckler's wife nudged him, pointing out Rose and whispering.

'Sorry there, Rose,' the well-meaning soul touched her arm and she felt the world close in around her and become very small again. 'We didn't know you in the new get-up.'

Talk. There had been talk, of course there had. Everyone knew. Everyone in the town would be laughing at her when she got up to sing. Especially the song the two lads had talked her into. What had she been thinking of? Was there any way out of it now? If she started to walk out of the bar she would have to crush past everyone and they would all know she was running away.

'Right, now we're ready, folks,' Liam called. 'First up is, Rose,' he subtly left out her surname. 'Can we have a big hand now, she's coming up to sing, "I Will Survive" by Gloria Gaynor.'

People shuffled and strained to one side and a path cleared. In front of her was the stage. To the left of it was Christian, waving her down, and in front of the silver curtain were six men in white showband suits, standing sideways to fit onto the tiny raised square.

Jesus. Backing singers.

But she barely had time to think about that. The town

was ready for her. Her town. She walked up the aisle of smiling faces towards her grand goodbye.

Mayday had been horrified when he saw Moses's hair.

'Eeeew! What have you *done*? You look like a balding cat!'

Moses growled.

'Oh bad mood.' Mayday had had enough of his surly landlord. Frankly, he was making him feel unwelcome. Mayday! An unwelcome guest! The very idea!

'Well, I don't care, I am not letting you go downstairs looking a fright. Where's your suit? You look terrible. This is your big night and you're *not* going to let us down.'

By this time, Mayday had taken a lethal-looking pair of sharp scissors out of his apron pocket (he had taken to wearing a pinny around the place, rose print with a frilly strap. He said it made him feel 'secure') and was brandishing them in Moses's direction.

'Sit down there, you ignorant lug, or it'll be more than your hair gets a snipping.'

Perhaps it was because he had addressed him like a bossy mother that Moses found, despite his dark mood, that he appeared to have lost the will to fight.

Twenty minutes later, he was sporting a new haircut, a smart pair of black trousers and a simple white shirt of Christian's. On his way down the stairs, Mayday squirted him with some Calvin Klein. He was a bag of nerves himself, never mind having to worry about that miserable little midget. Moses looked the part all right but Mayday knew, despite his commitment to the make-over as a form of spiritual enlightenment, it would take more than a dash of CK to lift this declining soul.

'At first I was afraid, I was petrified . . .'

Rose's voice echoed to the opening lyrics. It sounded small and weedy and cracked over the word petrified because, looking out at the silent mass of curious faces, that was exactly how she felt.

' . . . kept thinking I could never live without you by my side . . .'

Pathetic. Diabolical. This was torture, but she had to keep going. She had no choice. If she left the stage now it would be tantamount to making a scene.

' . . . but I spent so many nights just thinking how you did me wrong . . .'

There was Regina, sitting right in front of her, a nasty smirk streaked across her face. She should have chosen Crystal Gayle or, better still, not bothered at all. Everyone was looking at the backing singers wondering who they were and what Rose Fitzgerald thought she was at with them.

' . . . that I grew strong – and I learned how to get along.'

The disco beat kicked in and the boys behind her started to back her up, emphasizing certain words:

'So now you're BACK from outer SPACE, I just walked IN to find you HERE, with that sad LOOK upon your FACE.'

356

Christian, seeing what was going on, stood right in front of Regina and started to jig and whoop. No one else was doing much. It was too early in the evening and they weren't drunk enough yet to forget that this song pertained personally to the woman singing it.

'I should have CHANGED that stupid LOCK, I should have MADE you leave your KEY, if I'd have known for just one SECOND you'd be BACK to BOTHER me . . .'

The disco beat was beginning to get in amongst her and the lads behind were giving her confidence. Then Rose saw Moses. He was standing up by the bar and only half looking over. Like, here she was, spilling her guts out, in front of the whole town and that little shit was doing what? Ordering a drink? Could he not wait a few more minutes and show her a bit of support? She was moving to England, could he not just be a man and put the past behind and have some respect? She'd make him fucking listen to her, for once in her life, she'd make them all fucking listen.

So she put her back into it.

'GO ON NOW GO! WALK OUT THE DOOR! JUST TURN AROUND NOW – 'COS YOU'RE NOT WELCOME ANY MORE!'

She belted it out, turning the lads behind her into nothing more than a finger-clicking side-shimmying dance troupe. They became an accessory to her hip-grinding, finger-pointing power. The whole of Gorrib, in that moment, became nothing more than an accessory. The years she had lived here, the men she had loved, the family she had reared had brought her to this point. They were characters in her story, and now she was moving on. Letting go. And she did just that.

'WEREN'T YOU THE ONE WHO TRIED TO HURT ME WITH GOODBYES? DID YOU THINK I'D CRUMBLE? DID YOU THINK I'D LAY DOWN AND DIE . . .'

She ripped out the rest of the song at full volume and with soul. That miserable little shit was listening to her now. They were *all* listening. She lifted the roof with the glorious freedom of not caring, and sang it right out, believing every last word of this disco-diva anthem.

The audience was transfixed. Even Regina Malone, who had tried to interrupt by making a fussy move to the ladies' room. Christian had stood on her shoe and continued to grind his heel into it throughout, pretending not to notice her frantically prodding him in the back.

When it was finished, the room was silent. The six lads gave a little bow and left the stage. Rose was about to join them when Moses started to walk towards her, clapping. One by one, then ten by ten, the whole of Gorrib joined him until Rose was drowned in a tumultuous round of cheering, whistling and clapping. She bowed and smiled, but there were no modest blushes. Finally, at forty-five, her blushing days were over.

Rose didn't leave straight away as she had planned. She stayed on and enjoyed the rest of the evening. Took her goodbyes from the well-wishers and the gossips with equal charm and fortitude. Mags McGreavy and her 'girls' won in the end, singing the Supremes' 'Band of Gold'. They could have done without the fright wigs and the mini-skirts, but they were fine old things and deserved to be delighted at their age. Her mother-in-law got quite tipsy and hugged her saying, 'You're my lucky charm, Rose. What'll I do without you?'

She promised to call every week. Rose promised a lot of people she would stay in touch. By the time the night was ended she wondered why she was leaving at all.

Moses had avoided her for most of it. Ignoring her pointedly as if he had something to say.

When she gathered her bag and got up to leave he ran over.

'You're leaving?'

'Yes,' she said.

'No I mean to England. When are you going?'

'Wednesday.'

There felt like there was so much she had to say to him, and yet, she didn't really want to say anything at all.

'Next Wednesday?'

'That's right.'

He stood and looked at her. Just looked, right into her face. As if he were trying to puzzle something out. She held his eyes and looked back – defiant or defensive, she could not tell which.

'I'd best be off,' she said in the end. 'I'll call into Mags early in the week. If you're here I'll say goodbye properly.'

'I don't want you to go.'

He blurted it out like a child to his mother. Rose thought perhaps she should melt, but she didn't. She felt irritated.

'Well, I'm going Moses.'

'I'm coming with you,' he leapt straight in after her.

'Don't be ridiculous.'

She didn't even want to ask what had brought this on. This sudden surge of romance. Perhaps she had known it was there all along.

'I want to come with you.'

She put her bag down on the floor and eyeballed him.

'Look, Moses, I don't know what this is all . . .'

'I still love you Rose.'

She felt sick. She didn't want Moses to love her. Not like this. In this hurt, puppy dog way. She had been the bad bitch before, leaving him for Brian. Now he was doing it to her again. Except the last time she had pitied him. Now he was old enough to know better. If he was old enough to politely bat away her attempts at friendship, he should be man enough to say goodbye.

She hoisted her handbag strap up onto her shoulder. 'Too much has happened Moses. That was all a long time ago. It's too late. I've changed, and you've changed.'

But as she walked out of the door, Rose realized that the last statement was not true. Aside from the recent demise of his beloved mullet, Moses hadn't changed at all.

Epilogue

If there is one thing this job has taught me it is that there is no accounting for love. You can try and figure it out and, of course, we must all try. Sometimes you might be rewarded by a few helpful tips along the way, but you'll rarely find anything as tangible as an answer. If I said it was all down to luck, well then I'd be unemployed, but there is one thing for certain; the human heart sure has a way of putting it up to any of us looking for a challenge.

The truth is, I don't know what made Moses fall back in love with Rose that night. I'm pretty sure it wasn't me, and it *certainly* wasn't Mayday. If anything, we might have been at fault for fuelling her up with the gunpowder of her own gorgeousness to such an extent that she catapulted herself right out of his league.

Perhaps our principled ideal of true love became tainted, as it so often does, by the failings of the human ego. Moses wanted most what he sensed he couldn't have. Maybe that was what had driven his feelings for Rose all along. I like to think it was more than that, but then, maybe that's got more to do with my liking to have things all neatly wrapped up. Loose souls floating about gives one a messy conscience. I did the best I could at the time, but then, hands up!, I'm a control freak and in this game your best is only good enough if it gets results.

Moses did follow Rose over to England. Eventually, after Margaret died.

Rose was hard won. Doing a serious line with Kevin from Birmingham – the brother-in-law's friend who picked her up from the airport. Moses hung around the edges of her life, doing a bit of bar work, getting a gig now and then. He kept calling up to the sister's house, just burrowed himself into her life as an old friend from Gorrib. He kept in touch, but didn't push it. She was easy either way, didn't mind Moses hanging around as long as he didn't come the heavy. Then Kevin got killed. Car crash on the M4. It was tragic. Rose was devastated, naturally. This guy had meant a lot to her; had been part of her building a whole new life in England. She had spent a good year getting over him, and Moses had waited. Been a good friend. Then, almost without noticing it, Rose just found herself settling back into him like a comfy chair. They were fifty-odd, the pair of them. Too old for dramas. They never married.

Last year they tracked me down here, in Paris, and came over on a couple of cheap flights Rose had secured through supermarket points. We had lunch together in a small café near the Seine and we talked about that mad summer. 'Let's have a reunion,' we said. But we never did. To be honest it wouldn't have been the same without Mags.

I left the two of them walking along the Seine. Moses took Rose's hand and they stood and looked down at the river. They could have been young naive lovers, standing there like that. But they weren't. They were older, and not much wiser than any of us. I wondered if they were happy. They seemed easy enough in each other's company but then habit and history has a way of disguising itself as a kind of love. Maybe it's not the high-octane glamorous option I would have liked for them. But at the end of the day, people have to choose for themselves.

A MEMO FROM YOUR MAKER

REVISED HIERARCHY CIRCULAR

In light of recent confusion with regard to memorandums, applications for expenses and the such like becoming 'lost' in the system, the attached list is to be sent to all department heads and service unit directors, each of whom must take responsibility for circulating it amongst their individual field workers. I have enough to be doing sorting out world poverty without trying to decipher memorandums from cupids looking for fifteen euros to get into a lap-dancing club! So, do your jobs, people, and let me get on with mine.

Signed

GOD
High Commissioner
in charge of EVERYTHING

GOD
HIGH COMMISSIONER

at His left hand		at His right hand

DEPARTMENT OF COMPASSION AND PITY		**DEPARTMENT OF RENUNCIATION AND HOPE**

CEO	**MILITARY**	**CEO**
Mary (Blessed Virgin)	Saint Joan of Arc	**Jesus (Son of God)**
Chief Executive Officer in charge of Human Resources	*Officer in charge of God's Army of Angels*	*Chief Executive Officer in charge of Strategic Developments*
	Note. All applications must be made in writing to Rear Admiral St Brendan the Voyager, who is in charge of Transportation and Munitions	

DEPUTY CEO	DEPUTY CEO
Archangel Michael	Archangel Gabriel
Director of Human Healing and Empowerment	*Director of Conjugal Relations*

SERVICE UNIT DIRECTORS		SERVICE UNIT DIRECTORS
St James (job share)		St Andrew
Love and Fidelity		*Transition and Last Rites*
St John (job share)		St Peter
Love and Fidelity		*Divine Recruitment, Unity and Communion*
St Philip		St Matthew
Prayer and Contrition		*Petitions, Novenas and Indulgences*
James the Less	*SPECIAL NOTICE*	St Simon
Forgiveness	SECURITY STAFF	*Canonization and Sainthood (pending)*
St Luke	Please note that our gate staff have recently been issued with white bomber jackets and individual earpieces. In line with our new door policy and security regulations, anyone trying to get past the gate without a valid ticket or disrespecting standard uniform code by wearing 'trainers' will be dealt with accordingly.	Judas Escariot
Health and New Age policy		*Retribution*
St Jude		St Paul
Lost causes		*Finance and Penance*
St Thomas (doubting)		St Joseph
Manifestation, Visions and Miracles		*Industry and Fortitude*

ḣeaven knews

The only Newsletter with the OHF Official Seal of Approval

NOTICE TO ALL CUPIDS

I am saddened to inform you of recent abuse by cupids to their special privileges. Firstly, the Advisory Service Package, which allows you to call God up in your chosen image, has been most sacrilegiously misused by an alarming number of field workers. I will say no more except to attach a list of approved persons with whom the Heavenly Father is happy to have His wisdom associated. The following list is only a guideline, but it should give the more 'imaginative' among you some indication of what constitutes abuse of this bestowed privilege. We understand that, given the modern pressures on the gay community, it is tempting to choose some of the more colourful icons available to you. However, might I remind you all that Gay Pride is not just about big hair and handbags and that irony, cynicism or mere naked curiosity have no place in Our Lord's Army of Angels.

Thank you for your co-operation in this matter.

Archangel Gabriel

Approved people of genuine stature:

Barbara Cartland	Mother Teresa
Mary, Queen of Scots	Jackie Onassis
Saint Joan of Arc	Charles Dickens
Oprah Winfrey	William Shakespeare
Elvis Presley	Ghandi
Albert Einstein	

Recent requests that have been turned down:

Cher

The Marquis de Sade

Kylie Minogue

Freddie Mercury

Julius Caesar

All of the Borgia Popes

All of the Village People

Lucian Freud

Versace

CHAIRMAN'S NOTICE

The chairman is very disappointed with the poor take-up of redundancy packages offered last year. He would urge all saints who have been working for over one thousand years to step aside and allow newer saints the opportunity to serve Him. In light of many martyrs' reluctance to take up their Reward in Heaven, a new Perpetual Endurance Package is on offer, which includes a limited stint in Purgatory processing plenary indulgences for trapped souls. It is hoped this will help some of our more committed managers adjust to their eventual retirement in paradise.

Application forms are available from the department of Petitions, Novenas and Indulgences.

 LOVELY HAND-MADE CROSSES – Made to an exclusive Celtic design, these special-edition crosses are woven in genuine Irish straw by skilled seraphim. At only two plenary indulgences per cross, they make ideal accessories for any cloud. Contact: SaintBridget@heaven.com

---

SOUL FITNESS WITH MATT

Stuck in Purgatory and want to get out? Famous for his tireless commitment to punishment and penance, reformed alcoholic and registered martyr Matt Talbot has now set his methods of self-flagellation to the incantations of deceased monks. Using the latest technology, Matt will manifest himself to your personal plane and take you, step-by-step, through his guaranteed course for redemption. At just twelve plenary indulgences per eight-week session, this is an offer you really can't afford to miss. Contact:trussmeupandwhipme@heaven.com.

Acknowledgements

Alas, the time has not yet come that my genius has stretched to such an extent that I no longer require an extensive support network of people to enable me to write. So a special thank you to:

My mother, Moira. For the many months you self-lessly spent minding by firstborn while I wrote this book. That alone wasn't enough, you managed to amuse, inspire and educate both of us along the way. I will never forget the time you spent encouraging me in both my writing and my mothering. You are truly an extraordinary woman.

Other family members who pushed the boat out on this one with babysitting, prods in the back and big dinnery feeds were respectively: Renee Kerrigan, Deidre McGreevy and Angie Bracken.

Dee Hanna – for your invaluable advice on management structures on both Heaven and Earth. And for knowing so very much about saints!

My Dublin lap-dancing entourage who helped create the myth of 'Maurice'. Partners in crime Gai Griffin, Neill

Jones-Cubley, Johnny Ferguson, Vincent DeVeau, Erica Carroll, Paul and Aiofe Whittington and the talented Tish Curry for 'wig', make-up and all important beer belly.

P. J. Duffy for letting me root around behind his bar. Liam McHale for introducing me to what has to be the weirdest (and yet strangely wonderful) job in Ireland. Elaine Teigue, Carmel Tuffy and all of my friends in Ballina who kept me amused during those lonely-writer never-out-of-my-pyjamas months.

My gang of writers: Gai Griffin, Suzanne Power, Ailish Connelly and Marian Keyes for being at the end of those whingy/panic calls.

I just write the books. Other people stand behind me with a bit stick. Primary among them are my agent Marianne Gunn O'Connor, for your continued efforts on my behalf a million thanks, and my talented editors Imogen Taylor at Pan Macmillan and Alison Walsh at Tivoli.

Lastly and not leastly, my husband Niall for once again allowing me to plunder his seemingly bottomless reserves of support.

MORAG PRUNTY

Dancing with Mules

PAN BOOKS   £5.99

'*Irish American billionaire seeks bright, beautiful, independent, but above all Irish wife. Please send photo and 300-word essay about yourself to PO Box NY14786. Looking for genuine love. No time-wasting money grabbers, please.*'

Lorna has been twenty-five for nearly ten years and it's starting to show. Successful and sassy, her money's been spent on hard living and tough toy boys. She's hoping to pull her Ferrari into the last gas station before the desert.

Gloria is watching her hard-earned business go up the nose of her womanizing ex. Tired of life and not yet thirty, she's determined never to go back to poverty again.

Sandy has other things on her mind: this is the story that could make or break her career as a journalist – but will her long red curls win her a husband into the bargain?

Three women, one bolshy billionaire. Hopelessly romantic Xavier Big has whittled down the single women of Ireland and now he's coming over to choose . . .

Fast, feisty and highly colourful, *Dancing with Mules* is the laugh-out-loud, best-selling debut novel from Morag Prunty.

MORAG PRUNTY

Disco Daddy

PAN BOOKS   £6.99

*It's time to hang up your handbag and dance around
your glitterball!*

Ex-model Valerie never imagined that her short marriage to eighties
pop idol Jack Valentine would herald the end of her love life. Now
she's fed up with being propositioned by playboys and longs for a
safe, suburban husband who will look after her.

Record producer Sinead has an appetite for 'scruffy pop totty'.
She knows that they are never, on paper, ideal, but will she be able
to relinquish her desires and settle for a middle-aged man in a suit?

Magazine editor Karin is the author of 'Ireland's Most Eligible
Bachelor' list so, in theory, she should get first dibs at the pickings.
Trouble is, she knows they are lean and include a flicky-haired
Australian TV presenter and a businessman with a penchant for golf
wear and creative combovers.

When all three women are challenged to find a man to marry
before they all turn forty in the summer, they realize the time has
come to hang up their handbags and cut to the chase.

Sassy, snappy and endearingly funny, *Disco Daddy* is a refreshing
and entertaining novel about the search for Mr Right.

LOUISE HARWOOD

Calling on Lily

PAN BOOKS   £5.99

What do you do if your best friend is about to marry the wrong girl? Buy the matching bathrobes and keep your mouth shut? Or kidnap the groom on his stag night and hold him in a remote cottage in the Welsh borders until the wedding day has safely passed? Hal's friends know what they want to do, but they haven't reckoned on being overheard by Lily – who has already witnessed the devastation of her sister's wedding day, and is going to do anything she can to save this one – and Kirsty, Lily's friend, initially more interested in pulling the groom, but swift to take up the challenge.

Set in the wonderful countryside around the border town of Welshpool, *Calling on Lily* is a warm and winning novel about kidnap, deception, cattle prods and hoof picks, about falling in love and about how far you should go for a friend . . .

LOUISE HARWOOD

Six Reasons to Stay a Virgin

PAN BOOKS £6.99

Hopelessly romantic, thoroughly virginal, Emily knows Mr Right is out there somewhere and she's not sleeping with anyone else while she's looking for him.

Which means Emily is the most irritating person Caitlin knows. More than anything, Caitlin would love to prove to Emily how wrong she is and how she's missing out on the best years of her life. And Caitlin's got a pretty good idea who Emily's Mr Right is too. What could possibly be wrong in getting the two of them together?

But is he Emily's Mr Right, or Caitlin's? And does it matter if Caitlin is wrong? As the scheming starts to work and Emily finally begins talking the language of love, it's Caitlin rather than Emily who can think of at least six reasons to stay a virgin . . .

Light-hearted, liberating and wonderfully romantic, *Six Reasons to Stay a Virgin* is serious about sex – and no sex – about having principles and falling in lust and what it is that we're waiting for.

SARAH WEBB

Always the Bridesmaid

PAN BOOKS £5.99

*You know what they say: ALWAYS the bridesmaid,
never the bride!*

Amy is fed up. Her so-called friends, Jodie and ex-boyfriend Jack, have been having an affair behind her back; her career is on the road to nowhere, and she's about to turn the dreaded thirty.

Things couldn't be worse – or so she thinks! Then Suzi, her younger sister, arrives home with an Australian hunk and announces a May wedding. While Amy is still reeling from this shock, she learns that her best friend Beth is tying the knot too. In the same week! And guess who has to be bridesmaid? At both weddings! Amy is less than thrilled . . .

A real girlie page-turner that keeps you amused, entertained and guessing until the final page.

MEGGIN CABOT

The Guy Next Door

PAN BOOKS   £6.99

Melissa Fuller is late for work.

She is always late, but this time she has a serious excuse.

She's just rescued her neighbour from a violent intruder and in the process become sole custodian of Paco, the Great Dane – not the ideal accessory for a New York city girl.

Now Mel needs help, but she won't get it from her neighbour's only relative – ice-cool womanizer Max Friedlander. Max hasn't a compassionate bone in his body and he isn't about to give up his vacation with a supermodel just to help his sick aunt's annoying neighbour.

But if Max is to protect his inheritance, he needs a substitute to play the caring nephew and take over dog-walking duties from Mel. So when he calls in a favour from his old friend John, in theory, everyone's problems are taken care of.

In practice, they have only just begun.

The Guy Next Door is a wonderful, funny tale of love, office politics and mistaken identities from the author of *The Princess Diaries* – for slightly older but no less starry-eyed readers.

OTHER PAN BOOKS

AVAILABLE FROM PAN MACMILLAN

MORAG PRUNTY

DANCING WITH MULES	0 330 48491 5	£5.99
DISCO DADDY	0 330 48609 8	£6.99

LOUISE HARWOOD

CALLING ON LILY	0 330 48613 6	£5.99
SIX REASONS TO STAY A VIRGIN	0 330 48614 4	£6.99

SARAH WEBB

ALWAYS THE BRIDESMAID	0 330 41214 0	£5.99

All Pan Macmillan titles can be ordered from our website,
www.panmacmillan.com, or from your local bookshop
and are also available by post from:

Bookpost, PO Box 29, Douglas, Isle of Man IM99 1BQ
Credit cards accepted. For details:
Telephone: 01624 677237
Fax: 01624 670923
E-mail: bookshop@enterprise.net
www.bookpost.co.uk

Free postage and packing in the United Kingdom

Prices shown above were correct at the time of going to press.
Pan Macmillan reserve the right to show new retail prices on covers
which may differ from those previously advertised in the text
or elsewhere.